Spacemakers

A FORMER ENGINEER RECALLS HIS
ADVENTURES IN A FLYING FACTORY

LAYTON BUSHEL

Copyright © 2025 by Alastair Warren
All rights reserved.

No part of this publication may be reproduced, distributed, or transmitted in any form or by any means, including photocopying, recording, or other electronic or mechanical methods, without the prior written permission of the author, except as permitted by copyright law.

The story, all names, characters and incidents portrayed in this book are fictitious. No identification with actual persons (living or deceased), places, buildings and products is intended or should be inferred.

Any similarity to any other work or product is entirely coincidental.
This book is entirely fictional. It has to be, as it's set in the future.

First edition 2025.

Contents

Introduction	VII
1. Beginnings	1
2. The mishap	13
3. Ignorance is bliss	21
4. Space-bound	26
5. Adapting	34
6. Our first drain	44
7. Negotiations	48
8. The kidnapping	54
9. Deliveries	60
10. Amy	63
11. Tied up	67

12.	Joyce	71
13.	Not the man I was	75
14.	Deep space custard	78
15.	Time trouble	82
16.	Officer Smythe	89
17.	Facilities	92
18.	Muttley	96
19.	Custard busters	100
20.	Rocky	104
21.	Ideas	110
22.	Mines	115
23.	Lost in space	119
24.	Dogastrophe	122
25.	Undead Ned	126
26.	Deciphering	132
27.	String radio	139
28.	Handy Andy	145
29.	Moving house	149
30.	Moonpats	156
31.	Idle minds	160

32.	Fortunes	166
33.	Time of the signs	172
34.	Dreams	176
35.	Blakey	182
36.	Break time	189
37.	Hairbrained schemes	196
38.	Ghosts	201
39.	Nafwyres	206
40.	Boring times	212
41.	Changes	218
42.	Smythe and westerns	223
43.	Silence preferred	228
44.	Reunions	232
45.	The Moonbase	237
46.	Superdog	243
47.	The Bobberts	248
48.	Flickering flicks	254
49.	The visitor	260
50.	Re-homing	264
51.	Beachcombing	269

52.	Eye in the sky	274
53.	Nuts and vegetables	278
54.	Drainage issues	282
55.	Alien home	285
56.	Distant cousins	293
57.	Kebea	299
58.	Connections	303
59.	Ex-Dougals	309
60.	Seas end	314
61.	Upgrades	318
62.	Dances with wools	323
63.	Thursday	331
64.	Transitions	337
65.	Spirit having not quite flown	343
66.	The theft (nearly)	349
67.	Home and garden	353
68.	Cat capers	356
69.	Epilogue	360
70.	Zzzzzz... what?	366

Introduction

It's the late twenty-second century (in the book I mean, not now). A former engineer describes his adventures in flying factory, roughly a hundred years in his past. Yes, he's getting on a bit, although he doesn't look it (in his opinion). His son is even older.

Like most factories, this one wasn't built to fly. Unfortunately, things don't always go according to plan. Times were hard, so the staff there were told to build a really big spaceship. They were good at building such things and it would keep them busy for a while. Nobody at the site knew what the craft was for, as most of those who did were wiped out by time-travelling potatoes.

BEGINNINGS

It was a cold, miserable winter's day. The fallen snow was nearly half a leg deep. Icicles hung from the house guttering due to a blocked downpipe. I could see a small mound of snow moving about nearby, so I knew I'd found the cat. The trees were heavy with snow. They weighed enough anyway, so this wasn't helping. I had a stinking cold. Odd, because I couldn't smell anything. I had a cold, you see.

I must stop watching these old home movies. It's depressing. I'll go outside later and relax in my deck chair, in the warm summer sun.

I had a strange dream the other night. My wife and I were on the Moon, driving on the dusty Lunar surface in an old electric car. Strange, as my wife's been dead for decades. Little green aliens were chasing us, whizzing around in small, spherical, mostly transparent spacecraft.

As they flew overhead, they dropped bombs of washing-up liquid on us. I can't remember why. Soap bubbles were creeping in everywhere, mainly through the air vents. Strange, I thought. There's no air on the Moon.

My wife drove the aliens away, using the sausage gun. I don't think they liked supersonic sausages. Then I woke up. I found I'd sleep-walked into the bathroom and had been trying to eat the soap.

My son, John, was with me. I told him about it.

"Dad, you're a looney. You need to get that stuff out of your head," he said.

"Where would I put it?"

"How about that author recording thingy I gave you, almost a year ago?"

"Hmmm. I'll think about it," I said.

"That's the problem. If you didn't think about it so much, maybe you wouldn't keep having those weird dreams," John replied.

He had a point. My dreams were about things that had happened to me a century ago. He'd been nagging me to write a book about those days for ages.

"No time like the present," said John. "That recorder cost me quite a bit."

"A bit of what?" I replied. He didn't answer.

I looked for the recorder. I found it in a box marked 'Author recording thingy'. I took it out and examined it. It reminded me of an old reel-to-reel tape recorder, but without the tapes.

I decided I'd better get on with it. I've learnt not to argue with John, as he's older than me (I'll explain later). I still have my ancient diaries from the time, so I can refer to them if I have to.

My story starts roughly a hundred years ago, back in the late twenty-first century. I lived alone, in an ordinary detached bungalow. The house was part of a small group in a friendly cul-de-sac, at the edge of a small seaside town in the UK. I liked my house. It probably didn't like me, when I drilled holes in the walls to put up shelves.

The house suited me well. It was big enough for me and my daft projects, but not too big. I had a large garage, easily big enough for my car, a large workbench and some strong shelving. Tools hung on the walls behind the workbench. (They'd fall off if they didn't.) The house also had a basement. At the back of the house was a nice garden.

I got along well with my neighbours. I would sometimes help them out with small repairs, or lend them tools. They seemed slightly concerned about my daft experiments, but never complained.

I had an unusual car. I'd wanted something different, as modern cars all seemed much the same. The controls and features were almost identical on all models. Like many people I knew, I found them boring.

Few people bought new cars. There wasn't much point. A new one often had no advantages over an old one. Many dealers sold refurbished cars with new seats, carpets, pedals, brake parts etc.

One smart manufacturer started making replicas of much older cars. People liked them, as they stood out from the rest. They had more character than modern cars and sold very well. Other manufacturers soon did likewise, especially if they owned the rights to the older models.

I owned one of those replicas, bought second-hand. They had odd names, as the manufacturers weren't allowed to reuse the original ones. Mine was a Phord Korteener estate. The colour was Ford Sunset (a sort of orangey red, popular in the 1970s).

The car had a petrol engine when I bought it. I found that strange, as it had originally been electric. The previous owner had tried to make it as much like an original Mk3 Ford Cortina as possible.

That oily old engine wasn't running well. The previous owner knew nothing about engine management systems, so he hadn't fitted one. He'd argued that the original Cortinas didn't have them. Goodness knows where he got that worn-out engine and transmission from.

Finding petrol for it wasn't easy, or cheap. It had dreadful MPG and emitted black smoke from the homemade exhaust. That noisy lump under the bonnet would have to go.

The rest of the car remained in good condition, so I had it converted back to electric power. A man named Barry did the work. He owned a small company in a town around thirty miles from my home. He'd done many similar conversions, so he really knew his stuff. Barry did a good job with my conversion.

That car soon grew on me. It had the looks and interesting features of the older cars, without the noise or reliability problems. It was also much safer and lighter than an original Cortina. I could get loads of stuff in the back, which often proved handy. But enough about the car.

I worked for a branch of a large multinational manufacturing company. They had a factory around twelve miles from my home. The business was called Fiddler and Snitch. Not a good name, I thought. The site had previously been a quarry. Pine forests surrounded the place. Probably just as well, as the trees helped to keep the noise down.

I had been on holiday in the area several times before I started working for F&S. I had got to know some of the locals quite well. Shortly after one such holiday, I was made redundant. I couldn't find a suitable job anywhere near where I lived, so I looked further afield.

I still had a fairly recent local newspaper from the area where I'd been on holiday. In it, I spotted an advertisement for a job at Fiddler and Snitch. The site wasn't far from where I'd stayed during my holiday.

I liked the area, so I applied. They needed someone with general engineering experience and plenty of common sense. I wanted to attend the interview in person, but F&S wouldn't allow it. Video interview only. Odd, I thought.

They asked me some strange questions, then said they'd get back to me. Around three hours later, to my surprise, they made me an offer. I was suspicious. They seemed almost too keen. I said I'd think about it.

I knew some people in the area from my holidays, so I called them. They told me nobody liked working for F&S. They were a strange lot. Nobody wanted the job they were advertising. The position had been advertised for months. I was probably the only applicant.

I could see an opportunity, so I contacted F&S again. After much negotiating, we reached an agreement. I would take the job, but for much more money than they originally offered. I would work there for at least one year. They would have to pay my moving expenses.

I paid an unofficial visit to the F&S site about a week before starting there. I wanted to get an idea of what to expect. I'd done that with previous jobs and had always found the visits helpful.

I was shown in and given a visitor's pass. Someone accompanied me initially, but he got called away to do something urgent. That left me free to wander around on my own. I had no problem with that, as I could go anywhere I pleased.

The main buildings were unusually strong. They'd been built to withstand the frequent shockwaves caused by the previous owners doing quarry blasting. Just as well, as it would later turn out.

In the centre of the factory stood a huge building. It looked like a massive aircraft hangar, with huge sliding doors at one end. I think the former owners had used it for storing and servicing the quarrying machines. Outside the doors was a large area of concrete. Along the inside walls were workbenches and small offices. The central part was the main production area.

Car parking spaces surrounded the main building. Many smaller buildings and Portakabins were dotted around the site.

The pine forests hid the factory from the main road. That suited F&S well. They didn't want people watching what they were up to, although I don't think anyone really cared. I talked to a few people there, who told me about the place.

The American parent company thought they'd got a bargain when they bought the site. They didn't realise why until later.

The former owners had been ordered by the local council to cease all quarrying activities, due to many complaints over the years. Several local buildings had suffered from broken windows due to the quarry blasting, and farm livestock were getting stressed. The quarrying company was required to fill in the huge holes and make the site look natural again. They couldn't afford to do that, so they'd got out of it by selling the entire site.

Another branch of the American company carried out the work required by the local council. It took a while and was far from perfect. A council inspector turned up shortly afterwards to check the work. The local F&S management took him out for lunch. They managed to get him drunk enough to sign off the work without actually seeing it.

When the Americans bought the site, it included the surrounding forests and a private single-track railway line. It led to the local town. At the quarry end of the line were sidings and engine sheds. Several items of rusty old rolling stock, spare bogies and other things had been left there. Most of it lay out in the open, abandoned.

When I started at Fiddler and Snitch, I thought I'd got myself a good deal. Unfortunately, they hadn't told me everything. The buildings were basically sound, but there were many roof leaks. Buckets and large umbrellas were deployed inside when it rained. The main heating system hadn't worked for years. People told me they had to wrap up warmly during the winters.

Mr Fiddler and Mr Snitch were strange people. They were both ex-accountants, originally employed by the quarrying company. They balanced the books by not spending any more money than absolutely necessary. Equipment failures were common, due to poor maintenance or improvised repairs.

I put up with it for several months, fixing what I could. Most people appreciated my efforts. When I asked F&S to let me hire a cherry picker to fix the roof leaks, they wouldn't pay for it. I found it hard to believe the place could make money with such poor management. Most people hated working there.

Then I started checking for asbestos. I'd opened a can of worms. I found it almost everywhere, often hidden under sheets of other materials. Much of the roof had it, inside and out. Bits fell down sometimes, halting production. It was a potential health and safety nightmare. If I'd had a pound for every bit of asbestos I found in that factory, I'd have been rich.

I'd had enough. I made a video call to the company headquarters in America after our normal working hours, as I knew the F&S management wouldn't do anything. They sent two senior experts to meet me at the F&S site. The two ex-accountants complained but were brushed aside by the Americans. I felt good about that.

I showed our visitors around. They made notes and took photos. They interviewed many of our staff, who were happy to talk. Mr Fiddler and Mr Snitch were both sacked shortly afterwards.

The American management put me in temporary charge. Not bad for a man who'd only been with them for a few months, I thought. Although the two ex-accountants had left, the Fiddler and Snitch company name remained.

The Americans had a solution to our asbestos problem. A product existed in America called Asbestorot. It had only been on the market for about a year. It had good reviews.

They'd used it successfully on other sites. If a small amount was brushed onto an asbestos panel, the whole lot would be gone within a week. All that remained was a little sticky, smelly goo. The product contained strange alien bacteria that ate asbestos. They sent me some, in a large gas cylinder.

The idea of having that stuff in the air worried me. I'd been assured it was harmless to humans, but I wasn't prepared to take any chances. I temporarily closed the entire site and sent most people home. Important or delicate equipment was moved out of the main buildings and stored elsewhere. We covered large, immovable items with plastic sheeting.

Then I sent the remaining people home. I turned off the electricity supply at the main breaker supplying the building. Then I sealed all the buildings and flooded them inside with Asbestorot gas. After that, I went home too.

A week later, I returned to the site. I also called Ned, one of the shop floor workers, back to the site. Ned always volunteered when overtime was available, so I knew I could rely on him. Maybe he didn't like being at home.

Ned met me at the main car park.

"G'day, mate! 'Ere... what's that smell?" said Ned, as we approached the main building. Ned often didn't mince his words, although he sometimes shredded them. (He was trying to write a book.)

"A lot of it is Asbestorot," I said. "I've been told it's smelly when it turns to goo."

"Yeah... I read about that stuff. Don't always go well," he said. I thought it best not to ask why.

We walked into the main building.

"Strewth," said Ned, as we looked around.

Most of the roof materials were gone, except for the supporting structures. Interior panels were flapping about loose in the slight breeze. Panels were missing from some doors. Several shelves had disappeared, leaving things on the floor. Most of the floors were wet due to recent heavy rain, which had washed away much of the goo. The hot summer sunshine caused a little steam to rise from the floors.

We inspected the main building, attending to anything we thought dangerous.

"Nothing's working," said Ned, as he tried one of the light switches. I ignored him, while I thought about how to fix the roof. Then I heard a shout from Ned, who was out of sight.

"Hey! I know why nothing's working! Some bugger's turned the bloody power off! Soon fix that..."

"NOOOOO!" I shouted. Too late. I heard a loud 'clunk', as Ned turned the main breaker back on. There were flashes and bangs everywhere, accompanied by loud buzzing. It stopped when the main breaker burnt out.

The ancient fuse holders and switchgear had contained asbestos insulation. It had turned into an electricity-conducting goo, so the fuses were useless.

A moment later, there was a bright green flash. I heard a loud crash behind me. Ned came rushing in.

"What was that?" he shouted. I turned around. I found a steel toolbox in the middle of the room, in a puddle of Asbestorot goo. It hadn't been there before. All the goo in the room had a slight green glow, which faded away after a few minutes.

I cautiously approached the toolbox and looked it over. Ned kicked it. Nothing happened, so we inspected it more closely. Most of the contents were scattered on the floor, mainly well-used tools.

"What's this?" said Ned, looking at a strange object nearby. It was spherical and roughly four inches in diameter. It had rolled away from the toolbox, leaving a small goo trail.

Ned picked it up.

"Ow!" he said, as it fizzed slightly. He threw it across the room. The device started to whine, at a rapidly increasing pitch. It spluttered and emitted smoke. A few seconds later, it made a sort of farting noise and vanished in a bright green flash.

Neither of us said anything for a few minutes.

"What was that thing?" said Ned, eventually. I paused.

"It appeared from nowhere, then disappeared. I'm guessing it was a time travel device," I said. Ned looked at me strangely, but said nothing.

Ned found a few coins in the toolbox. He examined them.

"Holy dooley! Look at this!" he said, passing me a coin. It looked like a normal British coin. I couldn't see anything wrong with it, and said so.

"Look at the date," he said. It was two years into the future. The other coins also had future dates. "At least that confirms your time travel theory."

Ned's face suddenly lit up.

"We could sell these and make a bloody fortune!" he said. I disagreed.

"They'll be worthless a few years from now."

"Oh bugger."

We agreed not to tell anyone about the time travel ball. I didn't want a reputation for telling wild stories.

We put all the tools back in the toolbox. The letters 'R.W.' had been painted on one lid. We didn't know anyone with those initials. I hid the toolbox where I hoped nobody would find it.

Ned noticed that two fire alarm points were damaged. They'd probably been hit by falling roof bits. The alarm should have been sounding. It wasn't, because the old back-up batteries had swollen and were useless. I hated that system. It was over-complex, making tests difficult to do. People had stopped bothering with regular testing.

Ned and I tidied things up around the site as best we could, and then Ned went home.

I reported back to the American management. They told me they'd had trouble with Asbestorot in the electrics at another site. They apologised for not warning me.

I suggested that all the ancient electrical wiring should be replaced, throughout the site. What we had was barely legal. It was fried anyway. They agreed with me and authorised the work.

I brought most of our staff back onto the site to help clean up the mess. They did a good job, I thought. No Asbestorot remained. I thanked them for their hard work and attention to detail. Some looked puzzled. I wasn't sure why. Maybe they weren't used to being thanked for anything.

Local roofers were employed to re-roof the buildings. That put an end to the leaks. I also had good roof insulation put in. Solar panels were installed on the south-facing roofs.

All the old electrics were torn out. A brand new electrical system was designed and installed, from scratch. It met all the latest safety standards and suited our purposes much better.

I took the opportunity to install a large UPS system, as we often had power cuts in bad weather. A small, secure, watertight building was built, to house the batteries and electronics. It was located near a huge power transformer, away from the factory itself. I had a separate power feed set up to take electricity to a few Portakabins hidden in the woods. If the outside power went off, we'd be able to carry on as usual for a couple of hours using battery power.

We also had a better, simpler fire alarm system installed. I argued that all that expense would increase the value of the site.

The Mishap

It took us about two weeks to get everything fully up and running again. All that work and expense proved to be well worth it. The site was much better than previously. It looked better too, as Ned and others had repainted many inside walls. We had no more roof leaks and no more asbestos worries. The new, modern electrics and lighting were much better than before, with far more outlets than previously. No more daisy-chained extension leads.

I also got the main heating system working again. It was old but designed to last. New managers were hired, allowing me to concentrate on engineering issues.

Most people were much happier. The old sense of doom and gloom had gone, along with Mr Fiddler and Mr Snitch. New production equipment was bought, as what we had been using was slow, worn out and sometimes unsafe. We made better products, faster than before. Our reputation soon improved.

We didn't see the American management much at F&S. Few people recognised them when they visited us. They preferred it that way. They could make unannounced visits and catch people out. Sometimes people were caught doing 'homers' during company time. Nobody got sacked for it, though.

Our new managers were better than the previous ones, but they still made mistakes. They cut the advertising budget to save money. That proved to be a false economy. We soon ran low on orders. There were rumours of possible redundancies.

The American bosses held a big meeting to decide what to do. Nobody from F&S wanted to be there. Our UK managers were supposed to attend, but all found excuses (usually holidays) to get out of it.

Our youngest one, a spotty little herbert (called Herbert), signed himself off work for a few days. He claimed to be ill. It didn't work. He had to return, as no other F&S managers could be contacted. I think they'd all accidentally-on-purpose left their phones switched off. At least it proved the rumours that Herbert had terminal acne were false.

At the big meeting, someone mentioned that we were good at building small, custom spaceships. We had the expertise to do it well. It was suggested that we should build more spaceships, based on a standard design.

The American management eventually decided we should design and build one massive spaceship. That would keep us busy for quite a while. We could use it as a 'background' task. They would figure out what to do with it later.

Good spaceships were much in demand back then. Big, posh ones especially so. Somebody would be bound to want it. The managers expected it to sell well. If it did, we'd make more. Rough sketches and specifications were drawn up.

Two months later, all but one of those American bosses died in a dreadful space accident. Initial investigations found no clues, partly because they were looking in the wrong place.

Later investigations revealed that the spacecraft they'd been travelling in had collided with a sack of potatoes. Nobody could explain why the potatoes were there. It's just not the sort of thing you expect to encounter in space. People kept away from that area until the authorities declared it spud-free.

The one crash survivor had lost his memory. People looked everywhere, but they failed to find it. He also had amnesia.

When the new American managers were appointed, nobody in America told them about the plans to build the fancy new spaceship. They found out from us. None would admit that they didn't have a clue why it was being built.

They tried quietly asking our local management. That didn't work, as Herbert had suggested to the rest that it would be funny to just plead ignorance. It would serve them right for not keeping proper records of the meeting. We would just do as we'd been told.

The development and construction work continued anyway. We didn't want to upset the top company boss, although nobody at F&S could remember seeing him for about twenty years. Some thought he might be dead, but they couldn't prove it. He just looked that way.

Over the following two years, the spaceship took shape. A rather peculiar shape. Bits stuck out everywhere. Since nobody knew its intended purpose, they included everything they could think of, just in case.

Many useless things got installed. People kept thinking of more things to add. Every time they ran out of space in the spaceship, they just made it larger. They would worry about the outer skin later. Nobody (of any importance) asked questions.

The spaceship's main power came from some highly unusual objects. Another branch of our company had found them on the surface of Mars. They were cylindrical, mostly about a foot long and roughly an inch in diameter. A few were shorter and slightly fatter. They were semi-transparent and emitted a slight light-orange glow.

They were obviously manufactured. Nobody knew what those things were doing on Mars, other than just sitting there. Since some of our development staff had shown an interest in studying them, the strange glowing bars were passed to us. I don't think the Americans wanted anything to do with them. I forget why.

The bars were emitting some form of energy. We found it easy to harness. Tests were done to see how much they could deliver. The more power we extracted from them, the more they generated. They seemed to have limitless energy.

We used several to power the spaceship. A power unit was built inside the craft to house the bars and extract the energy as electricity. The system provided the electricity supply for the entire craft. They could provide much more energy than we were ever likely to need. Better to have too much than too little, we thought.

I started referring to the energy bars as Mars bars. Herbert soon put a stop to that. He didn't want people to think our nice new spaceship was powered by chocolate. It would give a bad impression. As we didn't want people to know what power source the craft used, we referred to them as MPBs (Martian Power Bars).

We didn't know how reliable the MPBs would be, so we allowed space for a second power source to be fitted. All the associated wiring and switchgear was installed, just in case. What that second power source would be, we didn't know.

Many people found the spaceship's interior more comfortable than the factory offices. Some set up new offices in the spaceship. They argued that its interior features needed to be well-tested. As more things were added, the spaceship's size increased. Our main factory shop floor area was huge, so nobody worried about the size of the craft.

More and more facilities were relocated into it, including the development laboratory. We started running the factory itself from the electricity supply and facilities within the spaceship, to save money.

We became almost independent of outside facilities. Large connectors connected the spaceship to the factory. We planned to disconnect them just before the launch.

We originally planned to use several types of propulsion but cut it down to just three. There would be the gravity drive system, the main space drive and the so-called 'sausage' drive.

The latter had been developed due to a misunderstanding. It involved firing sausages or other food products at extremely high velocities from the spaceship's rear to provide propulsion. We made a hole in one of the factory walls to allow for testing. People in a nearby village wondered why it sometimes rained burnt sausages.

Someone had suggested the idea to the development boffins. Most thought it was a joke, but they weren't sure. They developed and installed it anyway. The canteen staff couldn't keep up with the sudden increase in sausage demand. They invented a sausage substitute, which they found easier to make. Nobody complained (much).

A year later, the spaceship was about as good as we could make it. We didn't have an official name for it, so we gave it one, temporarily. We called it the Bovercraft, as we couldn't be 'bovered' to think of a proper name for it. It looked ridiculous, so we fitted the outer skin. It still looked a bit lumpy. Oh well. We planned to sort it out later.

We were rather pleased with ourselves. Then somebody asked how we planned to get it out of the factory. I'd tried asking the local management several times, but I couldn't get a proper answer. The Bovercraft had originally been small enough to get through the large factory doors, but it had grown considerably since then.

We developed a spherical force field 'bubble' for the Bovercraft. It would surround and protect it after it left the factory. It would activate once the craft was high enough above the ground. The drive systems were modified to allow for it, otherwise, the craft wouldn't have been able to go anywhere.

We installed a similar force field bubble around the factory itself, for security purposes. It originated from a well-hidden underground box just outside the factory grounds. Its power came from the small UPS building, well away from the factory.

Nobody could get through such a bubble. We set both to the same size, overlapping and locked together. We intended to reduce the size of the Bovercraft one before launch.

Eventually, we were given a launch date. We had a month to get ready. The factory doors were widened considerably, to allow the Bovercraft to leave. Three strong legs supported the Bovercraft. We planned to get it outside by floating it just above the factory floor, retracting the legs and then flying it out.

The management kept asking for launch simulations to be carried out. The simulations became increasingly complex. Clever software was written to check that everything was done correctly and in the right order.

Spotty Herbert thought himself an expert programmer. He wasn't. He kept interfering with the programming efforts. The programmers found it difficult to tell him to go away, due to his managerial position. He seemed determined to have things done his way.

A week before the planned launch, the American management turned up. They asked for a final, detailed simulation of the take-off procedure. They wanted to be sure that absolutely nothing could go wrong.

I was fed up with it. I'd worked hard for months. I'd done all I could to prepare. With the management's permission, I took the next few days off.

The next evening, the final simulation started. The Bovercraft's laboratory was unusually crowded. The boffins went through the well-rehearsed simulation. It started from the point where the craft had risen high enough above the ground for the craft's force field bubble to be activated.

Spotty Herbert looked nervous. Someone had seen him tinkering with the software after hours the previous day and had asked him about it (and been ignored).

The very realistic simulation took hours to complete. Everyone seemed impressed. By the time they'd finished, it was late into the evening. The managers left the Bovercraft. Some planned to stay in the disused factory offices, at least until the following day.

Spotty Herbert intended to drive home that evening, as he lived locally. He liked driving at night, which seemed odd to me. As he walked outside into the car park, he noticed the unusual clarity of the night sky.

The car park had lighting, but it seemed lighter there than usual. Herbert thought nothing of it, as his mind was on other things. He got into his souped-up little car and raced to the edge of the car park, where the exit should have been.

Then he stopped, with a short screech of tyres. He couldn't see anything ahead of him. He thought his car headlights were faulty. When he got out to check, they were fine.

He walked to the edge of the car park, where the tarmac stopped. He could see a dim reflection of his car's headlights in front of him. He walked right up to the tarmac edge and collided with something invisible. It seemed soft and spongy. He pushed hard against it, but couldn't get through.

Extra light seemed to be coming from somewhere. He looked around for the source. When he looked up, he gasped. Above him was the Earth. He almost fell over. He just stared at it, his heart racing. It was a beautiful but alarming sight. He thought he must be going nuts.

After a few minutes, he returned to his car and drove it back to his parking space. He sneaked back into the Bovercraft laboratory. When he checked the displays, he realised that his software tweaks were almost certainly responsible for what had happened.

Spotty Herbert had to own up. He handed in his resignation letter to the upper management, who were still on site. They eventually let him off, as he'd just learnt an important lesson. He had to work with the more qualified, experienced software engineers to undo what he had done. They explained why the 'unnecessary' code he'd removed was so important. Some of Herbert's changes were left in place for the time being.

Herbert's mistake cost him his reputation for a while. He told me later there's no such thing as a free launch. Two of our shop floor workers (a nasty pair) were winding him up about it for weeks.

Computer keyboards weren't the only type Herbert thought he was good with. He also fancied himself as a pianist. I don't think anyone else did. Some said his Bach was worse than his byte.

IGNORANCE IS BLISS

Meanwhile, I'd gone home. I didn't need to be present for the final launch simulation. I felt exhausted and needed a break. My engineering colleagues had assured me someone else could deal with any problems. I intended to return to work in time to watch the actual takeoff, planned for several days later.

It was a warm, sunny summer's day. I was in my garden, relaxing in my deck chair. I'd just cut my lawn and was enjoying a nice, cool drink. I planned to fix my newly rescued artificial cat later.

The chimneys on my house hadn't been used for decades. The cap had blown off one of the chimney pots sometime earlier. The crows had taken up residence in it. I'd meant to fit a new cap for ages but had never quite got around to it.

Those noisy birds were on my roof, making a dreadful racket. I threw a stick at them. They flew off, squawking loudly at me. I settled down again in my deck chair, feeling better. About two minutes later, I noticed a crow-shaped shadow whizzing across the garden. Then I heard (and felt) a 'splotch' on the top of my head.

I'd had enough. Time to deal with those pests, I thought. I got cleaned up and fetched my roof ladders from the garage. Then I looked for my normal extension ladders. They weren't there. I'd left them at work. I'd needed them for a job there a week earlier. I'd have to retrieve them.

I grumpily put my roof ladders back in the garage, fetched my car out and slammed the garage door shut. I locked the front door of the house and started driving to the factory. The car had got quite hot in the garage, so I opened the windows to let the fresh air in. I quickly closed them again when I noticed a dung spreader operating in a nearby field. Too late. What a stench. It took a while for the smell to clear.

When I arrived at the turnoff to the factory site, I was in a bad mood. I drove down the narrow, potholed track. When I reached the site, the factory wasn't there. I thought I must be dreaming, so I pinched myself on the leg. Yeeouch!

I got out of my car and walked to the site. A massive crater had appeared where the factory should have been. There couldn't have been an explosion, as I couldn't see any bits lying around. Besides, the hole looked too neat. I tried ringing the factory, hoping it might just be invisible (although I couldn't see how). I received no reply. If I'd had a personal worryometer, it would probably have exploded.

At the edge of the crater, I encountered an invisible force field. I couldn't push through it. Then the penny dropped. They'd taken off without me. Something must've gone wrong. They'd failed to reduce their force field size before leaving and had taken the entire factory with them. I knew the Bovercraft's oversized power source could probably do it. I calmed down a bit.

I drove home, not knowing what to think. I had considered myself reasonably popular, but perhaps I was mistaken. At least I could tell myself I was the first person in human history to own a set of extension ladders in high Earth orbit. At least, I assumed that's where they were. They could've been anywhere.

When I got home, I called the company's American headquarters to see if they knew anything. They knew many things, but nothing about the fate of our factory.

"We've been trying to contact F&S, but we keep getting told the lines are out of order," said one of the managers there. "The mobiles are all on voicemail too. What have you been up to? Are you doing some sort of maintenance you've not told us about?"

"You can't contact anyone, because the factory isn't there anymore," I replied, nervously.

"What's happened? Where is it? Has it been blown up, or something?"

"No, not *blown* up, but it is... erm... up. There's a huge, neat crater where it used to be. I think the entire factory is in space," I said.

"WHAT? You gotta be kidding me. What's it doing up there?"

"Probably wondering how to get down again."

I explained what I thought had happened and said that everyone would probably be fine. I suggested that since all communication with them had been cut off, someone would have to go into space and find them.

"I believe you have a couple of small spacecraft. Could I borrow one, please, to go and look for them?" I asked.

"Why you, not us?"

"With respect, I know the factory systems better than you. I'm better qualified to offer assistance, should they need it."

"Err, OK, you got it. I'll send a craft to you. The pilot will follow your orders. It'll be with you tomorrow, at your home," said the manager. "Let us know how you get on."

The next day, the small spacecraft landed in my garden. I grabbed my tool bag and a fully charged walkie-talkie, and then the pilot and I took off to search for the factory.

A man named Barry headed the general engineering team at F&S. He had done my Korteener conversion, in his previous job. We got along well. Barry's team usually did the maintenance and installation tasks, while I did the more 'interesting' stuff. I hoped to be able to contact him.

Once in space, where we thought the factory would probably be, I tried the walkie-talkie radio.

"Alan calling F&S," I said. Nothing. I had the wrong channel selected, which I quickly corrected. I hoped the pilot hadn't noticed. He obviously had, judging by the look on his face. I tried again. I thought I could hear a quiet reply in all the background noise, but I wasn't sure.

Meanwhile, another branch of our company had found them, using ground-based radar. They passed the factory's location to us. We headed towards it.

As we approached the factory's predicted position, I could see it ahead of us, floating in space. It looked strange, both familiar and unfamiliar at the same time. A semi-transparent spherical force field enclosed the entire factory. It looked like a giant soap bubble. Half the bubble contents (under the factory) were just soil. The factory looked upside down, with the building roofs facing the Earth.

We stopped nearby. I tried the radio again.

Barry answered.

"Where the (expletive) are you?" asked Barry, sounding shocked.

"Go outside into the car park and look up," I said.

He did. I waved at him through the spacecraft window. He waved back from the car park.

"Hang on... I'll let you in. If I weaken the bubble at one point, you should be able to get through," said Barry. He did, and we did, landing in the car park.

The pilot left me there and headed back to Earth. Barry and I had a long talk. We agreed not to tell anybody what had just happened, at least for the time being.

We forgot about the American pilot, who told everything to his superiors. Oops...

Space-bound

At first, few people noticed our departure from Earth. Those few kept quiet about it, to avoid panic. Everything seemed normal. We still had electricity, as it came from the Bovercraft's on-board power system. There hadn't even been a flickering of the lights to worry anyone. No 'we're-going-into-space' alarms had sounded, mainly because there weren't any.

A spherical force field bubble surrounded the entire factory. It wasn't easy to see, being almost transparent. Its size was still set to match the size of the one on the ground. We'd been running both most of the time for several weeks, testing them thoroughly. They were usually turned off at the beginning and end of each working day, so people could get in and out. The site bubble was handy for overnight security.

The Bovercraft's artificial gravity had switched on automatically. It was linked to the size of the craft's force field bubble, so the entire factory still had gravity. The boffins thought that if it worked well like that, it would be no trouble at all when used for just the Bovercraft.

When the unintended launch happened, most people were indoors. Some had gone home before the 'simulation', as it had taken place after working hours. A few had stayed to watch a football match on the massive TV in our canteen. They were wondering why they could no longer get a TV signal. Herbert instructed the boffins to slowly rotate the factory to a different angle, to put the Earth out of sight.

Most staff were unaware of what had happened, but rumours spread quickly. The management told everyone to remain within the factory buildings until further notice. Not a good idea, as the buildings weren't space-proof. Someone looked through a window and commented that the star constellations looked wrong for the time of year.

Earlier that day, interviews had been taking place for people to fill vacant positions aboard the Bovercraft. Some interviewees were still on the site and were still being given the guided tour.

The management were panicking. They'd never before experienced anything like what had just happened. They tried slowing down the clocks, to buy themselves more time. Some had been sneakily doing this anyway, to get more work out of people. They sped them up again during the night. Most people owned wristwatches, so few got caught out. It had become annoying.

Soon, the brown stuff hit the fan. People were noticing odd things. The stars looked much clearer than usual and no longer twinkled. The Moon looked bigger and clearer than normal. The weather forecast had been bad, yet not a cloud could be seen.

I advised the management to tell everyone what had happened and where we were. They agreed, somewhat sheepishly.

An announcement was made over the Tannoy system that everyone should gather in the main building.

I was told I'd have to be the one to tell everyone what had happened, as it was my idea. I objected, as it wasn't my fault. I eventually agreed, as long as the managers were there to back me up.

With everyone assembled in the main building, a senior manager announced that I had something to say. I stood in front of the crowd and explained what had happened. Spotty Herbert hid somewhere, out of sight. After a brief pause, it got noisy. People panicked. They had been taken away from everything and everyone (outside the factory) they had ever known.

"How do we get home?" someone asked, angrily.

"Don't panic," said one manager, looking panicky. "We can still go home whenever we need to. All we need to do is land where we took off from. With any luck, nobody will notice."

"That's unlikely," I said. "We've probably been spotted on radar. I suggest we hide behind the Moon for now, where Earth can't see us. Anyone tracking us will see us moving away from Earth. That'll give us time to come up with a plan."

The management agreed. I didn't tell them that the American headquarters already knew we were in space. We had been difficult to find, as our bubble tended to absorb radar.

As we headed for the Moon, I went outside and watched. We had rotated slightly, so the Earth was visible again. It seemed to get smaller and smaller. The colours were all wrong. I knew about the Doppler effect, but I'd never encountered it like this before.

A short while later, we landed on the dark side of the Moon. I hadn't expected us to actually land there. We had brought a huge amount of soil with us under the factory, so it puzzled me that the lunar surface was at the same level as our car park.

Seeing the lunar surface out there just beyond the factory limits alarmed people. Most, like me, had never left Earth before, let alone been to the Moon. I found it exciting, but scary. Someone said he could see one of the old Apollo landers out there, but he was clearly drunk.

Amongst the factory workers were a group of people who had formed the F&S Astronomical Society. They had a good telescope set up at the edge of the car park. Our former quarry site had been ideal for them, being far from the light pollution that often plagued amateur astronomers.

They thought it was brilliant. The images they saw through the telescope were incredible, compared to what they were used to. The usual atmospheric distortion was completely gone.

Nobody could go home. Some interviewees were still with us. As there weren't many, the management decided to employ them all, starting as soon as possible. Important positions aboard the Bovercraft were assigned. People needed to be kept occupied, so everyone was given something to do.

We got busy, testing the Bovercraft's systems and correcting problems. We still had access to the rest of the factory, so fixing any issues we found wasn't difficult. People had a considerable incentive to do things properly.

The management set up a chain of command for the operation of the Bovercraft. The captain would be Mr Smythe. Being an ex-military man, giving orders was second nature to him. He was a tall, slim man with a big moustache. He tried to look down on people to make himself look superior, sometimes standing on his toes slightly to gain height. He stopped doing that when he noticed people trying not to laugh at him.

I wasn't convinced Smythe was the right man for the job, but nobody else wanted it.

The deputy captain was a shorter man, called Simon. Most people liked him more than the captain. They found him much easier to talk to, and he didn't shout at them. If you wanted to get something done, it was often easier to ask Simon first. Simon liked good ideas.

I became heavily involved in fixing the Bovercraft's problems. Sometimes there were design issues, which weren't always easy to fix, but most were just silly things. I found it hard to believe what some people had done. Still, I found it rather fun sometimes. Knowledge is power, as they say. People usually appreciated my help.

Over the following days, it became increasingly apparent that nobody knew why the Bovercraft had been built. I asked all the managers individually, but they were clueless (as usual). Most assured me that somebody would know. Nobody did.

I urged several to tell our American masters on Earth where we were and what had happened. None would listen. I think they were afraid of being sacked. We couldn't have contacted Earth anyway, from the Moon's dark side.

Meanwhile, our parent company had been trying to keep things quiet. They knew we were fine, but didn't want to admit that an entire factory had vanished. A neat, half-spherical crater had appeared at the former quarry site where the factory had been, protected by a spongy, invisible barrier.

A few local contractors had visited the site, found the huge crater and contacted the police. They, in turn, had contacted the American owners. The contractors were asked to sign the Official Secrets Act, even though they didn't legally have to, as a way of keeping them quiet.

Company people from America soon arrived at our launch site. They wanted to see for themselves what had happened. They had to explain to the local police why the factory wasn't there. The fences had to be repaired, as only the four corners of the original fence remained.

The Americans were surprised to find the crater filled in. The area inside the force field looked like the surface of the Moon.

Back in our factory, Captain Smythe didn't like the situation. He wasn't authorised to do anything yet. It seemed to him that nobody was in charge. It went against his military training. He'd tried to keep quiet, but it had all become too much.

He approached the management and asked that he be given command of the Bovercraft, at least temporarily. They readily agreed. If something went wrong, they could blame Smythe.

The captain felt better. Now he could use his authority to get things done. He announced over the Tannoy system that he was in charge. That amused me. Anyone could have made such an announcement. Nobody challenged him, though. He was welcome to the job.

He announced that if anyone knew the Bovercraft's real purpose, he or she should tell him or his deputy, Simon. A difficult, but necessary announcement to make. Pointless, as it turned out, as nobody had the slightest idea what the Bovercraft had been built for.

Smythe started wearing his military green ex-army jumper. He thought it would give him a more 'I'm in charge' look. Meanwhile, he announced that the Bovercraft should be prepared for action, whatever that action might be.

The captain set about familiarising himself with the Bovercraft and its crew. He visited each department and talked with the senior staff members. He started with Amy, the chief medical officer.

Amy liked animals. Not surprising, really, as she was a qualified vet. She had only come on board to attend to someone's pet Labrador. She had assured the management that she could do the job, as she had (almost) become a nurse before training as a vet. Nobody else on board had any medical qualifications, other than compulsory first aid training. They had little choice but to employ her.

Sue was the chief science officer. She certainly knew her stuff, but she lacked confidence. She'd been verbally bullied during her school days, and this still affected her occasionally. She'd told her school friends that she'd seen a ghost while her family had been on holiday. They'd stayed in a hotel that some believed was haunted.

Nobody believed her claims that she'd talked to a ghost. Some kids called her names like 'Woo-Hoo Sue' and 'Clair Voyant'. Sue later became a science teacher. She would never tolerate bullying.

Sue was quite a large woman, with long blonde hair and blue eyes. Some said she had an above-average centre of gravity, but this was never tested. (Yes, she had a large head.) Some referred to her as 'Eleven-of-nine'. I can't remember why. She got along well with most people.

Barry, the chief engineer, knew a great deal about cars. He'd done a lot of work converting older vehicles to electric power before he started working with us.

Unfortunately, he didn't know much about spaceships. The subject never came up at his interview, roughly a year earlier. Fortunately, the other engineers were able to teach him. He could learn things quickly. He had a genuine interest in technical things and how they worked, so he was soon up to speed.

The chief negotiator was a young fellow known as Angry Charlie. The post had been created by one of the top managers shortly before the potato crash, to try to force him to calm down. Charlie was his son. He could never sit or stand still for long and was always fidgeting. He was on all sorts of pills. Too many, some thought.

The cleaners shouldn't have been with us. Nobody had told them we were about to leave Earth, so they were stuck with us in the factory. They cleaned just about everything, just to keep busy, and soon ran out of cleaning materials.

I suggested to the management that we needed a health and safety person. We had much new and untested equipment, and I had noticed several unsafe practices being repeatedly carried out. They tried to find someone, but nobody with us had the necessary qualifications. The matter was soon forgotten.

One extra person had ended up on board, called Phil. He was an oversized zookeeper, there by accident. He sometimes wore thick glasses. Odd, because he didn't need them. He'd heard that glasses were good for someone's eyesight and assumed they'd be good for his. Phil was a big fellow, so nobody wanted to argue with him.

He'd wandered off during a guided tour, as he hadn't been guided well enough. He had several bumps and bruises, as he kept walking into things. With glasses like those, I wasn't surprised. Phil always wanted to help people with things, but nobody would let him (he could be quite clumsy sometimes). He felt a bit down.

ADAPTING

Captain Smythe soon felt more at home. He liked being in charge and telling people what to do. Most people did what he asked them to. Others would tell him to push off (or words to that effect). He had to keep reminding himself that he wasn't in the military anymore.

The bridge layout looked like a set of an old science fiction TV series. Right at the back, on a slightly raised platform, was the captain's chair. Smythe could see the entire bridge from there. It made him feel superior.

He found the chair extremely comfortable. It would automatically adapt itself to suit anyone about to sit on it. Smythe declared it the most comfortable chair he had ever sat on. Nobody bothered to tell Smythe that the automatic settings could be overridden and set manually.

It had several handy controls integrated into the armrests. Perhaps too handy. The small control panels weren't originally recessed, so Smythe found pressing the buttons too easy sometimes. He accidentally set off the fire alarm twice. Barry had to replace the 'Alarm Test' pushbutton with a rotary switch.

Smythe demanded that extra padding be fitted around the switch panels.

In the middle of the bridge were two rows of control desks. Comfortable swivel chairs were provided for the operators. Various displays and controls were fitted into the desks. Some positions just had blanking panels fitted, to allow for future expansion. The front row was a little lower than the rear one.

The large rectangular window in the front wall was intended to look out into space. It gave us a nice view of an interior factory wall. Fortunately, a large screen could be lowered in front of it to display images from the various remote cameras.

Near the back of the bridge were two doors. Close to one of them, a shiny brass plate had been fitted to the wall. It had ornate designs around the edges and some fancy text. It read 'Spacecraft name here'.

Smythe wanted to do some proper testing. He got everyone to man their positions, and then we took off. We positioned ourselves behind the Moon, facing it. Being ex-military, he wanted to test the Bovercraft's armaments first. He ordered that the Moon be targeted.

"Fire!" said the captain.

"Where? I don't see anything..." said someone, clutching an extinguisher.

"Shoot at the Moon, you fool," shouted the captain. We did. Several new craters appeared on the lunar surface, along with a big hole in the main factory building wall. Nobody could remember which craters were the new ones.

We were going to do it again, but the management wouldn't allow it.

Smythe was told that if he did, the cost of repairing the building would come out of his pay. The armaments would have to be set up outside the building if they were to be used again.

It had been several days since we left Earth. Some people found what had happened quite exciting. Most just wanted to go home. It wasn't fair to keep people away from their families for so long. After much nagging, the managers decided we should return to Earth.

The boffins in our development laboratory had been doing the piloting so far. Nobody else knew how to operate the equipment. It worried them. None had ever (intentionally) piloted anything in Earth's atmosphere before, let alone a factory. Re-entry into the atmosphere worried them.

I thought they were being daft. I told them so. We could move around in any direction we wanted to, relative to the Earth, using our gravity drive. We didn't need to go fast. I said we should locate the UK, go into geostationary orbit where we could see it and then slowly descend towards it.

They still looked nervous.

"Look, I'd do it myself if I knew how. If it's just a matter of using a joystick, any fool should be able to do it," I said. Me and my big mouth. One of them, a keen gamer, produced a joystick and plugged it in.

"OK, smartarse, let's see you do it," he said. He ushered me to the chair. I sat down and nervously grabbed the joystick.

I did my best. The boffins controlled our speed while I kept us heading directly towards our base. It wasn't too difficult, apart from one near-miss with a commercial aircraft. We landed the factory exactly where it had originally been. Our positioning accuracy amazed me. It didn't seem to be my doing. It looked like we had never left. We switched both bubbles off, and then almost everyone went straight home.

Many people resigned. They could find nothing in their employment contracts about space travel. They no longer trusted the company. It took us a while to get our staffing levels back to normal and to train the new people.

Staff were given time off if they wanted it. I took advantage of the chance to escape the place for a while. Simon lived in the same town as me, so he gave me a lift home, as my Korteener was still in my garage. His car wasn't big enough for my extension ladders, so I had to return for them later.

The next day, I sorted out my crow problem. I removed the sticks and other rubbish from the chimney, and then fitted a new cap to it. The crows complained loudly at first but gave up after a day or two. I was glad I couldn't understand crow. The language would've been terrible.

I settled down in my garage workshop to repair my cat. He was a rescued, artificial cat. I'd rescued him from a bin a few months earlier. I'd been walking past a house several streets away when I'd seen a soggy tail hanging out of a wheelie bin. That alarmed me. I walked over to it, to investigate. When I lifted the lid, I found what I now call Robocat.

I'd asked the owners if they would mind if I took him. They were happy to let me have him, and gave me his remote too. They told me he'd caught fire, so they'd put him out with a foam fire extinguisher. He hadn't worked after that, so they'd thrown him out and bought a new one.

I'd taken him home, cleaned him up thoroughly and then put him aside. It was time to start the repairs, so I got busy. I fitted some replacement batteries that I had lying around, plus some other bits. I soon got him working. He looked just like a real cat (apart from the scorched bit where the original batteries had overheated). Most of the time, he behaved like a real cat.

Having a programmable cat meant he couldn't just go and live with somebody else, as my earlier (real) cat had done. He could be turned off when I wasn't at home.

I kept a close eye on him for the next couple of days. He seemed normal most of the time, but he sometimes did odd things. I'd programmed him to return home in the evenings, but he occasionally seemed to forget.

I sometimes found him in my garden, motionless. He'd been in the middle of doing something when his batteries had run out of power. When I'd repaired him, I'd fitted batteries with a lower capacity than he originally had. I corrected that. Whenever he returned home, he was supposed to curl up and 'sleep' on a special mat (which I bought), which would recharge him.

Robocat became reluctant to return home on time. We'd had a thunderstorm several days earlier. There must've been a lightning strike on the power lines. I heard a deep rumble, quickly followed by a REEEAAARRROWWW!'. Robocat should've been recharging, but I couldn't find him. Then I looked up. I saw him hanging upside down from the ceiling by his claws, above the charging mat. His hair was standing up (or down). He wouldn't let go of the ceiling until I switched him off with the remote.

Sometimes he wanted a saucer of milk. Goodness knows why. It took me a while to find out where it had all gone. I eventually discovered he'd been spraying it from his back end, all over my garden fence. That stuff stinks when it dries out.

I'd been getting complaints about the pong. Some said I should take a bath. I said I didn't need to. I'd already got one. Pressure-washing the fence fixed the pong problem. Robocat got no more milk after that. If he wanted some, I'd give him a nice bowl of wood preserver.

After a few weeks, we were contacted by our American masters to see if we were fit to go back into space. Herbert told them we were.

An urgent message had been received from an alien planet. Our assistance had been requested. Our factory had the resources they needed and was capable of space flight. Herbert said we'd do our best.

That pleased the captain. At last, we had a proper task to do. We kept our bubble configuration the same as before and took off again during the night. Then we headed for the alien planet.

After a week of travelling, someone noticed our faster-than-light drive wasn't active. Oops. By the time we reached the alien planet, they'd fixed the problem themselves. I forget what it was. It took us about an hour to return to Earth. We landed back at F&S, as before.

We couldn't pronounce the name of the alien planet. Sue asked what we should call it. Smythe just said, "Eh?". Nobody argued with him, so we called it Planet A.

Travelling to other planets was quite straightforward if you used the space tunnels. Not all planets (such as Planet A) could be reached that way. Those tunnels acted as shortcuts through space. As long as the special hardware at each end had been positioned and configured correctly, they could allow a space traveller to travel huge distances in a short time. Not many people understood how they worked.

Someone on a TV channel had called them 'space drains', as a joke. They had interviewed an unusual drainage engineer. She'd been using them for years. A woman called Lorraine, from Spain, who went mainly down the drains. A reference, I think, to an old musical. Probably My Fair (-ly humming)

Lady. Having no sense of smell proved to be handy in her line of work. The name stuck. People just called them drains.

Setting them up could sometimes be tricky, as a new drain was not initially secure at the far end. It could be a long way from the intended position. Somebody had to use it to reach the far end, and then position and configure the equipment. It sometimes took ages to do. One spacecraft had yet to return, after being sent years ago to set up the far end of a new drain.

When we landed on the Moon after our unintended maiden flight, the factory had settled at ground level. I found that puzzling. I thought it would be sitting on an unstable mound of soil and be likely to fall off or disintegrate. I visited the laboratory to ask the boffins about it.

One of them told me they had anticipated possible landing problems, as there were foundations, soil, etc. under the factory. During the time between our leaving Earth and our first Moon landing, they'd devised a solution.

Anything the factory's force field bubble came into contact with when it landed would be instantly transported into the hole in the ground where the factory had originally been. Since both bubbles were the same size, the amount of material moved would exactly fill the hole. When we took off again, that material would instantly return to its original position. It would look like we were never there.

This brilliant solution had been devised mainly by the triplets. They were part of the development team. All three were quite clever individually, but when they worked together, they seemed to share a telepathic link. It allowed them to do incredibly complex things that nobody else could do.

Spotty Herbert had been involved with that idea, too. He may have been young and inexperienced, but he still had some good ideas. I never asked how their solution worked. I knew my relatively tiny mind could never understand it. I was just happy that it worked. I hoped I'd never have to fix it.

I settled down and started trying to fix an old machine in one of the factory buildings. I needed some extra tools, which I'd left in my Korteener. I walked to the car park to fetch them.

We had an odd selection of cars in our car park. Some said we had odd people. Simon had an old, small car. He used to say he'd bought it from a car dealer close to a famous French cathedral. He called it the 'Hatchback of Notre Dame'. (Yes, it's an old joke, but it still got a few laughs.) I didn't believe him, as it was right-hand drive.

One of the cars there was owned by a man we called Ron. He wasn't the youngest of people. He didn't like to be called Ronald. To him, it sounded too much like Ron-old. The 'old' bit didn't appeal to him, so we just called him Ron.

Ron didn't work for us originally. After we returned from our first space flight, one of our engineering staff quit. We needed to replace him.

Ron applied. He'd come across as a bit strange. He'd mentioned on his CV that his grandfather had been a time traveller. That hadn't gone down well at his interview. He didn't get the job.

When he'd arrived for his interview, he'd parked his car in our car park. He hadn't had it long. He'd bought it from a dishonest car dealer a week earlier, at a bargain price. Ron thought he could fix almost anything. He'd taken a chance on the car, as he liked the look of it.

Unfortunately, the risk backfired on him, much like the car. It had an old petrol engine, which he'd been told (falsely) was an electric replica.

When he tried to leave after the interview, the car wouldn't start. He had to leave it in our car park. It leaked oil and smelled of petrol. Ron had no sense of smell, so he hadn't noticed.

Ron was supposed to get it removed, but none of the local garages would touch it, for safety reasons (they claimed). He'd have to fix it himself in the car park.

Barry, being an expert in converting cars to electric power, felt sorry for Ron. He offered to help him convert it to electric power. Ron couldn't afford to pay much for parts, so they had to improvise. Barry found an old scrap motor lying around. He thought it would work as a replacement for the existing engine. He told Ron that if he could get it working, he could use it.

Ron worked hard on that motor. He gave it a complete overhaul, even fitting new bearings and repainting the casing. It looked and ran like new after that. Barry was impressed with Ron's work. Ron's attention to detail had been excellent.

Between them, they got the conversion done. The car worked well after that. There was little doubt about Ron's engineering expertise. Barry wanted him on his team, so Ron was employed shortly after that.

Captain Smythe owned an unusual vehicle. He'd won it in a competition. He could choose almost any car he wanted, so he'd asked for a hover car. He'd wanted it metallic blue, with a sunroof, a spoiler, a powerful motor and a top-quality stereo system. (Why would you want a spoiler on a hover car?)

When it finally arrived, it was metallic blue and had the extras he'd wanted. It was much bigger than he'd expected. It had large wheels, brushes on the underside and a big tank on the back. Smythe became the proud(?) owner of a road sweeper. Someone had written the order down wrong. He'd got a Hoover car.

He went ballistic at first. Such custom models couldn't be changed, so there wasn't much he could do about it. It wasn't all bad, though. The powerful motor enabled him to (almost) reach motorway speeds. It was comfortable, with a good stereo system.

The local council sometimes asked him to help with the street cleaning, as he could do it in half the time it would normally take. He had to wait for wet days to avoid stirring up too much dust.

Our First Drain

Not long after our return from Planet A, we heard (unofficially) that we were to set up a new drain. This was puzzling. The plumbing at our site was old, but it still worked well. I wasn't aware of any major issues with it. Neither was Barry, who usually got lumbered with the plumbing tasks. Nevertheless, Barry made sure we had plenty of pipes, joints etc. in stock, just in case.

When the official notification came through, it wasn't what we'd thought.

Our parent company in America had won a contract to set up a new space tunnel. These were commonly known as drains. We'd never done one before, so Barry and I did some research. It seemed quite straightforward.

We were chosen because we could take all the equipment required to set up the far end in one go. Normally this would require several spacecraft, or several trips.

We could probably have got all the equipment into the Bovercraft itself, however we had become accustomed to taking the whole factory with us everywhere we went. The system was working well, so we could see no reason to change it. Being able to relocate an entire factory to another site at short notice was a huge advantage for our business.

We were instructed to relocate to America and land close to the company headquarters. The Americans tried to keep everyone away from our landing site. They told the US mail not to deliver that day, but the message never reached the local postman.

The postman was leaving when we arrived. He looked up, to see us descending towards him. As he wasn't looking where he was going, he veered off the road and got stuck. He got out and legged it, just as we landed.

A few minutes later, the postman walked slowly back to his van, to find the rear half missing. What had originally been the middle of his van was resting on the ground, along with much of the post.

Barry and Ron spotted him and went to help. They knew they shouldn't laugh but couldn't help it. Ron fetched a large trolley from the factory. We lifted the back end of the half-van onto it and secured it to the trolley. The van was front-wheel drive, so the postman drove it back onto the road and out of the way. Barry and Ron covered the whole lot with plastic sheeting to keep the rain off.

Goodness knows how the postman explained it to his boss. How do you lose half a van? The US mail had to send someone to collect him and what was left of the post.

We settled down and started preparing for our task. Our management advised us not to leave the company grounds unless absolutely necessary. Nobody took any notice. Large signs were erected near our car park exit, telling people to 'keep right' if driving and to try not to upset the locals.

The Americans supplied us with everything needed to set up the far end of the new space drain. They set up the local drain entrance themselves. They aimed it at the intended destination, as per usual practice. It was supposed to end about twenty-five light years away.

All seemed well, so we restarted the factory bubble, took off and headed down the new drain. When we reached the other end, we weren't where we expected to be. I suggested returning to Earth and trying again, but Captain Smythe wouldn't have it. He wasn't the type to give up easily.

It took our boffins about two days to figure out where we were and what had gone wrong. The Americans had used Imperial measurements and we had used metric. (Some people never learn.)

We configured the equipment at the drain exit and slowly dragged it to where we thought it should be. It wasn't easy to shift. It needed a lot of power to move it such a distance.

The whole task should have taken us a day or so, but it took us much longer. Smythe wanted us to move faster, but Barry advised him not to. He was worried it might overstress our main power system.

After we completed the task, Barry insisted we wait a couple of days before returning home. He and his team needed to check over our power and drive systems. Everything seemed fine. Then we discovered we'd taken the drain exit to the wrong planet.

Nobody knew about that planet before. We found it uninhabited and rich in valuable rare metals, so it wasn't all bad. Our company still got paid. We had no more drain contracts for a while.

After we took off from America, the missing rear part of the postman's van reappeared there. Nobody would believe the postman's story. We heard that he'd welded the two halves back together himself, then filled and painted over the joins.

It didn't look quite right. The van appeared slightly shorter than it had been originally. The US Mail couldn't legally sell the van due to the poorly done 'cut-and-shut' repairs. The postman had to keep it for several more years. He falsified the annual inspection records until the van became old enough to be officially scrapped.

He hated that van. It kept creaking and squeaking, mainly due to his poor welding. His poor joins in the wiring didn't help either. He wondered why people kept hooting at him. He'd got the wires for the rear indicators crossed over.

While we were in America, two of our more troublesome shop floor workers caused considerable trouble with the local law enforcement. They nearly caused several accidents. They drove on the wrong side of the road and argued with the traffic police.

They used to do welding work in their previous employment, at a shipyard. Some said their faces could 'sink a thousand ships'. One ship did sink, due to poor welding. How they managed to get jobs at F&S was beyond me. They were known as Wide Bertha and Big Con (Connie).

They both took a liking to Phil. Phil, being a big fellow, wasn't normally afraid of people, but he kept well away from those two.

NEGOTIATIONS

We returned to our UK base, landing exactly as before. The precision of our landings impressed me. One of our boffins explained that when we landed, the factory bubble locked onto the one at the site, ensuring a precise landing.

We planned to stay for a month or two. We would do normal manufacturing work, as if we had never left. It would give us time to settle down. There were a few small contracts in the order books, but nothing urgent.

I drove home, feeling glad to be back. When I reached my house, I found the padlock from the gate to my garden lying on the ground nearby, broken. I feared the worst. However, my front door was still locked and undamaged. The garage also looked fine. All the windows were secure. I could find nothing missing.

As I walked around the outside of my house, everything looked normal. Then I remembered my old, obvious security cameras. I'd soon identify the padlock pulverisers. I looked up at one of the cameras. It wasn't there. The thieves had stolen my cameras!

Those cameras were quite old. I'd deliberately used obvious ones as a deterrent. Later designs were self-contained, having built-in recording devices. Mine were too old for that. They transmitted the images wirelessly to recorders in my house, under the stairs.

I had good footage of the thieves. Those cameras were designed for industrial sites, so they had a good transmitting range. I was still getting pictures from them, so the police soon caught the thieves.

The crows had noticed my return. They started waking me up early in the mornings, making a racket outside my bedroom window. I couldn't sleep through that noise. I had to do something about it, so I constructed a removable barrier from thin plywood and soundproofing material, mounted on a wooden frame. My plan was to fit it neatly inside the window opening on the inside, to reduce the noise.

I put it down in the bedroom, leaning it against the wall. I'd switched my cat back on, as he'd been turned off during my absence. I soon wished I hadn't. He got under my feet and tripped me up. I fell heavily onto my newly-made soundproofing board, which snapped in half. Oh well. At least I could say I'd broken the sound barrier without even leaving the house.

I had to go back to the F&S site to fetch something. It wasn't all that important, so while I was there I took the opportunity to explore the nearby forests, as it was a nice day. There were parts of the F&S site that I hadn't even been to. Some people walked their dogs there at the weekends.

Then I remembered the private railway line. The company had acquired it when they bought the site. Few amongst us knew about it. I don't think anyone had bothered to explore it. The former owners had used the line to transport quarried products to the local town.

I drove my Korteener along the narrow road to the start of the railway line. The line had been disused for years. It looked it, as did the remaining items of abandoned rolling stock in the sidings. There were weeds everywhere.

Two small electric railway locomotives remained at the site, which had been used for shunting. They interested me. When I returned to the factory the next day, I asked the local management if I could have a tinker with them. Maybe I could get one going. I think they thought I was potty, but they still let me work on it after hours.

After much work, I got one locomotive working. I used the best batteries and parts from both. (Those batteries were heavy. I nearly did my back in.) I drove the locomotive down the line for a short distance and then back. I checked the batteries. They were fine. I charged them fully, secured them properly and drove the locomotive to the local town.

It was a slow yet peaceful trip, with nice scenery. The end of the line had been fenced off behind the buffers after the sale to F&S. I found a gate had been fitted in the fence. It wasn't locked.

I took the opportunity to do a little shopping in the town. I put my shopping in the locomotive and then drove it back. Then I transferred my shopping to the Korteener. Later, I let the management know what I'd been doing.

The two nameplates from the working locomotive were missing. They'd probably been taken as souvenirs by quarry staff. I made replacements. I carefully painted 'Ivor' on them and fitted them to the locomotive. I added a little oil and dirt to make them look more authentic. Nobody was any the wiser.

Ivor proved handy if we needed things from the town. It wasn't quick, but there wasn't any traffic to worry about. A few trusted people were told about it and allowed to drive it. They liked Ivor. Some of our staff didn't have car driving licences, so it was handy for them. I often had to remind people to put the batteries back on charge after each trip, as some forgot.

Since our first space flight, we hadn't had time to properly adjust to our new situation. Nobody had envisaged that our entire factory would go into space. Factories weren't designed to do that. We would have to make changes.

As things were quiet, we took the opportunity to get better organised. The boffins and Barry's team created proper manuals for the important stuff. People received training where needed. We disposed of many useless items (gardening things, half a dozen Spacehoppers, spares for machines we no longer had, etc.).

After several weeks, we felt much better prepared. We (perhaps foolishly) thought we were ready for almost anything. Smythe wanted to do a few tests and exercises we couldn't do on the ground, so we quietly took off during the night and went into Earth orbit.

We did our tests. Captain Smythe appeared to be enjoying himself, devising hypothetical scenarios to test our reactions. I considered it a pain at times, but with hindsight, I think it was worthwhile.

We still didn't know why the Bovercraft had been built. Nobody cared anyway. The single survivor of the potato crash had partially recovered, but he still had amnesia, so he couldn't tell us.

Just as people were starting to relax and enjoy themselves, we received a message from our head office. We were to hurry to a solar system where two planets were on the brink of war. At least, their inhabitants were. They needed neutral ground for negotiations, and we had some.

We went there and positioned ourselves midway between the two planets. Barry weakened our bubble at one point, just enough to allow the two visiting spacecraft through. We moved our cars out of the way, so they could land in our car park.

The negotiations were to take place in our conference room. Our visitors were shown to their seats. The talks began.

The two races looked alike, yet strange by human standards. They took on human form for our benefit, but it took some concentration. If they weren't careful, they would start to sag in their chairs and flow over the sides.

They had adopted English for communication, as neither wanted to speak the other's language. We didn't have any of those 'universal translator' things you used to see in old science fiction.

The two races had names we couldn't pronounce. They were the second and third alien races we'd encountered, so we called them the Bees and the Seas. They didn't seem to mind.

The two parties were soon shouting at each other and making strange noises. The smell was terrible. Simon called in Angry Charlie, as he could shout louder than any of them. Charlie sat down with them.

He took some pills to calm himself down. He also gave some to the diplomats, who were staring at him, curiously. They also calmed down. The word 'Placebo' had been written on his pill bottle, in big letters. He'd meant to look it up, but he had never quite got around to it. He thought it was the name of the manufacturer.

With help from Charlie, our visitors worked out their differences. Charlie gave each group some of his pills, as they seemed keen to have some. They were supposed to copy them, but they didn't. We had to supply them with those pills for years afterwards. Something in them had them addicted.

I wondered what would've happened if they'd needed to use our toilets. The doors had no 'Ladies' or 'Gents' signs. I'd meant to attend to the matter, but I always had other things to do. It wouldn't have mattered much with them anyway.

Phil always wanted to help when he could, so I gave him the task of fitting the signs to the toilet doors. A simple task, I thought, well within his abilities. If I'd known he was illiterate, I'd have given him signs with the usual pictograms, rather than words.

He resorted to trial and error, often the latter. That caused predictable problems. It would've been simpler if he'd just asked somebody.

He got it done eventually, although some signs were the wrong way up. Simon asked him to put them all the same way up. Soon, they were all the wrong way up. He said it was for Australian visitors. Phil meant well. I wasn't going to argue with him. I quietly fitted them the right way up when I had the time. I also rubbed off the small smiley faces Phil had pencilled on the corner of each sign.

The Kidnapping

Not long after the peace talks, an odd rumour started going around the factory. Apparently, one of the daughters of a top manager had disappeared. Some people thought she'd been kidnapped. The manager in question used to work at the F&S site, before the sacking of Mr Fiddler and Mr Snitch. He'd had frequent arguments with them, before moving to the American headquarters. Our local management told us to quietly investigate the suspected disappearance.

It took us quite a while to discover any details. Reports were often conflicting. I tried to track down the source of the rumours. I failed, but was almost certain that they originated on our shop floor. The one thing that was consistent was the missing person's name. It was Lorna.

We started investigating her whereabouts, but could find no sign of her. I tried using the old Internet. I sent some emails. All that came back was spam. We put it in the fridge.

I asked around to see if anyone knew what she looked like. Several people thought they knew, but no two descriptions were the same. Maybe they weren't all describing the same daughter.

Simon eventually found a picture of her on an office wall. Her father had used that office. Then I remembered we had a Lorna working for us somewhere. The face in the photo looked familiar, so I searched the factory myself.

I found her working alone in a small, almost forgotten office. She was sitting at a computer, doing general typing work.

"Hi Lorna," I said. "We've been looking everywhere for you."

"Why?" she said, looking surprised.

"Rumours have been going around that you'd been kidnapped."

"I can assure you I haven't been."

"So I see. How long have you been stuck in this office?" I asked.

"A few weeks now. I like it here. It's nice and quiet."

"Wouldn't you prefer to be with other people, on the shop floor?"

"Erm... not really. I don't like it there anymore."

That concerned me. Lorna usually didn't say much, but I could still remember her happily chatting with other people. Something was wrong. I had my suspicions, but I needed evidence.

I asked her about her father. I wanted to know why she'd never mentioned him. She said she didn't want to use her father's position to get a job, so she'd kept quiet about it. Her surname had changed after her (brief) marriage.

I reported back to Smythe. He announced over the factory Tannoy system that 'we' had found her. I also told him about my suspicions. Smythe agreed with me. I asked a few people on the shop floor if they knew anything about it.

We had two problematic women working for us. They were known as Big Con and Wide Bertha (the same two I mentioned earlier). They'd been causing trouble for some time and had no respect for anyone. They were often close to being sacked, but they always got away with it somehow. I heard rumours later that they'd only got their positions by intimidating other interviewees into withdrawing, and by lying on their CVs.

Several shop floor staff told me that Lorna had been verbally bullied by those two. Ned was the most outspoken.

"I feel sorry for that poor Sheila," said Ned. "Those two used to wind her up."

"What sort of things did they do?" I asked.

"They kept pinching her stuff, then laughing at her. One of them stole her tucker. I think they ate half of it."

"What else?" I asked.

"I saw one of them cut the mains cable on Lorna's machine. Big flash, there was. Stupid sod. Lucky the cutters had plastic handles."

"Lucky for them, not me. I had to replace the cable."

"Lorna hates it here. She's been keeping herself to herself. They bullies call her 'Lorna the loner'. I think they've got kangaroos loose in the top paddock," said Ned.

Our management had wanted to sack them for some time, but they couldn't. Employment laws were strict back then. I wanted them gone too. They often broke things, which I had to fix. They usually did it on purpose. I called them the 'damn busters'. It irritated me. Production was frequently delayed until I completed the repairs.

Simon and I started investigating. We hid tiny cameras near where the troublemakers worked. We recorded them laughing and joking about Lorna. They had started the kidnapping rumours themselves and had even worse things planned.

We took the evidence to our management. They immediately terminated the employment of our two troublemakers. They got the sack (half each). Captain Smythe got the job of telling them. He'd wanted to do that for some time. I think he was the only person they were scared of. He hated bullies and really let them have it.

They were gone within minutes. I removed their biometric data from the door entry systems to stop them from getting back in. Smythe had a long talk with Lorna afterwards. He asked her to tell him immediately if anything like that happened again.

Lorna seemed much happier after that. She spent less time on her own. I sometimes saw her working in the main production area, assembling things.

While we were still home at the F&S site, our management asked us to look after some international visitors for a couple of days. Someone would have to show them around. Captain Smythe claimed to be too busy, so Simon got the job.

Simon had been quieter than most when he first started with us. That changed after a few months, as his confidence increased. He became much more sociable. His sense of humour became very apparent. If a practical joke was going on, it often involved Simon. He could wind somebody up with a completely straight face. I could never master that.

Simon started showing the visitors around. They included a tall man, wearing a ten-gallon hat. Simon politely told him he didn't need to wear a hat indoors, but was ignored. Simon joked later it was to hide the shape of his head.

Simon was in a slightly silly mood. Every time the hat-wearer seemed to be about to say something, Simon would start speaking. He soon got bored with that and deliberately paused.

The man spoke up.

"Say, boy, you seen any of them haggis critters around here?"

"No, can't say that I have," replied Simon. A slight grin appeared on his face. Sue was standing at the back of the room, behind the visitors. She tried to get his attention and silently mouthed "Noooo!!!" at him, but to no avail. Simon couldn't let this one go.

"The land ones mostly died out about two centuries ago. They were hunted almost to extinction to make sporrans. I think there might be some in the lake, though," continued Simon.

"What lake?"

"It's not far from here," said Simon. "It's called Loch Ankie."

"What in tarnation would they be doing in a lake?" said our visitor.

"Swimming," said Simon, with a straight face. "They're sea-haggises, you know. You can see them in the water at night because they glow in the dark."

"I never saw no lakes when I came here," said the visitor.

"That's because it's hidden," said Simon.

"Hidden? Where? How do you hide a lake?"

"It's hidden in the sea."

"I never saw it..."

"You wouldn't. It's underwater." He paused.

"I think you're having me on!" said the visitor.

"Ah sure am!" said Simon, loudly.

Our visitor turned around, looking for support from the others. They just laughed at him. (I think he was French.)

I heard a rumour about him later. Apparently, he'd gone to where this 'lake' was supposed to be, in a boat, at night, searching for sea-haggises. He'd seen lights under the water. He threw a wooden spear at them. He missed, of course, but the frogmen carrying out an urgent repair to an undersea cable were furious.

Deliveries

I was having a day off, at home. It was about mid-morning and I hadn't had much breakfast. I could feel my stomach rumbling. Time for some beans on toast, I thought. I started heating the beans, in the microwave. Then I remembered the toaster had packed up several days earlier.

I wished it had packed up and left. It nearly set fire to my kitchen when it refused to pop the toast up. I suppose it served me right for buying a cheap toaster. It would have to go back. Meanwhile, I made my toast using a fork and a hot air gun.

I would have to select a carrier to return the toaster. I hadn't done that for a while. Fierce competition between parcel delivery companies often resulted in daft gimmicks. Most failed. Some tried using small robots for deliveries, but they were easy targets for thieves.

Some tried using drones. They often used cheap ones or forgot to charge the batteries. A couple fell from the sky and got robbed. A few were shot down by disgruntled homeowners living near the delivery depot, who were sick of the noise.

One delivery company tried using a robot kangaroo. It had a zip-up pouch, for local deliveries. It was quick as it bounced along. It wore boxing gloves to scare off potential attackers. The local council complained, as the bouncing was causing pavement damage. The kangaroo had to walk after that.

Later, the same company started using the walking kangaroo for milk deliveries. Some called it a Cowaroo.

It fell over when it walked into a pothole. That damaged the 'walk' mode, so it reverted to bouncing. People complained that they'd asked for milk, not butter. It's a good job cows don't bounce like that.

In the end, I chose the cheapest carrier. It was a cheap toaster, after all.

At F&S, we did many large deliveries, often between planets. Stuff often got left on wooden pallets in the car park. It should've been kept indoors, but sometimes wasn't, as it never rained inside the bubble. People became complacent, cutting corners.

On one planet we visited, that attitude caught us out. We'd been there several times before. The planet had a lower atmospheric pressure than Earth. We were normally careful to manually equalise the pressures inside and outside the bubble before turning the bubble off. On this occasion, we didn't. I think everyone assumed that somebody else would do it, so nobody did.

We had some delicate cargo with us. When the bubble was switched off, much of the cargo was damaged. A few factory buildings were also damaged. Some had shattered windows. One Portakabin suffered badly. A few people outside the Bovercraft complained of hearing problems. There wasn't anything we couldn't fix, but we learnt a lesson. After that, the engineers added safety interlocks to make it difficult to turn the bubble off if the inside and outside pressures weren't near enough equal.

We needed to repeat the entire delivery at our own expense. The managers weren't pleased. From then on, we stored anything fragile in a specially prepared building, capable of withstanding sudden changes in outside pressure.

I remember somebody coming up with a 'clever' idea for transporting goods to our home site very quickly. He suggested that we just land on the goods. That would send them instantly to our home base.

It wasn't a good idea. Nobody would have been able to get at the goods due to the bubble at the site, which had to be permanently active while we were away. We also had no way of knowing what was going on at our home base while we were on another planet. If we'd taken off too early, the results could have been disastrous.

I think it was Phil's idea. He meant well, as usual. I sometimes found Phil a little gullible. During his time working at the zoo, one of his colleagues had tried to persuade him that the trombone had been invented by giraffes. They said that giraffes used trombones to confuse elephants. Then they hid the trombones high in the trees, where the elephants couldn't reach them.

Phil wasn't convinced. There weren't any trees in the giraffe enclosure. A short while later, someone tried to convince him that the penguins spoke Japanese during the night and that the monkeys were trying to hypnotise him. Phil was normally quite docile, but this nearly got him arrested for GBH. Nobody would go near him for a week.

Amy

Amy had been on board the Bovercraft when we took off on our first (unintended) flight. We were legally required to have at least one medically qualified person with us at all times, so we needed to employ somebody. Since she was the only suitable medically trained person on board, Amy got the job.

It was often a lonely job. Early plans to employ additional medical staff had been forgotten. She had the entire medical department (and all that fancy equipment) to herself.

Amy had many years of experience as a qualified vet. She had only come on board originally to microchip someone's black Labrador and give the dog a check-up. Amy could find nothing wrong with the dog, mainly because she couldn't catch him.

The last time the dog had been taken to a vet, he'd left there feeling sore and incomplete. He could smell a vet (or a doctor) from some distance away. Maybe it was the smell of hand sanitiser. He didn't want to lose anything else, so he kept well away from Amy.

Amy had trained to be a nurse before becoming a vet. She'd done all the training, but she hadn't done the final exams, due to being ill at the time. She switched to veterinary work shortly after that. Her employment with us was conditional on her passing her nursing exams as soon as possible, and then studying to become a proper doctor.

She had become accustomed to dealing with animals, rather than humans. Animals can't tell you what's wrong with them. She sometimes forgot to ask people about their symptoms.

Amy studied hard and learned quickly. It wasn't long before she felt up to dealing with almost any medical emergency. She wanted to try out the fancy equipment on somebody, but nobody seemed to be ill.

Amy was a nice person. She genuinely wanted to help people. She started going around asking people how they felt. People avoided her, for fear of being diagnosed with something. She gave up trying. She used her spare time to revise for her nursing exams, which she soon passed.

Amy was a little shorter than most and quite thin. People joked that if she turned sideways, she would disappear. I thought that was rather cruel. I would sometimes take the time to talk to her, after first assuring her I had no ailments. I think she appreciated my company. I could answer her technical questions about the equipment.

One day, a man turned up at her medical facility. She immediately told him to lie down on the medical bed.

"But..." he complained.

"Just keep still," said Amy.

"But I only came here to..."

"Shush!"

He shushed, looking worried. He decided to wait and see what happened.

She carefully examined the displays, determined to discover his complaint. After about ten minutes, she gave up and asked what was wrong with him.

"Nothing!" he replied. "I only came here to deliver this letter!"

"Oh, I'm so sorry," she said, looking embarrassed. "I thought there was something wrong with you."

"Maybe that's why I had so much trouble getting this job," he muttered.

"I didn't mean it like that."

He handed her the letter, told her not to worry about it and left. Amy made a point of talking to her patients after that, rather than trying to discover their ailments from scratch.

I remember visiting her at her medical facility one day when I was bored and a little drunk. I asked her if she'd got anything for a hangover.

"Beer usually works," said Amy, with a grin.

"I mean, do you have anything to get rid of one?"

"Well, if one were to jump off a cliff, that would get rid of one," she said. She was clearly in a silly mood, like me. Before I could reply, someone else walked in. The visitor was a larger-than-average woman (or so she thought), who wanted to know how to lose weight.

"If you hide it somewhere safe, you'll soon lose it," I said.

"Alan, be quiet!" said Amy, with a sort of annoyed half-grin. She spoke more directly to the visitor.

"Do you have any scales?" asked Amy.

"Do you think she might be turning into a fish?" I said.

"Alan! Stop it!" Amy looked a bit cross, so I thought I'd better leave. I'd have to find my own hangover cure.

Phil, the former zookeeper, got along well with Amy. He also liked animals. He boasted that he could get them to do things that nobody else could.

He told Amy about what he'd done at one of his many former jobs. He'd worked on a farm, where his physical strength often came in handy. While his boss was on holiday, Phil had been left to look after the sheep and several new sheepdogs. Phil wanted to train the dogs.

Then he had a 'better' idea. He planned to train the sheep instead, and not bother with the dogs. Things didn't go as he'd planned. The sheep became more confident and managed to herd the dogs into the pen. The dogs became scared of sheep, so they had to be re-homed. Phil lost his job.

Tied up

We had become good at what we were doing. We had completed several major contracts on time and well within budget. Our general technical expertise and experience had increased considerably. With that in mind, our American masters trusted us to set up more space drains.

All were completed without issues. Our technical staff devised new equipment, specially designed to make setting up new drains much easier. We became good at it. Our prices were competitive. We soon earned a good reputation.

Ours wasn't the only company setting up space drains. Our competitors usually managed it without problems, but not always. On one occasion, our main rival ran into unexpected difficulties.

They'd completed several similar projects before without trouble, yet this one was driving them nuts. The drain starting point seemed fine, but the far end couldn't be set up properly. The problems were causing delays.

Only small spaceships could get through. One larger spaceship had been stuck in it for weeks. There seemed to be a restriction somewhere. The far end of the drain was short of where it should have been. They'd tried everything they could think of, but had failed to find the problem.

They were in trouble. The agreed completion date wasn't far off, so they reluctantly asked us for help. We agreed to investigate but warned them it wouldn't be cheap. They accepted our price, on the strict understanding that if we failed to fix the problem, we wouldn't get paid. We set off, keen to find fault with our competitor's work.

Smythe thought it best to go to the far end by conventional means, as we had a faster-than-light drive. It took us a while to get there, but we knew we'd have become stuck if we'd used the new drain.

We found the far end. Apart from being slightly short of where it should have been, it looked fine. We couldn't find any hardware or configuration issues.

Simon came up with an idea. Our newly designed equipment allowed us to visualise the drain from the outside. We used it to follow the drain exterior back, looking for issues.

We soon found the problem. The other company had made several navigation errors when positioning the equipment at the far end. They'd been moving it about all over the place. They had no way to visualise the drain, so they couldn't see they'd tied it in a knot. Trying to pull the far end equipment to the correct position had tightened the knot.

We untied it and set everything up the way it should have been. That released the stuck spacecraft, which appeared from the drain exit. We returned to Earth (via the drain, to prove that it worked as it should). We received more money from our competitor for getting them out of trouble than we would've done if we'd won the contract ourselves in the first place.

We occasionally encountered older races, who didn't approve of those space drains. They seemed to look down on us for using such 'primitive' technology but were too polite to say anything. Their technology was far more advanced than ours. They didn't need space drains.

We went home again, for another rest. We did that quite often. The management didn't mind, as we were making good money. I went back to my house.

I needed something to do. I understood modern electronics well, so I decided to modify Robocat. I wasn't always able to reach the phone in time (we still used landlines back then), so I modified the cat.

He would find me quickly if the phone rang. He would make 'purrr-purrr, purrr-purrr' noises and his eyes would light up bright blue. A bit scary in the dark, I thought.

I wanted to do more checks on him, but I couldn't find my multimeter. I looked everywhere for it. No sign of it. I couldn't understand it, as I rarely took it out of my workshop.

I wondered if my smartphone might have moved it. I disliked that thing, but I needed it sometimes. Some smartphones were quite big. Many could fly, usually to a charging point, to recharge themselves. They became known as dronephones. Some could carry small loads. Mine could.

I found my phone and checked its logs. It wasn't guilty. The house windows were closed, so my multimeter couldn't have been taken by anyone else's phone. It made no sense.

I ended up buying a nice new multimeter. This time, I took the precaution of fitting a tiny tracking device inside the battery compartment.

There were plans to ban smartphones. Only basic 'dumb' mobile phones would be allowed. Smartphone addiction had become a recognised medical condition. Those things were much too clever and sometimes scared people. Phones occasionally flew off through open windows, for no obvious reason. Nobody knew where they went.

I found Robocat in my garden the other day, face-to-face with another artificial cat. Both used the same basic software. They were going through the same cat-like behaviour pattern, albeit out of sync. They'd become caught in a software loop. When I turned off the scorched one (mine), the other one ran away.

Maybe I should've bought a Robodog. The company that made them had tried making all sorts of animals. They stopped making cows, as nobody had any use for them. You can't get milk from a robotic cow, although someone was daft enough to try. (Does a vending machine count?) They even made a robot elephant. It destroyed much of their factory before they could turn it off. It didn't get past the prototype stage (or their main gate, fortunately).

Another thing they didn't quite get right was a robot dog with a built-in radio. They called it a Golden Receiver. It received more criticism than anything else. The sound came from the back end, to avoid affecting the microphones in the ears. They put the antenna in the tail. Not a good idea. You don't want a wagging antenna in poor signal areas. Real dogs wouldn't go near it.

JOYCE

We were back on Earth. I happened to be talking to (spotty) Herbert, our youngest manager, about things in general. We discussed health and safety, as there had been several avoidable accidents in the preceding weeks. I reminded him we still needed a health and safety person. I suggested it was probably a legal requirement.

He agreed, so we started advertising for someone. We needed somebody well-qualified, who would be prepared to be away from Earth for weeks at a time. Finding someone suitable wasn't as easy as we expected. We ended up advertising worldwide.

After much searching, we found a candidate in Australia who matched our requirements. Our all-female interview panel had long felt there were too many men among our staff, so they picked a woman.

Joyce's qualifications were excellent. Her previous employer gave her a good reference, so she got the job. She got along well with everyone she met before her interview. I've always thought that to be a good sign.

I think her looks might have helped her a little too. She was slightly taller than average, slim and relatively young for someone so well-qualified. She was a long-haired redhead, with brown eyes and too much makeup (in my opinion).

Joyce told me later she had personal reasons for wanting to get away from Australia. She'd divorced her racing driver husband several weeks earlier. She used to call him the Ozzard of Whizz. The stress of always worrying about him had been wearing her down. The last straw was when she'd caught him with another woman, shortly after winning a race. You could say that he won and lost on the same day.

On her first day, Joyce was sent to see Amy, who gave her a thorough check-up. They got along well. Amy had been spending much time on her own in her medical department. She needed a good friend.

Joyce was allocated an office in the factory buildings, plus a disused Portakabin as temporary accommodation. She soon settled in. After a couple of weeks, we noticed new safety signs appearing all over the factory. She also organised the inspection and calibration of the laboratory (and other) equipment.

She persuaded me to do the portable appliance testing, as I had already passed the required exam. At least, she thought she had. I'd been doing it anyway, but I didn't tell her that until much later.

I thought there would be fewer accidents after taking her on. When I checked with Amy, she told me the number of minor accidents had slightly increased. The new patients were almost always male, with minor head injuries. They had been walking into things when Joyce passed by. A smile from her was often followed by a 'crunch' or an 'ow!'. Amy told me she suspected that Joyce might be doing it on purpose, for a laugh.

Amy didn't like Joyce doing that. I think she was slightly jealous. She advised Joyce to stop wearing makeup and to try to look as dull as possible. Joyce didn't like it, but she complied. To her surprise, it worked. People found her easier to talk to after that, so she stuck with it.

Joyce had a greater sense of humour than most people. She had been involved in several harmless practical jokes in her previous employment, although we didn't know that then.

After a month or two, the silly stuff started. Her accommodation and her office were on opposite sides of the factory. People would see her walking to work each day.

She liked attention, and this was her chance to do something daft. Each day, as she walked to work, she would look a little more silly. She would revert to normal once she got to her office.

The changes were quite subtle at first, but they soon became more obvious. She started wearing brightly-coloured wigs. Her footwear was different (often louder and heavier) each day. Then came the light-green moustache. It got her the attention she wanted and plenty of laughs, so she continued. She made at least one more change each day.

By the time Simon spotted her, she was wearing a bright purple wig, blue waterproof trousers and red braces. On her head was a white crash helmet on the wrong way around. It had eye, nose and mouth holes cut in it. She'd painted it to look like a panda's head, with drawn glasses on. Her flippers slapped loudly on the smooth floor as she walked.

Simon had been told to stop her. He was supposed to tell her off, but he couldn't. He advised her to dress normally, which she did after that. Simon was pleased that he'd found a fellow joker.

Joyce really knew her subject. New safety procedures were written, which prevented several injuries. She gained considerable respect from people, although she got a bit carried away at times.

Some projects were delayed due to her safety concerns. She was usually right, but sometimes it went too far. Some people called her Joist, because she held things up. Simon had a quiet word with her about it. They agreed that difficult health and safety decisions should only be made by him or the captain.

People liked Joyce. Sometimes people would turn up at her Portakabin after normal working hours, to discuss (they said) health and safety issues. She put up with it at first, but she soon found it annoying. She had me put up an obvious CCTV camera outside her Portakabin, with a red flashing light on it.

Then she stuck a big sign on the Portakabin door, with a black exclamation mark on a filled yellow triangle. The words under it read, 'Warning – occupant likely to explode without warning'.

I remember seeing someone walk up to the door, read the sign and then quietly walk away.

NOT THE MAN I WAS

Several years before I started working for F&S, I had fallen on hard times. I was unemployed and getting little money in benefits. The bills were becoming a problem. (It occurred to me that one way to reduce the Bills would be to stop naming people William. But I digress.)

I was short of money. Various unofficial odd jobs earned me a little. I sometimes fixed things for people, but it was often hard work for little gain.

Then I came across an advertisement in a local newspaper. Volunteers were needed to take part in medical experiments. The company wanted to develop products that could slow down (or stop) human ageing.

Such things always worried me. Some unfortunate volunteers had suffered greatly due to similar experiments. I found the money being offered very tempting, so I eventually decided to risk it.

I considered myself quite healthy, even for a thirty-five-year-old. I thought it would be nice to not get any older, so I signed up for the trials, not seriously expecting them to work.

There were several to choose from. They asked me which one I wanted to try.

"All of them," I said, jokingly, as I badly needed the money. I didn't expect them to take me seriously.

I was unconscious when they administered the stuff, as one of the tests needed me to be. When I woke up, I found out they'd given me the lot. I felt stupid and demanded extra money. They reluctantly handed it over. I asked if they were insured, but I never got a proper answer.

Other people signed up for those trials too. Some suffered from side effects. They claimed against the company, which had forgotten to get us to sign disclaimers beforehand. The company tried to get us to sign the papers afterwards, but were told where to go. They went out of business not long afterwards.

I looked in the mirror several weeks later and noticed a few grey hairs on my head. I knew it would happen sooner or later, but I still found the discovery alarming. I guessed that either the experimental products had all failed, or I hadn't actually been given any of them. Maybe I was the 'control' subject. I didn't feel any ill effects, so I soon forgot about it.

A year or so later, I remembered the grey hairs and looked for them. When I looked in the mirror, I couldn't find any. My hairline didn't seem to be receding as much as before. I also realised that a slight ache I'd had for years had vanished. Odd...

By the time I started with F&S, I'd long forgotten about it. That was until I noticed someone from the personnel department looking at me strangely. I asked her what was up. She pointed to the ceiling. Then she said that according to the company records, I was forty-one. I looked about thirty, maybe less. I pointed out that some people age faster than others, but she didn't accept that.

That worried me. I thought about inventing a story about a new experimental hair restorer. Then I thought better of it, as I knew it wouldn't work. I disliked lying to people. Besides, I didn't have experimental hair.

I eventually said I was taking part in secret experiments with semi-permanent wigs. She wasn't technically minded, so I managed to 'blind her with science' to the point where she gave up.

Phew. She left us after we returned from our first trip into space, so I was off the hook. I started adding a little grey to my hair from time to time, to make myself look older. I also avoided letting Amy examine me unless absolutely necessary.

Not long after that, an old school friend contacted me. She had been trying to organise a sixth-form reunion and had managed to track me down. She sent me a recent photo of herself and some of her friends. I recognised them, but they all looked older than me.

I wanted to go, but I felt it wasn't worth the risk. People were bound to ask why I looked so young. I reluctantly declined the invitation, giving some rather feeble excuses.

I took more care of my appearance after that. I tried cutting my own hair to give the false impression of a receding hairline, but I couldn't maintain that. It looked odd after a week or two. I also bought cheap reading glasses, removed the lenses and fitted plain glass instead. I used them occasionally for close-up work, even though I didn't need to, if I thought anyone might be watching me.

I kept well clear of opticians, even when they offered me free eye tests.

DEEP SPACE CUSTARD

We'd been hearing rumours. Strange things were happening in a remote part of space. People from several other races we knew had been there, but none would tell us about what had happened to them. They just advised us to keep away from there.

Our upper management sent us to investigate. They thought it would be good for the company's image if we fixed the problem. I could hear Captain Smythe muttering and cursing as he passed me in the corridor, as we'd recently returned from that direction.

There were no space drains to take us there, so getting there by conventional means took us weeks.

During the trip, we took the opportunity to get a few overdue tasks done. Barry's team carried out routine maintenance and repairs. Others practiced using the equipment and generally tidied the place up.

The Labrador got more exercise than usual. Many people wanted to take him for walks, but they weren't so keen to clean up after him. Amy still couldn't get near him.

The boffins upgraded our scanners, so we'd be well-prepared when we reached our destination. We couldn't scan through the factory walls, so the boffins placed additional remote sensors near the bubble limits.

Before we left Earth, some of our boffins had been experimenting with gravity. It had occurred to them that it might be possible to send messages by modulating gravity waves. They had done several successful test transmissions.

As we approached our destination, they noticed something strange. The gravity wave detector was detecting signals that weren't theirs. There appeared to be information in the signals.

It took them a while to decode and translate the information. Other races had received our experimental transmissions. They weren't pleased with us. We had caused considerable interference with their communications. We had to apologise and cease our experiments.

When we reached our destination, we stopped and looked around. We saw nothing unusual. Our amateur astronomers also found nothing, even with the telescope.

We tried our new scanners. After much searching, we still found nothing out of the ordinary. We were about to give up and go home when the scanners detected something. A large, fast-moving object could be seen heading our way. It looked round, mostly flat and slightly wobbly. Smythe, sitting in his captain's chair, asked to see it on our main display.

We couldn't believe our eyes. It looked like a massive custard pie, about a hundred yards in diameter. Smythe assumed it to be somebody's joke, so he did nothing about it. Then it hit us.

The outside of the force field bubble looked a right mess. Smythe thought it best to leave the area. As we turned around to go home, another pie hit us.

Navigating with our bubble covered with custard wasn't easy. We couldn't just go outside the bubble and wipe the custard from in front of the sensors. We didn't dare collapse it either, as to do so would have exposed the factory to space and huge quantities of custard.

As we approached Earth, Smythe told Barry, our chief engineer, to find a solution. The bubble would have to stay active until we removed the custard. Barry suggested that we could wash off the mess if we went underwater.

We picked a quiet location over the sea, where we hoped nobody would see us. Trying to submerge didn't go well. The bubble power had to be turned up considerably to keep the water out. The bubble generator soon overheated, so we had to stop. We eventually found that as long as we used our own gravity within the bubble, we could roll over and over on the sea surface and wash the bubble clean.

Someone wanted to know why we couldn't have just hovered over the sea, upside down, and turned the bubble off. Surely the custard would've just fallen into the sea. I explained that anything not secured would have fallen in too, including our cars, as our artificial gravity would have been off.

I discussed the matter with pie victims from other races after we got back. They were hard to track down. They wouldn't admit to anything until I explained what had happened to us.

There seemed to be no defence against those pies. Missiles, energy beams etc. just went straight through. Cleaning up after a pie hit took ages. Nobody went there twice.

Someone attempted to destroy an approaching pie by firing a time-delayed missile at it, but they got the timing wrong. It went straight through the pie and exploded just behind it. The craft got blasted with custard. That part of space became known as the Custard Zone.

Our management asked Smythe to provide a written report on what had happened to us. He refused. The incident seemed to have affected him more than anyone else. Some thought something custard-related in his past might be responsible. We never did find out what. Maybe he had a custard allergy. Simon ended up writing the report.

There were reports of custard slicks washing up on beaches. It washed away eventually, but some people complained that their fish tasted of custard. Nobody could explain why. We said nothing.

TIME TROUBLE

We spent much of our time travelling around the galaxy. Boredom became an issue on long trips. There were plenty of dull, monotonous tasks to do, but nobody wanted to do them. Smythe always had something he wanted done. People soon learnt not to ask him.

Simon found an old, full-size piano keyboard at a car boot sale. He got it cheap, as it didn't work. I fixed it for him. He knew I probably would when he bought it. He planned to learn to play it. It would keep him busy when he had nothing else to do. Fortunately, it had a headphone socket. I think he hoped to impress Joyce, although he never said as much.

Those long trips gave our boffins more time to work on their (sometimes daft) projects. They were always trying to improve things, even when they didn't need to be improved. Some people just can't leave things alone.

The boffins wanted to upgrade our main drive system. They were aware of the effects of our speed on the passage of time and thought they had compensated for it. They had to be careful we didn't end up arriving before we left. I think they were rather enjoying themselves.

Unfortunately, they forgot that the artificial gravity system and the laboratory were fed from the same power feed. If their experiments used a lot of power, they sometimes affected the artificial gravity.

The effects usually weren't noticeable. Nobody complained, unless they were trying to lose weight. Scales became impossible to calibrate. Some were chucked in the skip.

Major modifications to our primary drive system had been carried out. The boffins claimed the changes would reduce our travelling time dramatically. Extensive simulations had been done. It was time to do some real tests.

I wasn't entirely happy with the changes, so I carefully documented them. I took many photographs before and after the modifications were done. I wanted to make sure the changes could be reversed if necessary.

When the time for the first proper test arrived, many people were in the laboratory or the bridge to watch. The boffins powered up the drive system. They used a low power setting initially, then slowly increased the power. Everything looked good. We were going much faster than usual. They increased the power. We soon reached speeds previously thought impossible. The control desk operator's hair began to stand up.

Suddenly, we heard a sharp 'BANG!', accompanied by a bright flash from the control desk. The operator fell backwards off his chair. We accelerated rapidly and kept doing so. We couldn't slow down. Sparks were coming from the control desk. Nobody could get near it without getting zapped.

We watched the monitors. A green glow had formed ahead of our protective bubble, getting brighter. The bubble became egg-shaped, pointed at the rear.

Our artificial gravity went haywire. Some people floated about, while others couldn't get off the floor. We were out of control.

Just then, Phil stumbled in. He had his ridiculous glasses on, so he couldn't see properly. He tripped over a cable, pulling a mains plug from the wall socket. It fed the control desk. We slowed down rapidly and stopped. Barry got up off the floor, put lots of masking tape over the desk plug and labelled it 'Do not use'.

For the next week, Phil felt very pleased with himself. Smythe ordered that the experiment be abandoned, permanently. I felt it wasn't his decision to make. My photos came in handy for returning the drive system to normal.

The new parts were removed from the control desk. I took them and hid them away. Barry wired the power to the artificial gravity system to a separate feed after that.

The injuries kept Amy busy for days afterwards. Our great speed during the experiment had taken us a considerable distance from Earth, so it took us months to get back home.

We didn't want anyone else to discover the failed experiment, so the boffins tinkered slightly with time during our return journey. It would look like we had only been away for a week.

Someone went to check on the dog. She found him asleep in his basket. He'd slept through the whole thing.

We were close to home. Captain Smythe and I were talking. Just general topics at first, but he appeared to be leading up to something. He told me he wanted us to be better armed. I said we'd look silly with more arms. He wasn't pleased. Little sense of humour, that man. I said I'd look into it.

I spoke to Simon first. He wasn't happy about us having more weapons. He wondered if a way could be found to defend ourselves without destroying anything.

When we spoke to the triplets, they proposed a solution. Maybe they could devise something that moved the target slightly back through time. That way, we'd have more time to escape, with no harm done. Simon gave them the go-ahead to develop something.

A month later, they showed us a small prototype device, which they'd called a 'time bomb'. It looked like a black cannonball, only not as heavy.

One of the boffins picked it up.

"We're rather pleased with it," he said. "You just set the time delay to activation, like this," he said. He inserted a small screwdriver into a hole in the device. He turned it until the 3-digit display read '2.00'.

"Then you set the amount of time to send the device back by." He inserted the screwdriver into another hole.

"Like this... hang on... this doesn't feel right." I heard a crunch. The display changed to 'FFF'.

"Oh no!"

"What's wrong?" I asked.

"I think I've broken the control."

"Then switch it off," I said.

"I can't. The switch is part of the control I've just broken. It'll go off in under two minutes!"

"Give it here," said Simon. He grabbed it and ran off. He passed Smythe in the corridor.

"Stop running!" shouted Smythe.

"Sod off!" replied Simon, loudly. He ran to the car park and threw the device as far as he could. It bounced along the tarmac, coming to rest against a sack of potatoes.

Smythe caught him up.

"You can't talk to me like that!" said Smythe. Simon was exhausted. He pointed to the device.

"That's a time travel device. It'll go off at any moment," replied Simon.

There was a bright green flash, and then the potatoes and the device were gone. So was part of the tarmac.

"That thing has just sent a sack of potatoes back to goodness knows when," he said, still breathing heavily.

Smythe's face turned pale. He realised what had probably happened to them.

"Nobody must ever know what just happened here. Don't tell anyone," he said. "Management must never find out."

I had caught up by then, so I heard what Smythe had said.

"You're not to make any more of those things. Their development must stop immediately," said Smythe. We understood his reasons.

Smythe didn't know that several earlier prototypes still existed. Nobody dared to tell him. The boffins hid them carefully, where they thought Smythe would never look.

I talked with Ron shortly after that. I remembered the matter of his grandfather being a time traveller coming up at his interview. People had laughed at him at the time, but I knew him well enough by then to know he wasn't a nutcase. I asked him about it.

He told me his grandfather was an enthusiastic inventor in his younger days. He'd invented something that allowed him to see into the past. Then he'd found that if he reached into the window of the device, he could pull small items into his present. It wasn't easy, as it took a lot of power to bring through anything big. Foolish too, I thought. He could have lost his hand.

Old 'retro' electronics products were popular back then. Ron's grandfather planned to take small items from the past and sell them in his present.

He hoped to take small radios from a 1960s electronics shop. He would leave money on the shop counter to pay for them. He would also leave a note explaining that the radios were needed urgently.

It seemed like a good plan. He had everything set up ready. The money and the note were ready, in a large envelope. Ron's grandfather activated the machine and positioned the time window near the back of the 1960s radio shop during the night. As he tried to take a radio from one of the shelves, lightning struck the power lines near his workshop.

There were bright green flashes everywhere. His arm tingled. He grabbed the radio, pulled it through to his own time and threw the envelope through the time window. Then the machine blew up, leaving him with a blackened face.

When he'd calmed down, Ron's grandfather looked at the radio. It looked new, mainly because it was. The styling looked slightly odd for the time. He'd never heard of the make before. A quick check on the Internet revealed nothing about the manufacturer. He tried the radio. It worked well.

Ron seemed relieved to be able to tell his story to someone who wasn't going to make fun of him. I assured him that I believed him, even though his story did seem rather unlikely.

I remember another time-related project that didn't go well. It wasn't anything to do with our factory, but it happened at roughly that time.

The UK government had decided to update Big Ben, to make it digital. It was in their manifesto at the last election. Many people had become unfamiliar with the old-fashioned circular clock face idea. It tended to be just the very old who liked it.

The contractors tasked with the job made a right mess of it. They covered the original clock faces with round screens, displaying the time. The displays stuck out a bit, so they looked odd. Almost everyone hated them. Several variations were tried, including a sort of digital cuckoo clock.

Vulture clock, more like. It sounded terrible. I thought it sounded like an elephant with its trunk caught in a mangle. I suppose it needed to be loud. The designs were all hopeless. The project went well over budget. It soon became known as Big Bill.

Before the work could be finalised, a general election resulted in a change of political party in government. The new government ordered that Big Ben be returned to how it used to be.

I remember sales of flowerpots going through the roof.

OFFICER SMYTHE

I was talking to one of our factory workers one day. He told me he used to work in a police station. Smythe had worked there too. Things hadn't gone the way Smythe had hoped. I wanted to know more, so he told me all about it.

Shortly after leaving the military, Smythe decided to become a police officer. They were short of people at the time and the pay was good. He thought the job would suit him well.

He used to watch a lot of old TV 'cop' shows. That had given him a distorted idea of what real police work was like.

He did the police training, read the manuals, memorised the procedures and passed the exams. Eventually, he became a proper British police officer. He looked quite intimidating as he walked his beat, looking for any signs of trouble. He tried to do everything 'by the book', often arresting people for very minor offences. He would never let anyone off with just a caution.

The police cells were soon full of people he'd arrested. Most didn't understand why they were there. He used more police notebooks than all of his colleagues combined. They gave him a replica pocket watch, so if anyone asked him the time, he could tell them. They set it for GMT, in July. Nobody he met dared to tell him that his timepiece was an hour out.

Few crimes were committed on Officer Smythe's beat. There were so many people in the police cells that hardly anyone was left to commit any crimes. Housing and feeding all those 'criminals' became quite a problem.

On one occasion, he spotted a group of men innocently chatting on a street corner. He approached them, thinking they must be up to something. One of them knew him and said, jokingly,

"'Ello... 'ello... 'ello... what's all this then?"

Smythe arrested him for impersonating a police officer. Someone took a picture of that street corner and changed the street name in the photo to 'Letsbe Avenue'. It was an old joke, but it still got pinned on the station noticeboard.

His colleagues soon became sick of Smythe. They wound him up whenever they could. They hoped it would make him sick of the place, and he would leave.

They created several new station procedures, which became increasingly silly. They watched and chuckled quietly as Smythe tried to carry them out.

Someone wrote a procedure for walking down the corridor. It included the assertion that having both feet off the ground (e.g. when running) counted as flying. 'Flying is not permitted within the station premises', it said. It included a complex formula for determining the optimum walking speed. It was based on the walker's height, stride length, shoe size, inside leg measurement and how long it was until tea time. Smythe soon smelled a rat. Someone had hidden a dead one in his locker.

There were other pranks, too. They fitted a small, round mechanical clock into his police helmet. They'd wanted to use a cuckoo clock but thought better of it. They said it would make his life easier, as he wouldn't have to tell anyone the time. They'd used an old helmet and hidden his original one. It was a wind-up in more ways than one.

He didn't find out about the clock's alarm until it went off as he walked his beat. He rushed around, trying to find the source of the ringing. He thought a shop burglar alarm had gone off.

When he realised it was all in (or above) his head, he removed his helmet. He tried to silence the alarm, but the button wasn't there. He tore the clock out of his helmet and angrily binned it. He thought he could hear people laughing somewhere nearby (they were). They were also laughing at the small blue flashing light that sometimes popped up on the top of his helmet. It appeared when he ran and disappeared when he stopped.

After he returned to the station, someone got hold of his helmet and fitted a round piece of white card in the hole where the clock had been. It had a message written on it. It read, 'Normal service will be resumed as soon as possible'. Smythe requested (and got) a new helmet, which he had to pay for. He was quietly fuming, especially when his original unmodified helmet reappeared. It still had his name in it.

The police sergeant told Smythe to take a two-week holiday. When Smythe got back, he found the station deserted. The cells were empty. They'd moved and not told him where. It took him a week to find them. The sergeant had another long talk with Smythe. Smythe resigned shortly afterwards. His police experience had taught him some important lessons.

He'd become well known in the local area, so his next job had to be in a different town, about fifty miles away.

FACILITIES

As I sat at home one evening watching a boring old film on TV, my mind started to wander. I couldn't remember seeing any films with toilets. They didn't seem to exist in the world of fiction unless they were vital to the plot. Maybe the superhero characters in science fiction films had four-dimensional super-bladders. They'd be able to keep it all in for a month. A visit to the toilet could take hours. (Best not to think about it.)

We had no such problems at F&S. In the early days, we only used the old factory toilets. Most were in a poor state. As the Bovercraft improved and modern facilities were installed, most of us used them instead. We argued that they needed to be well-tested. We didn't want the toilets to fail in space. They were much better and mostly self-cleaning.

We replaced our old factory fire suppression system after we returned from our first space flight. The old system no longer suited us. The factory used to rely on an outdated sprinkler system. A big diesel engine powered the water pump. Nobody could remember if it still worked. Having diesel fumes in our air whilst in space would have been problematic.

The water supply for the sprinkler system came from a huge stainless steel water tank. It had remained empty since the system was decommissioned. Ron had plans for it.

A smaller water tank had been fitted in the factory grounds to supply potable water while we were in space. Sometimes the water ran out. We kept some extra in large plastic containers, just in case.

Ron wanted to reuse the huge, disused water tank for potable water. Herbert liked the idea. He let him go ahead with the work. Ron cleaned the inside of the tank thoroughly. He welded extra supports on the outside to strengthen it. He sealed the top, to stop water from floating out if the artificial gravity failed. He also fitted a vent near the top, which automatically opened when water was added to or taken from the tank.

Initially, we just used the water from the tank to flush the toilets. Later, with suitable treatment and filtering, it was declared fit for general use. The tank was refilled whenever we got the chance, usually by Phil.

There were two septic tanks in the factory grounds. They had to be emptied occasionally. Someone thought we should just dump the unwanted 'stuff' into space. The idea horrified Smythe. I agreed with him.

Electricity came from the Bovercraft's main internal power source.

We fitted a large oxygen storage tank on the site as a precaution. We rarely needed it, as we recycled most of our air. Ron added reinforcing around it as a precaution, due to the risk of exposure to space.

We originally had a small greenhouse. It wasn't much use in space. Most plants died. We found it more hassle than it was worth, even with artificial lighting, so we got rid of it. Landing on an Earth-like planet and collapsing the bubble gave us a quick (and sometimes welcome) air change.

One of the vacated offices served as a small library. We had proper books in there, as not everyone liked electronic media. Operating manuals and procedures were kept in there too.

We converted one of the larger offices into a gym. It had all the usual gym equipment. We could also vary the artificial gravity in the room. Fit people sometimes turned it up and weaker people turned it down. Barry's team bolted all the equipment securely to the floor.

The gym's artificial gravity would automatically reset to 'Earth normal' if no movement was detected in the room after a few minutes. Not so handy if you're asleep on the ceiling. After a couple of mishaps, Barry altered the gravity control so that any automatic changes to the gravity happened slowly.

The Bovercraft had a small cinema. We mostly watched old Earth films. Someone had acquired some alien material. Barry and Sue were tasked with converting it to a format suitable for our cinema equipment.

Barry had a thing for Sue. He'd meant to hand it over but had forgotten where he'd hidden it. I think he'd put it somewhere 'safe'. He never told me what it was. They got along well.

Once Barry and Sue had converted the alien material, we tried it. It looked strangely interesting, but the plots seemed odd. We couldn't understand the dialogue, as it hadn't been translated.

It amused some of our alien visitors. They told us that the films were running at the wrong speeds, and some sections were running backwards.

We didn't need as much heating as you'd imagine. The bubble would let light through, yet reflect heat well. We didn't lose much to the coldness of space. The downside was that we couldn't benefit from the warmth of a planet's sun if we were on a planet with a hostile atmosphere. We couldn't risk collapsing the bubble under those circumstances.

If the inside and outside pressures were similar, we could weaken the bubble at one point to allow suitably suited people or vehicles through. Alien races often liked our electric cars. We sold them quite a few. Some wanted my Korteener, but I always refused.

We originally had solar PV panels on some of our factory roofs. We took them down. They were useless when we were travelling between planets. Our energy source had a seemingly limitless supply of energy available. The solar panels were redundant. We donated them to our American colleagues at the company's headquarters. Many of those American employees had solar panels on their houses a short while later.

Sue seemed very interested in the MPBs used in our main power supply, so Herbert allowed her to 'borrow' a small one. She spent much of her spare time studying it. She wanted to unlock its secrets. She usually kept it in her quarters, on her bedside table. It glowed slightly, so it became a handy nightlight for her.

Our reliance on those MPBs as our main energy source worried me. All that power had to come from somewhere. I felt certain it wouldn't last indefinitely.

Muttley

I've mentioned the dog a few times, so I think it's time I told you more about him. He was a young black Labrador, belonging to one of our staff. He'd been called Muttley, after an old cartoon character.

Penelope owned him. She worked in our HR department. Most people called her Penny. She wore a gold-plated pendant on a thin necklace, made from an old 'One Penny' coin. The coin had a hole drilled through it near the edge, so it could be attached to the necklace. She claimed that the year on it was the year of her mother's birth.

Muttley was a good-natured dog. Most people liked him. He'd been given too many food scraps, so he had a slight weight problem. Penny couldn't (or didn't) do much about it. He would sometimes sneak into the canteen and sit by someone, with his tail wagging slightly. He'd look up at him or her with a soppy look, sometimes drooling. He got fed, of course.

He'd been 'done' a few months before we left Earth for the first time. There were unusual (to him) smells in that vet's office, which he would never forget. Amy had a trace of that smell, so he kept well away from her.

We occasionally had alien stowaways on board. Muttley usually sniffed them out. Most had never seen a dog, so they ran away. Muttley thought it was a game and gave chase, barking. We often just left him to it. It gave him some exercise and discouraged further potential stowaways. He never harmed any of them. He just wanted to play.

On one occasion, Muttley caused an unintended injury. Penny knew we were expecting important alien visitors, so she kept him with her in her office, on a long lead. She'd attached it to one arm of her chair.

Muttley got a whiff of the visitors as they walked along the corridor outside the office. He wanted to give chase. Penny held him back until she thought the danger had passed. She closed the door and then continued with her work at the computer.

Suddenly, Muttley heard something from far down the corridor. He ran towards the door. It wasn't closed properly, so he managed to get it open. He paused briefly and then ran off down the corridor.

Penny's chair was on castors, on a solid floor. (There had originally been a carpet, which Muttley had ruined by 'digging' holes in it.) She was towed rapidly out of her office, still seated. She shouted at Muttley. He ignored her.

She managed to grab hold of a doorway as she whizzed past. She stopped herself, falling awkwardly. The plastic chair arm attached to Muttley's lead snapped off. Muttley continued running, with the chair arm trailing behind him. It got caught on something, stopping him abruptly. He was startled, but otherwise fine.

Joyce happened to be passing. She spotted Penny on the floor and rushed to help her back into her chair. Penny was clearly in pain, having just sprained her ankle. Joyce recovered Muttley, took him back to Penny's office and shut him in. Then she wheeled Penny to see Amy, who attended to her injury.

Penny was limping for several days after that. Some people used to refer to her as 'Penny-lope'. That became 'Penny-limp' for a while.

Muttley wasn't always popular. On one occasion, we were watching an old musical in the Bovercraft's cinema. We heard a scratching sound on the door, from outside. Penny was with us, watching the film. Muttley must've followed her. She let him in, thinking he'd be no trouble. People made a great fuss of him.

Things were fine at first. Then he smelled food. Some people gave him bits of popcorn. He couldn't get enough of it. He also stole some ice cream. We had to finish or hide any remaining food. Penny took Muttley to the central aisle and told him to 'sit'. He did.

We continued watching the film. All seemed fine until one of the actors started singing. Muttley started howling. It happened with every song. Penny escorted him from the cinema by his collar. He sat just outside and continued howling. Some people found it amusing, but the film had to be re-shown later.

Sometimes Penny gave Muttley a bone as a special treat. When he thought nobody was looking, he'd bury it somewhere outside. At least, we assumed he had. Nobody knew where.

After a while, people noticed that things were going missing. They were mostly unimportant things, but not always.

Several people were under suspicion, but nobody could prove anything.

I had a hunch. I had an old, damaged telephone handset lying around. I was never going to fix it, so I charged it up, rubbed a little cheese on the back and left it lying around. Sure enough, it disappeared.

I rang the handset. I searched the entire Bovercraft, but I couldn't hear it anywhere. When I went outside and listened, I could just about hear something. I followed the muffled sound to a patch of dead grass near the bubble edge. The sound was coming from underground. I dug up the handset. I found several doggy tooth marks on the casing.

I looked around and found several other burials. Most of the missing items were there. We watched Muttley more carefully after that. He got much more exercise, to keep him occupied.

Joyce and Penny eventually persuaded Muttley to follow them to Amy's medical facility, using a combination of play and food bribes. Once she'd gained his trust, Amy gave him a proper check-up. She found nothing wrong with him.

Custard Busters

The Custard Zone, as some called it, remained a problem. Pie hits continued to disrupt interplanetary trade in the region. Most people avoided the area and went around it, but that took longer. Simply getting out of the way didn't work. It wasn't easy to avoid a MK2 laser-guided custard pie (as some called it). Victims didn't know why they had been custardised.

Victims from many affected planets got together and held a meeting. They created a three-dimensional map. It showed all the known points in space where the attacks had occurred. Many assumed the one planet in the centre of it all to be the cause of the trouble, but nobody would go there to confront its inhabitants, for obvious reasons.

The disruption to trade in the area annoyed our management. They told us to investigate (again). Smythe's objections were overruled. We were soon on our way back there. Ron had his own solution to the problem. He wouldn't be there. He avoided the trip by being on a 'pre-arranged' course elsewhere.

Meanwhile, the senior members of the crew were on the bridge. They were discussing custard-evasion strategies. Sue sat at her desk, listening intently. She tried to speak up, but she couldn't get a word in edgeways. It irritated her.

"May I say something...?" said Sue, in her usual quiet voice. Nobody reacted. She tried again, louder than before.

"If I could just point out something..." Still no response, so she stood up and faced them.

"WILL YOU LOT SHUT UP for a minute!!!" Silence.

"Well, what is it?" asked Smythe, looking startled.

"I kept a sample of the custard from the last time and asked the lab staff to analyse it. Those pies weren't always so big. It should be possible to create a machine that could shrink the pies to their original size, making them harmless to us," she said.

Nobody else had any better ideas. Smythe told Sue to organise the design and construction of the custard-busting device.

She worked with the boffins on the design. Barry and his team built the new machine. They fitted it to one of the external factory walls. As we approached the Custard Zone, we prepared it for use.

We waited where we had been hit previously. Within hours, a massive custard pie could be seen heading our way. We let it get close and then fired the new weapon at it. The pie shrank to about eight inches in diameter. It bounced harmlessly off our bubble.

The pies kept coming. That enabled us to locate the source. As we approached the offending planet, we tried to open radio communications with the people there. They appeared to be ignoring us. We kept trying, but to no avail.

Then Barry remembered the experiments with modulated gravity waves. He asked for the equipment to be reconnected. When we tried it, we found we could talk to the people on the planet.

They didn't want to talk to us at first, just telling us to go away, in rather poor English. Charlie got involved and eventually managed to persuade a few of them to meet us. One of their spaceships came up to us and landed in our car park.

We had a long talk with them. Charlie asked why they were so keen to keep people away. They told us they'd been attacked by aliens several centuries earlier. Those attackers had plundered their planet for precious metals. It had taken them years to drive the invaders away.

Since then, they had avoided contact with other races and had done everything possible to keep them away.

I asked why they hadn't responded to our radio messages. They explained that radio communication was difficult on their planet, due to something unusual in their atmosphere. They used gravity waves instead.

They explained about the pies. Food shortages were a serious issue on their planet. Their solution was to develop a way of making soft things, such as food, much larger.

They had set up an experimental radio receiver in space. It had picked up some of our early radio and television transmissions. The material included old black-and-white comedy films, where custard pies were thrown at people. They seemed to be an effective, yet non-lethal weapon. It also explained how they could speak in our language.

They didn't like anyone getting anywhere near their planet, so they fired giant custard pies at them. I never figured out how they stopped the pies from freezing solid in space.

By the time we left, we were getting along well with them. We agreed not to tell anyone else where they were, although many people had already worked it out. They would stop throwing custard pies (or anything else) at passing space vehicles, unless they were known to be hostile. Charlie assured them that most races were friendly. If hostile aliens were around, somebody would let them know.

Talking of pies... Our factory canteen had originally been well staffed. Good cooks used to make our lunches for us. After our first trip into space, most left us. Much of the kitchen equipment became rarely used. We tended to stock up the frozen food store with ready-made meals. We could easily microwave them when needed.

We consumed large quantities of pies. Sometimes a group of us would get together in the kitchen to make a large batch. I would occasionally bulk-buy boxes of nice locally made pies from the nearby town. I'd bring them back in my Korteener estate.

If I had a pound for every box of pies I bought, I'd soon have been overweight.

Rocky

We had just completed an important contract for the UK Space Agency. Our task had been to install and configure a lunar observatory. It would be remotely controlled from the UK.

A few weeks after its commissioning, it detected a large object, apparently heading for Earth. Few people believed the data at first. Many simulations had been done to test the system before it went 'live'. Some thought a simulation had been left running accidentally. Others blamed a calibration error, although that seemed unlikely.

Later observations and calculations by other countries confirmed that something big was heading our way. It showed no signs of being powered, so it couldn't be a space vehicle.

A small, fast spacecraft was sent to investigate. Images sent back showed it was a huge asteroid. Someone gave it a name, to stop people from using the word 'asteroid'. He called it Rocky. The name stuck.

Anyone who could leave Earth did so. Most didn't have that kind of money, and nobody would lend them any. The prices for transportation off the planet went sky-high. Many people, particularly the older generation, just accepted that the impact would happen. They chose to make the best of the time they had left. Some just assumed that 'somebody' would deal with it and didn't worry (much). There were the inevitable groups of asteroid deniers.

Someone suggested setting up a new space tunnel directly between the surface of the Earth and that of another planet. It might've worked, but there wasn't enough time to set it up. Getting so many people from around the world into one tunnel in so little time would have been impossible.

Large international conferences took place. Most attendees were scientists or scared politicians. They usually ended badly.

UK House of Commons held a debate. Some MPs were standing, due to a lack of seats. Many crazy ideas were suggested. One daft MP suggested moving the Earth out of the way, down a giant space tunnel. Some wanted to blow Rocky to bits.

The debate became very loud. The Speaker managed to keep control for a while, shouting,

"Order! Order!" from time to time, but it didn't work for long.

"I'll have an ice cream," yelled one of the honourable members.

Things soon degenerated. There were scenes never before seen in the House of Commons. One (dis)honourable member from the opposition benches crossed the floor, amidst much cheering. He hit another honourable member and crossed the floor again. The speaker had him removed from the House.

MPs stopped calling each other 'the member for' anywhere. The main broadcaster terminated their live television feed.

Others didn't, getting huge viewing figures. Two 'horrible' members ended up in hospital.

We ferried as many people as we could from Earth to other planets. We had to do something, yet this took up valuable time. We knew the scientists on Earth had thought of everything they could, including trying to deflect Rocky. They were stumped.

We had the most advanced spaceship on Earth and some clever people on board. We organised a meeting of our entire staff, hoping some genius would come up with something.

Sue had another of her ideas. She often had ideas. Sometimes they actually worked. She didn't like to speak up, but she forced herself, as nobody else had a viable plan.

"Excuse me... I think I've got an idea," she said.

"Go ahead..." said Smythe, listening intently.

"I realise we can't destroy the asteroid from the outside, as we don't have enough explosives. But what if we could blast it apart from the inside?"

"How do we do that?" asked Smythe, looking sceptical. He appeared to be about to dismiss the idea.

"Just a minute," said Barry. "Sue might be onto something. If you contain an explosion, that makes it more effective. We could start by cutting a tunnel to the centre of the asteroid. Then we position the explosives inside, set them up for remote detonation and fill the tunnel up."

"Hmmmm... interesting," said Smythe, rubbing his chin. "How do you propose to make the tunnel?"

People muttered and mumbled for a while. The triplets talked amongst themselves at a considerable pace. That went on for about five minutes. Eventually, one of them spoke up.

"We think we have a plan. With our protective bubble, we could become a massive boring machine, transporting material away from the asteroid. At the moment, every time we land anywhere, the displaced material is transported to our launch site. It's returned to its original location when we leave. We propose to change this system. Anything our bubble comes into contact with would be instantly transported to another location and left there. It would enable us to act as a huge tunnelling device."

"Perhaps we could create more tunnels, to weaken the asteroid," I suggested. "Some above the central one, some below. We might be able to split the asteroid in two."

"Where do you suggest we put all that displaced material?" asked Barry.

"We think it should be deposited in space, beyond the Earth. Hopefully, it will continue on its original path and travel away from Earth."

Smythe approved, so we got busy. It took a few days for the engineering staff and the boffins to modify our systems to make the plan work. We positioned equipment beyond the Earth to receive the displaced material.

We did a quick test by landing on the Moon and then taking off again. A new crater appeared where we had just been. We went to where the material was supposed to end up. A semicircular chunk of the Moon had appeared there, floating in space. It was far enough away from Earth not to cause any problems.

We had little time. Smythe knew several arms manufacturers from his military days. He arranged for as much explosive material as possible to be brought to us, using another spaceship. (We didn't want to land on the Earth, as that would have taken a chunk out of it and dumped it in space.)

We found Rocky and cut a tunnel right to the centre of it, from the leading edge towards the back. Our tunnelling speed was limited, due to the huge amount of power needed.

Then we carefully came back out again. We made several more tunnels above and below the first, right through, to weaken and slightly lighten the asteroid.

The spaceship carrying the explosives positioned its cargo in the middle of the first tunnel. We were given control over the remote-controlled detonating device. The spaceship left quickly. Then we reconfigured our systems again to allow us to retrieve some of the removed material and block up the entrance to the central tunnel.

We were ready. Earth-based and lunar observation posts would monitor events and let everyone know what happened. We had no time to lose, so we moved away to a safe distance. Smythe issued the command to set off the explosives. We watched.

At first, nothing seemed to happen. We'd forgotten about the time it would take for the signal to reach the explosives and the time it would take for the light to reach us.

We saw a brilliant white flash. The material we had refitted in the tunnel end facing the Earth blew out. That in itself might have slowed the asteroid a little. At first, it looked like nothing else had happened. Then we noticed the asteroid had split. The two halves were slowly moving apart. We named them Rocky 1 and Rocky 2.

The observation posts confirmed there were two objects instead of one. It took a little time to calculate the two separate trajectories. One half would miss the Earth. The other half, although less dangerous, would still be a big problem. Barry suggested that if every available spacecraft, including us, were to give it a push, it might just be enough to deflect it away from Earth.

As there wasn't time to devise an alternative plan, we went straight to the half still heading for Earth. The boffins reconfigured the bubble again to make it as strong as possible. We used all the power we had to try to deflect the half-asteroid by pushing against it. We kept this up for as long as possible. Our propulsion system was overheating, so we had to stop. By then, several other spaceships had arrived to take over from us.

Luckily, it worked. Half the asteroid missed the Earth easily. The other half just skimmed the atmosphere and bounced off into space. Some small pieces fell into the Earth's atmosphere and burned up. We felt like heroes. Sue received a medal from our American masters. (No, Muttley wasn't jealous.)

Like most of us, Sue didn't want any publicity. We were told to keep quiet about it. An 'official' version of events appeared. It bore little resemblance to what had actually happened. Several uninvolved people got the credit for it. We weren't happy, but we couldn't risk saying anything. Nobody would have believed us anyway.

When things settled down again, Smythe got us to find the piece of the Moon we had displaced with our test. He wanted it put back on the Moon in its original location. Captain Smythe was a keen golfer. He knew you should always replace your divots.

IDEAS

In my many years of existence, I've come across more crazy ideas than most. There's always somebody who thinks their brilliant idea or invention will change the world. Few ever do. Here are some of them.

Someone invented a product he called Gnashguard. It was designed to protect teeth from decay by covering them with a thin, tough protective coating. Fine, in theory. The inventor had tested it on his own teeth, with impressive results. The reviews were good. It wasn't long before it appeared on sale throughout the country.

Unfortunately, the inventor forgot something. Human nature. The product could only work properly if the teeth were thoroughly cleaned first, using the materials provided. Many people didn't bother. Tooth decay continued under the coating and couldn't be stopped. Others got their teeth glued together, as they didn't follow the instructions properly. Many accidentally pulled their fillings out.

Dentists were kept busier than usual, removing the stuff. Fortunately, it glowed in ultraviolet light, so they could see if they'd missed any.

Then there was the company that made my Robocat. They'd designed him well. He's very realistic and behaves like a real cat most of the time. The latest ones can clean themselves like real cats do. Mine doesn't. The less said about that, the better.

They made dogs too. Then they got a bit carried away. They wanted to make models based on comic book superhero characters, but ran into legal trouble with copyright and trademark issues. They had to create their own characters, complete with a series of comics to go with them.

The comics were rubbish. Few kids bought them. They were pretty worthless until years later, when they became rare and collectable.

They tried Flush Gordon, who did plumbing in his spare time. That idea went down the toilet. Spiderelephant got them into a tangle. They tried Megadonkey, but they made an ass of it. They had high hopes for Superwalrus but eventually admitted that the idea was never going to fly. Daft lot.

Our younger boffins also had some odd ideas. They invented luminous toothpaste. It made your teeth glow brightly for a week. If you were in the dark without a torch, you just had to open your mouth.

They also built a translator unit for Muttley, so they could talk to him. It didn't work. We didn't need a machine to tell us what Muttley wanted. He hadn't the slightest idea what the thing was for. Dogs don't think like that. He thought it was just another toy and chewed it up.

The triplets came up with something better. They created a machine to enable a person to 'think' a design into existence. If they wanted a custom part made, they usually needed to design it using CAD software on a computer and then make it. They hoped to save time.

An odd-looking hat, connected to a computer, could detect the wearer's thoughts. The equipment could be used to create and edit an object on the computer screen easily, using thought alone. Another machine made the object.

It wasn't perfect. If the wearer became distracted, the results could be unpredictable. One test subject was thinking about doughnuts, and the system made one, from plastic.

Barry asked what would happen if the user fell asleep and started dreaming. The idea amused them. They just had to find out. Oh dear. They should've known better.

One of the boffins volunteered to be the test subject. The others made him comfortable and fitted the hat to his head. He tried to sleep. Not so easy, in the middle of the afternoon. The two people who were supposed to be watching him got bored with waiting for him to fall asleep, and dozed off.

Some odd things came out of that machine before it caught fire. The smoke alarm woke them all up. Only carefully selected people were allowed to try it after that.

Not all the ideas I came across were completely daft. Having glassless windows may have seemed loopy to some, but it did work most of the time. Force fields were used instead of glass. They weren't cheap. People who had them fitted to their houses had to have backup window security, like strong shutters, for when the power failed.

We didn't have glassless windows in our factory, let alone in the Bovercraft. We had to use other materials. The Bovercraft had very tough windows, for obvious reasons. Our factory buildings weren't so tough. They hadn't been designed with space travel in mind.

When time permitted, we replaced all the factory windows with spacecraft-standard ones. We fitted them much more securely than the originals. All the factory doors and window frames were reinforced or replaced. The buildings had been built to withstand the shock waves caused by quarry blasting, so they were unusually strong.

All doors and windows were set up to automatically close securely if the air pressure outside fell below a preset level.

With the work mostly completed, we carefully inspected all the factory buildings. We fixed any remaining problems. If the bubble were to fail while we were in space, we could be in trouble if the buildings leaked.

Joyce insisted that we keep spacesuits in every building. They were hung on the walls in obvious places. She felt there were bound to be a few leaks (in the buildings, not the spacesuits). Atmospheric pressure sensors and displays were fitted in every room. They were set to sound an alarm if the pressure dropped too low, accompanied by bright red flashing lights.

With the work completed, Captain Smythe wanted it put to the test. Some managers were worried, but he insisted that we needed to find any problems as soon as possible, not wait for a real emergency.

We were approaching Earth, having just made a routine delivery to another planet, so Smythe took the opportunity to do his test. He ensured that everyone was aboard the Bovercraft. Then he checked that all the building windows and doors were secure and locked. Once back in the Bovercraft, he slowly lowered the atmospheric pressure within the bubble while we watched for problems. All the atmospheric pressure sensors in the buildings could be monitored remotely.

Most factory buildings withstood the test, right down to zero pressure outside. One didn't. We'd forgotten about an old, disused Portakabin at the edge of the factory. It exploded, sending bits everywhere. We never bothered to replace it. We later removed the two remaining Portakabins from the site, as both had leaked like sieves during the test. (Joyce had to use another building after that.)

After the test, people had more confidence in working in the factory buildings while we were in space.

Mines

Our force field bubble's reliability proved to be excellent. As the technology was reasonably straightforward, there wasn't much that could go wrong.

The bubble controls and displays had been relocated to a desk on the bridge, along with new safety systems. Operating procedures had been written, then checked and approved by Joyce.

Our bubble deflected things well. It felt soft if pushed on. Nothing ever got through it unless deliberately allowed to. It protected us from almost anything.

As far as we knew, we were the only people using that technology. Other spaceships had to be careful to avoid small objects in space. We could shove our way through asteroid fields if necessary. Some astronomers (especially ours) got upset when we made a hole through one of the rings of Saturn. Oops. We learnt not to do things like that in the future.

We heard about a planet in a distant solar system that many people on Earth wanted to visit. There were rumours of ancient, abandoned, advanced technology there. Many had tried to visit the planet, but few had returned. Nobody had managed to land there.

That system had a large sun. Observations from our lunar telescopes suggested that one of its planets might be habitable. Our astronomers were keen to learn more.

We discussed it with a couple of friendly alien races. They told us what little they knew about the place. We heard that an advanced civilisation had once lived there. They had all died out thousands of years ago. Nobody could tell us why. There were active space mines still orbiting the planet.

We were told that the mines were no longer under proper control, as the ground-based control systems were long gone. The mines were all out of position. Each mine seemed to be doing its own thing. It seemed amazing that the mines were still active after so long.

Our upper management told us to investigate, just before going on holiday. Rotten lot. We had better scanners than anyone else, so we headed towards the system. No space drain existed to get us there. We had to go the slow way. At least we'd avoid the Foodies (more about them later).

We approached the alien solar system, found the planet and headed for it. Captain Smythe told us to scan for mines (like we needed to be told). We found one and carefully approached it. It came to meet us, warning us to stay away. Goodness knows how it knew our language. We retreated until it lost interest in us and returned to its original position.

We spotted another mine some distance from us, approaching a passing asteroid. It positioned itself in the asteroid's path and blew it to bits. We thought we could explode our mine using our weapons, but it just evaded anything we fired at it. Whenever we tried to approach the planet, the mine got in our way.

Barry suggested using our sausage drive as a weapon. Smythe just laughed at him, but I backed him up. The mine had clearly been programmed to avoid high-speed projectiles, but what about sausages? We had nothing to lose by trying, so Smythe gave in. We thought it would be funny, anyway.

The sausage drive had no targeting system. It wasn't designed as a weapon. We just had to guess. Most projectiles missed, but one sausage hit the mine. It blew up. Its designers didn't seem to have anticipated sausage attacks. Some bits hit our bubble, but they just bounced off. This impressed and amused Smythe. He told Barry to fit a targeting system to the sausage drive and wire it into the bridge controls.

We had fun for days, blowing up the mines with sausages. We tried other things, too. Rice pudding wasn't much good, but cabbages worked well. There were bits of food and mines everywhere. When we couldn't find any more mines, Smythe told us to clear up the mess. We did our best. Our bubble wasn't bothered by it, but other spacecraft would have been. You don't normally expect to find bits of food orbiting a planet.

We took the opportunity to land on the planet and look around. We found evidence of a long-gone, highly advanced civilisation almost everywhere. Recovering some of the technology for our own use wasn't possible. Thousands of years of corrosion and decay had destroyed most of it.

In several ruined buildings, we found small gold boxes containing small glass cylinders. We guessed they must be information storage devices, so we took them. We took lots of video footage of what we found there.

Whatever killed those people appeared to be long gone. Vegetation had taken over. Most buildings had collapsed. Only those made from large bricks or stone blocks remained partially intact. Some animal life remained, mostly things that looked like insects, plus a few other small crawling things.

We were careful to decontaminate anything we brought back, including ourselves, before we headed home to Earth. Our boffins were determined to find out how to read the information on the glass cylinders. They spent much of our return journey time trying. The tiny bits of information were much smaller and stranger than they expected. Reading it wouldn't be easy. They weren't sure that our technology was up to the task.

LOST IN SPACE

As the months passed, our confidence in our abilities grew. We were good at what we were doing. We thought we could do just about anything. That attitude nearly caught us out.

Problems had developed with two space drains. Spaceships would enter a drain, but fail to emerge from the other end. Those drains had been fine for many years, yet spaceships using them were disappearing. Nobody knew why. Someone sent a small, unmanned craft into one end of a suspect drain to investigate. It reappeared at the other end with no problems. People were baffled.

We were told to investigate. When we arrived at one of the drain entrances, we activated all our sensors. Cautiously, we went in. We got roughly halfway through, then the readings went haywire. Nobody knew what had happened. Some people went outside into the factory grounds to see for themselves. They saw other spaceships nearby, flying around in all directions, obviously lost. Sometimes one would seem to run into something soft and then bounce off it.

We seemed to be inside something big. Only blackness and other spaceships could be seen. No stars. No obvious way out. We wandered around like the others, trying to escape, but we soon realised we couldn't.

Barry remembered we had equipment that could see the structure of a space drain from the outside. We'd never tried it inside one before. It had never been necessary. Barry tried it anyway.

The inside surfaces of whatever enclosed us appeared on our displays. We looked for a way out. Instead of finding two exits, we found four. We picked one and headed into it. Our equipment told us we were back in a normal space drain. All our sensors worked normally again.

Much to our relief, we emerged at one of the drain exits a short while later. We were near a planet that wasn't our expected destination.

From the outside, we followed the drain exterior back to roughly where we had previously been, watching for problems. When we got there, we could see a massive bulge at the intersection of two crossing space drains. It appeared to be slowly growing. Its shape changed randomly. It looked alarmingly unstable.

We went back to one of the drain entrances and went in. When we got to the bulge at the centre, we contacted all the other space vehicles. We told them to follow us precisely. Then we led them into one of the bulge exits, into a normal drain and to freedom.

We contacted the authorities on the four planets affected. We advised them not to allow anyone else into those two drains until further notice.

Space drains were odd things. Although the ends could be fixed in space, the middle parts were free to float about all over the place. They often did. We found out later that space drains tend to attract each other. These two must've merged at the point where they crossed.

We had to collapse and deactivate both drains. Then we waited a while for space to settle down. When we restored the drains, we split each into two halves so they couldn't overlap. The midpoint area became a crossroads. It allowed travellers to transfer to a different drain if they wished to.

We returned to our UK base, feeling quite pleased with ourselves. The new 'crossroads' area, having four drain entry or exit points, became a magnet for Foodies.

Foodies were people who used to wait in small spaceships near drain entry or exit points. They would ask people who passed by for food. They'd used up almost all the resources on their own planets. Some had resorted to begging from other races. We felt sorry for them, but they were becoming a nuisance. Nobody dared to go near any of their planets for fear of being robbed of everything they had.

Dogastrophe

I went home again. I did that quite a lot, as I lived there. Robocat had been behaving well. Some people weren't so lucky with their artificial pets.

A nice local couple I knew had bought an artificial dog a few weeks earlier. It was an old English sheepdog. I say 'old' because it was an outdated model. They'd found it sitting, almost forgotten, in a far corner of the pet shop, gathering dust. They'd felt sorry for it and bought it. Being a discontinued model, they got it cheap.

That dog couldn't see well. It had to rely on other senses. I think it used ultrasonic echolocation, amongst other things. It weighed more than a normal dog.

Its owners sometimes threw an old tennis ball for it to fetch. That was usually fine, until one of them threw the ball into the swimming pool, briefly forgetting they had an artificial dog. Then the phone rang. The dog got forgotten. Meanwhile, it jumped into the pool to retrieve the ball.

The street past their house runs slightly downhill. I mention this because of what happened next. The dog grabbed the ball and, being heavy, sank to the bottom of the pool. For some strange reason, it decided to bury the ball. It started digging. Eventually, it dug right through the bottom of the pool and into the mud. It wasn't long before the pool water took on a muddy brown appearance.

All that digging drained the dog's batteries, so it remained down there. It released its grip on the ball, which floated to the top. A few hours later, its owners went looking for it. They couldn't find it anywhere, although the pool water looked brown. When they spotted the tennis ball, they realised where the dog was. Their neighbours, downhill from them, complained about unusual puddles forming in their lawn.

It took a day or two for all the water to drain from the pool. They lent their neighbours a water pump, to help drain their waterlogged garden. A thick layer of mud remained on the bottom of the pool, with a mud-coloured, dog-shaped lump standing in the middle. They let the whole lot dry out before trying to tackle it. They chiselled the dog from the dried mud, carried it out of the pool and charged it up. Then they started washing it.

That didn't go well. With the muddy dog wet again and recharged, it could move. It suddenly ran straight through the front door. The dog couldn't see well even when clean, and the mud made things worse. The shattered door had a roughly dog-shaped hole in it. The dog ran off, down the street. It stopped outside a neighbouring house and shook itself, as dogs do. Their neighbour's newly washed car got splattered with mud.

The supposedly waterproof dog wasn't designed to withstand being under several feet of muddy water. I visited them shortly afterwards. The dog detected me approaching, ran towards me and went 'Moooooo!!!'.

It nearly scared the living daylights out of me. The muddy water must've got into its audio circuits. People in the neighbouring houses didn't like it, especially during the night. They said they could hear it at the far end of the street. One of the dog's owners said he planned to rename it Daisy. Then he started singing at me...

"Daisy, Daisy, give me your answer... moooo!" Oh dear.

As it was several years out of warranty, he tried tinkering with the dog's circuitry himself. He managed to make it go 'Meeow!'. At least it wasn't as loud. He said he'd fix it properly later, but he didn't bother. It wouldn't wake him (or anyone else) up during the night. It would also be easy to identify if stolen.

Robocat didn't give me much trouble, but he wasn't perfect. I found him in my garden one day, motionless, stuck nose first in the ground. A new hole had appeared in the fence. He must've tried to jump the fence but not had enough power. When I found him, his batteries were flat. I cleaned him up and recharged him. I planned to fix the dent in his nose later, or maybe buy him a new one.

He needed some slight adjustments. I needed my multimeter. I couldn't find it. The original one still hadn't turned up, so I'd lost two multimeters.

I remembered the tracking device I'd fitted in the newer one. I felt sure I'd find it, but found no sign of it. I rigged up a very sensitive receiver but still received no signal. It didn't make sense.

We had many stray dogs in the area where I lived. They didn't know what to make of the artificial ones. They kept well clear of them, especially the old English cat-dog.

I put up strong fences around my garden to try to keep the dogs out, as they'd sometimes chase Robocat up a tree. He sometimes stayed up there until his batteries ran out. Then he'd fall. I put old mattresses around the base of the tree. The dogs sometimes raided my bins, looking for food and scattering rubbish everywhere. I don't mind dogs, and most were friendly, but some weren't.

If I had a pound for every stray dog that visited me, I'd have needed a bigger garden.

Undead Ned

Not all planets were reachable by drain, so we were sometimes away from our base for weeks. Everyone found accommodation somewhere, either in the Bovercraft or in disused factory buildings.

Watching films in our cinema became popular during those long trips. We built up a huge film collection. Most production staff took the opportunity to work overtime and earn extra money. The astronomers built a large remotely controlled telescope and set it up at the edge of the bubble. It sent live images to computers in one of the offices. That kept them amused for hours at a time.

The rest of us found various ways to amuse ourselves. Simon and Joyce spent a lot of time together. They claimed there were health and safety issues to discuss, but most of us knew better. They would sometimes devise silly schemes to wind people up.

Smythe disapproved. The pranks were always harmless, though. I remember one occasion when we had to dispose of a large quantity of food colouring. It would change colour, depending on the room temperature. They added the whole lot to the main water tank, with predictable results.

Occasionally, Simon would bring out his electronic piano keyboard and play some pieces for us (mainly the black and white pieces). He had learnt quite quickly, so it wasn't too bad most of the time. Joyce said it sounded better when he plugged the headphones in.

Simon started playing a piece of classical music. Joyce was nearby.

"What's that supposed to be?" she remarked.

"The Nutsqueezer," said Simon.

"Surely you mean Tchaikovsky's Nutcracker?" said Joyce.

"I've not quite cracked it yet," said Simon. "Besides, it wasn't his nutcracker. He'd borrowed it from his neighbours because he couldn't find a hammer."

Simon had hoped to impress Joyce with his piano playing. He tried playing a simple version of Für Elise (Beethoven) to her. Then she showed him how it should be done. Simon was a little embarrassed, but impressed. He argued that his version was about Beethoven's cat, Furry Liz.

Joyce's piano-playing skills far exceeded Simon's. She'd kept that quiet until then. She'd been waiting for an opportunity to wind him up. She started giving him piano lessons. I think she was quite impressed with his progress.

Sometimes a group of us would get together after working hours to play games. Usually cards, Scrabble or other board games. The usual group consisted of Simon, Joyce, Barry, Sue and myself. Sometimes Lorna would join us. We occasionally asked Smythe, but he always refused. We knew he would, but we had to ask.

We got bored with the normal games after a while. Some people invented new ones. We created a space version of Monopoly. Simon disrupted it by printing huge amounts of extra Monopoly money. He hid it about his person. He always looked fatter than usual at those games. No wonder he kept winning. We always found more money when the game finished than at the start.

Sue came up with some interesting ideas. I'd never believed in ghosts, but she did. She sometimes held a séance, or something similar. Since we were in space, we didn't know what to expect. Strange things often happened on those occasions. Many were just pranks by Simon and Joyce.

Occasionally, we were joined by Ned. He worked on the factory shop floor. He seemed interested in spooky things and sometimes attended Sue's séances. During a séance, she would try to contact the spirits of the dead.

One of those séances didn't go well. We all joined hands and started the procedure as usual. Sue's behaviour sometimes started Joyce giggling, so we'd have to stop. Until then, Sue had never managed to contact anyone.

That didn't happen this time. Sue started acting very strangely. She looked around at us.

"What's happening? What am I doing here?" said Sue, looking distressed. "Why do I sound like a Sheila?"

Her séances had never worked before, often due to certain people messing around. I looked at Simon, who shook his head. Joyce wasn't even smiling, so this had to be real.

"Who are you?" I asked, carefully.

"I'm Ned, you drongo. Don't you recognise me? What's going on? I think I wanna chunder," said Sue.

"We're holding a séance," said Barry, tactlessly. "What happened to you? Are you dead?"

"Not sure. I was working at my bench on the shop floor when everything went black. Then I found myself here," said Sue.

I rushed off to find Ned, fearing the worst. Everyone else shuffled around to complete the circle again. Ned wasn't on the shop floor. Everything on his bench looked tidy, as usual. On my way back, I checked in the cinema. I found him there, looking through our collection of films. I told him to follow me.

"Hello, cobber! What's the rush?" asked Ned.

"You'll see," I said.

We arrived back at the séance. When Sue saw Ned, she looked scared. Really scared. She almost fell off her chair.

I managed to calm her down. Then I asked her the date. It was several days into the future. I thought it best to halt the proceedings. We all separated and Sue returned to normal.

While I'd been looking for Ned, his 'future ghost' had remembered that just before he died he'd looked up, to see a large chunk of the heating system getting rapidly bigger. Then everything had gone black.

Simon, visibly scared, told Ned to keep off the shop floor for a week or so, while we did some checks. There had been much strengthening work done to the roof not long before, to make it more spaceproof. Some things had been moved for better access.

We checked everything. Most things were fine. When we checked above Ned's bench, we discovered that the heavy heating unit above it hadn't been bolted back in properly. The pipes were still disconnected. Checking its security dislodged it. It fell heavily onto the bench, causing much damage. Fortunately, Ned wasn't there.

We thought the episode with Ned was over. It wasn't. Ned didn't look right. He had become semi-transparent. His skeleton and internal organs sometimes became visible. He looked quite scary.

Ned went to see Amy. She tried to scan him with her fancy medical equipment, but most of it wouldn't work on him.

"Use a torch," said Ned, trying to be helpful.

"It's OK... I'll keep trying..." She did. She failed. She eventually called Simon, who brought a strong torch.

"How do you feel?" she asked.

"How do I feel what?"

"I mean, do you feel unwell?"

"Well, I've got a few aches and pains," said Ned. "Nothing serious."

"Let me be the judge of that!"

Amy asked Simon to leave the room, then examined Ned using the torch.

"Do you mind if I take photos?" asked Amy.

"Of what?"

"Your insides. They could be useful in the future."

"Sure... fill yer boots," replied Ned.

Amy fetched a camera, photographed Ned's innards and showed him the images on a large monitor. Ned's appendix operation site could be clearly seen, along with other repairs.

She added the photos to his medical records. She also suggested some dietary changes and reassured him that his general health was fine.

Ned returned to normal after a few weeks. His aches and pains eased too.

Sue had another 'party trick'. She would get a group of unmarried people together. One of them would throw a handful of Scrabble tiles into the air and let them fall on the floor. The letters that were the right way up could be rearranged to spell a person's name. She suggested that the thrower might one day marry someone with that name.

It always worked with Sue around, but it rarely did when she wasn't. I tried it myself, after a little nagging from Amy. The letters formed the name Lisa. They had even fallen in the right order. I tried it again on a different day. Again, the name Lisa appeared. Sue said she had a strong feeling about this one. That worried me. I liked being single.

Deciphering

When we returned from the planet with the mines around it, we brought back several boxes of small glass cylinders. We'd guessed they were data storage devices.

Our boffins were keen to get at the data. They started work enthusiastically, but reading them proved much more difficult than expected. Under high magnification, they could see patterns of tiny dots on each of the thirty-two internal faces just under the surface of each cylinder. They assumed the dots were binary data.

They copied the dots into a computer. Whatever they tried, the data made no sense. It appeared to be meaningless gibberish. They made little progress in months. Some found it rather depressing.

Sue had been as keen as anyone to discover what data those cylinders contained. So far, she'd kept her distance from the boffins. She didn't want to get in the way. When she heard they weren't getting anywhere, she decided to pay them a visit.

When she appeared in the laboratory, she saw two boffins staring at a display. It showed a magnified view of one of the cylinder surfaces. She asked them about it. They told her they couldn't make any sense of the data. They'd tried every algorithm known to Man (or alien).

Sue stared at the image. She thought the dots looked a bit rough. She asked if she could increase the magnification. They didn't expect her to find much, but they let her have a go anyway.

She looked closely at the dots and progressively increased the magnification, up to the machine's limit. A big smile appeared on her face.

"Look at this," she said.

What they saw startled them. Those 'dots' were symbols. Sue left them to it, feeling quite pleased with herself.

I often find that a fresh pair of eyes, looking at a problem from a different angle, can reveal something that's been overlooked. This was undoubtedly one of those cases. The two boffins still felt like total numpties, though. They muttered and mumbled, then resumed their work.

They found that each symbol consisted of a pattern of straight lines of equal length, bounded by an undrawn square. They copied the images of the symbols onto their computers, meaning to decode them later.

There were thirty-two different symbols. Sometimes the first symbol of a group was larger than the others. They thought it might be like a capital letter, but they weren't sure. They didn't know which symbols were letters and which were numbers.

More weeks passed with little progress. They couldn't see any pattern in the arrangement of the symbols. They didn't even know in which direction to read them.

Eventually, they went to see Captain Smythe. They managed to nag him into letting us return to the planet where we'd found the cylinders.

When we got there, we checked for space mines. No complete ones could be seen. However, there seemed to be quite a few mine parts floating around in space. Smythe accused us of not being thorough enough with our cleanup operation the last time we were there, yet I was sure we'd cleaned up almost everything. It made little sense.

We landed in a park, in the middle of what had been a large city. Many people were keen to explore. Everyone took cameras with them.

We split up into several groups. One group explored the city centre and another the abandoned residential streets. Other groups investigated any important-looking buildings they found.

Almost all the buildings were in ruins. Only the strongest had survived, albeit with the roofs missing. Most doorways were still intact, which seemed odd to me.

My group investigated the streets in a residential area. In some ways, they looked much like typical streets on Earth. There were pavements, roads and the remains of terraced houses.

I entered a house and looked around. The plant life had taken over in the outer rooms. In an inner room, I found some gold items lying on the floor, in the dust. I picked them up. Some looked like coins, some like rings. Some had symbols engraved or embossed on them, in the alien language.

I went outside again and looked at the stone doorway. A single symbol had been carved into it. I looked at the adjoining house. It had a similar, but slightly different, symbol. I thought they might be house numbers. I put that idea to our group. We split up and walked along a few streets, carefully noting all the symbols on the house doorways.

One group discovered what had once been a vineyard, in a large garden. I joined them, as I wasn't far away. There were grape vines everywhere, and the grapes looked ripe. It seemed strange to me, to find grapes there that looked identical to an Earth variety. Perhaps foolishly, I tried one. It certainly tasted like a grape. I wanted to have some more, but thought better of it.

There were traces of wine-making equipment lying around nearby. Empty bottles were scattered everywhere. Our group sneaked bucketloads of grapes back to our canteen, being careful not to be spotted.

When we got together again, we compared notes. We worked out the order of the symbols. We checked several more streets, which confirmed our conclusions. We also discovered that some longer streets used two symbols for some houses. All symbols were photographed.

One of the other groups discovered what must have been a museum. Some exhibits were still present. A few glass panels lay on the floor nearby, with alien symbols etched onto them. They photographed everything. They also found a scientific section, with diagrams and drawings etched onto glass panels.

Another group discovered a library. There were many small gold boxes. Each contained carefully arranged groups of glass data cylinders, just like the ones we had found earlier. There were the remains of the reading machines. We photographed the machines, internally where possible, before taking the cylinders. Someone tried to pick up a machine. It fell apart, smashing on the floor.

There were also some printed books on glass shelves. It was hard to tell what the books were made of. They fell apart if anyone tried to pick one up. Two of the group went back to the factory and brought back scanning equipment. It allowed them to scan the interiors of the books without disturbing them.

We were there for about a week. We took huge numbers of pictures and lots of video footage. When we felt there wasn't much else to discover (and we'd taken all the grapes), we returned to our factory and left the planet.

The boffins got busy, trying to piece it all together. A week later, they'd made little progress. Sue couldn't resist paying them another visit. She walked into the laboratory and sat down in a chair on the far side of the room from them. She sat and watched them, keeping quiet this time and grinning slightly (she had excellent hearing). Occasionally, someone would look at her, mutter something and then continue the discussion.

Eventually, they all stopped talking and walked over to her.

"All right... what is it?"

"What have you figured out so far?" said Sue. "Do you know which symbols are numbers and which are letters?"

"No..."

"I think they're all both," said Sue.

"Uhh...?"

"I reckon the numbers are the ones in a group that start with a larger symbol and the others are letters. I think the same symbols are used for both numbers and letters. The size of the first character tells you which is which. You have the order of the numbers from the house numbers on the streets. The houses with two-digit numbers have a big first symbol followed by a smaller one."

"Yes, that's true..."

"Since you have thirty-two symbols, they may be base thirty-two numbers rather than base ten."

Sue also suggested that single, isolated symbols might be numbers. She'd been thinking about the symbols. She had developed her own theories. She'd kept her ideas to herself, assuming the boffins would be well ahead of her, not realising the reverse was true.

After a little more discussion, they agreed that Sue would work with the boffins on the decoding from then on.

After a week or two, they had made progress. The data started to make sense. Several large groups of symbols in regular patterns were noticed. They proved to be digital images. There were fascinating digital photographs, showing how things had been thousands of years earlier. The images also included diagrams.

After a couple more weeks, they were really getting the hang of it. They wrote computer programs to make the decoding easier. They also built special reading hardware. It wasn't long before we discovered some quite advanced theories and inventions. We put them to good use. That increased our technical lead over our competitors. We patented some of the ideas.

Meanwhile, others analysed the grapes. They were pronounced safe to eat. We planned to make some cheap 'plonk' with them, but we couldn't resist eating them. We soon scoffed the lot. The planet we'd taken them from became known (briefly) as Planet Plonk. Captain Smythe disapproved, so someone suggested we call it the 'Planet of the grapes'. Smythe didn't like that either, so we ended up calling it Planet Dee (officially).

We weren't sure what to refer to the former inhabitants as. Some suggested Dees, some said Deeites and some suggested other names. We couldn't agree on a sensible name, so we called them Plonkers. We were being silly, of course. Smythe disapproved, yet the name stuck.

STRING RADIO

Barry and I were on the bridge. I had just completed some adjustments to one of the displays. We used it to view space tunnels when we needed to.

"I wonder if any drains exist naturally," said Barry.

"Yes. I call them *rivers*," I replied.

"Very funny. I meant space drains."

"I don't know. I've never looked for any," I said.

With Smythe's permission, Barry started looking for space drains. He looked all around us for a considerable distance but found nothing.

"Well, that was disappointing," moaned Barry. I thought about it.

"Maybe they're not all as big as the ones we're used to. There might be much smaller ones. We're just not looking for them," I suggested.

Barry reset the controls. As he did so, something unexpected appeared on the screen. It looked cracked, or covered with thick cobwebs.

"Good grief!" said Barry. There were tiny space tunnels almost everywhere, of varying diameters. "I wonder where they all go."

"Let's follow one and find out," I said. Smythe was watching.

"I suppose you lot want to go tunnel chasing?" he said. Barry and I both looked at Smythe, with big, silly grins.

"Yeah... why not?" said Barry.

"Oh, all right. Just don't take us too far away from where we're supposed to be," said Smythe.

We were close to Earth, so we followed one of the more obvious ones to its origin. It started at a site in southern England, near the top of a mountain.

The tunnel end had somehow fixed itself to the site. We landed nearby and walked to the tunnel entrance. It started about three feet off the ground.

It wasn't visible to the naked eye. Luckily, we had portable equipment with us that allowed us to see it.

The tunnel entrance was about four inches in diameter. It intrigued Barry. He picked up a small stone and threw it into the tunnel. It travelled about twenty feet along it, then fell through the side and onto the ground.

Lengths of rusty metal were lying around nearby. They were the remains of what had once supported a national AM radio transmitter.

Barry had an interesting idea. If the tunnel had been there when the transmitter still operated, strong radio signals would have entered the tunnel. If the other end of the tunnel was far enough away, and if we could find it, perhaps we could listen in to the old radio transmissions.

Barry told Simon. Simon was very interested. He had a collection of old radio jingles, some quite rare, and many other old recordings. Barry had a massive collection of vinyl records, mostly from the 1970s. Some people called them the Boogiemen. They convinced a sceptical Captain Smythe to let us follow the tunnel, to see if we could find the other end.

Before we left the site, I noticed an old dronephone lying in the grass nearby. It seemed like an odd place to find one. Then I spotted another. We soon discovered dozens more. All were dead, as the batteries were flat.

A large mobile phone mast had been erected nearby. As we walked towards it, we found hundreds more phones. They must've been attracted to the signals from the masts when they escaped from people's homes. We collected bucketloads of them and took them back to the factory. Then we resumed our tunnel investigations.

We took off, found the tunnel end again and carefully followed it into space. Once out of Earth's atmosphere, we picked up speed. The tunnel didn't bend about much, so we were able to keep track of it without too much trouble. We locked our sensors onto it and followed it for around a hundred light-years. It ended on the surface of an uninhabited planet.

We found the planet's atmosphere breathable, but a bit smelly. Simon had an old radio, which had been restored to working order. (Guess who had to restore it.) This would give him a chance to test it properly.

Simon fitted some improvised batteries to his radio. He switched it on. He scanned through the long wave band, then the medium wave. At a wavelength of around 247 metres, he picked up a radio station broadcasting pop music from the 1970s. This amused us greatly. We both recognised the music, although the sound seemed a little distorted.

We had good-quality audio recording devices that could record continually for months. We set one up on the planet, along with a solar panel, a battery and Simon's old radio, to record the radio station.

We revisited the planet a few months later. We were worried that the local wildlife might have got at the equipment, but it hadn't. Maybe the sounds had driven the local creatures away. We set up a second recorder and returned to Earth with the first one. We managed to filter out the distortions in the recordings.

On our way back, Barry made a copy of the recordings. He broadcast it over our Tannoy system for several days. He had expected complaints, but there were none. Almost everyone wanted more. The old news and traffic reports were interesting, and the jingles were amusing. People liked the music. Yeah, man. Groovy.

Barry and Simon set up an online radio station on Earth, from which we broadcast what we'd recorded. It went down much better than we expected.

We discovered that many small space tunnels started near sources of strong electromagnetic radiation, such as radio transmitters. We set up several similar recording systems on other planets.

I hated the popular 'music' of our own time. Some groups seemed to have forgotten what notes were for. I remember one lot that called themselves Shakywaddlywaddly. They sang old material, very badly. All were severely overweight and out of tune. They attempted a few concerts but had to stop. They had to pause for about ten minutes between songs, due to exhaustion. One of them lost weight from practicing too much. He had to leave the group. The 'Flab Four' had to give it up, for health reasons.

I'd been working with Barry one day, trying to improve the quality of the recordings from the 1970s. On my way back to my quarters, I bumped into Phil. Well, nearly. I wondered how he could see anything at all through those thick glasses. They made his eyes look enormous. He asked me if I could look at a light in his room. It had been flickering for months. I said I would, as long as it wasn't too bright. He didn't get the joke.

I still had some tools with me, so I accompanied Phil back to his quarters. While Phil searched for the lamp, I looked around his main room. I expected the place to be dirty and untidy, but it wasn't. Everything looked neat and clean. Pictures hung on the walls, mostly of wild animals in their natural habitats.

I noticed a framed certificate on the wall. It stated that Phil had completed a survival training course roughly five years earlier. When Phil returned, I asked him about it.

"Phil, this course you've done... was it in Australia by any chance?" I asked.

"Yes," he replied. "How'd you know?"

"Just a guess. There can't be many places left where you could do a course like that." He'd also hung the certificate upside down. Perhaps he did it on purpose.

I got to work on his faulty lamp. I found a loose wire, which I fixed. Phil thanked me and I left. I had been tempted to tell him the truth about those glasses, but I thought better of it, for self-preservation reasons.

That reminds me. Phil didn't like the dark much. He'd complained to me several times about the corridor lights in the Bovercraft. Many were failing.

I did some checking. I discovered that Sue had purchased them from an online auction site. She thought she'd got them at a bargain price.

The lights were cheap because they were rubbish. They were intended for occasional home use only. Most of the ladies liked them, partly because they were slightly pink.

I hated them. So did Barry, who refused to install them. They looked cheap and nasty. He gave the job to our apprentice. Our apprentice was keen to learn, but he often just got in the way.

He had an annoying habit of leaving tasks half-done and then starting something else. We referred to him as Zoddoff, because he often did. Nobody called him that to his face, though, except on one unfortunate occasion. I'll tell you about that later. We found his real name difficult to pronounce.

He didn't always do things well. He didn't get enough proper supervision, often being left to get on with things on his own, so it wasn't his fault. He wasn't with us for long.

Zoddoff fitted the lights as best he could. There were temporary blanking panels where proper lights were supposed to go. Those cheap lights were non-standard and didn't fit. He'd resorted to just glueing them to the blanking panels using hot glue and then wiring them in. When they went wrong, they would get hot, the glue would melt and they'd fall off.

Since Phil wanted the lights replaced, I gave him the task. They were low-voltage units, so he couldn't get electrocuted. I showed him what to do. He had to remove the blanking panels with the old pink lights attached and disconnect them. Then he would connect a nice new light, designed to fit the space, and then slot it into place. Easy. I watched him do two, then left him to it.

As I walked off, I heard a loud crash. I turned around, to find Phil on the floor. The pink lighting unit hung by its wires. It had fallen on his head. I took him to see Amy. I told her that Phil had been struck by lighting.

Phil continued with the rest later, being much more careful. He stuck a small smiley face sticker on the corner of each one he completed.

HANDY ANDY

Nobody wanted to do the boring, routine tasks. Some things weren't too bad, such as emptying the bins. Others were messy or smelly. Most companies would get outside contractors to come and do the work. That's not so easy when you're in space. We had to do the tasks ourselves.

Our management expected everyone to do their part. They drew up a rota, but some people still managed to evade their duties. Excuses included illness, claiming that a sick relative had just died, the budgie had exploded, etc. One person's house had (apparently) been struck by lightning three times in the same year. Strange how all the photos looked the same. We discovered later that it wasn't even his house.

That clearly couldn't go on. Many people argued that they'd never had to do such things in previous jobs. We had to do something, so two androids were bought to do the unpleasant tasks. Both were designed specifically for use in hazardous environments.

They were realistic and performed well. Some people thought they were too realistic. It could be alarming to discover that the 'person' you had been talking to for half an hour wasn't a real person.

One early manufacturer created a model they called Andy Roid. They sold well. Other manufacturers wanted in on the act and created 'compatible' android parts. Parts were often interchangeable between models from different manufacturers, as the original interfaces had become an unofficial standard.

People could build androids to their own specifications. Sometimes people built silly ones by mixing up parts from several different models. They looked very odd. An android often found it difficult to walk in a straight line with legs of unequal lengths. After a few years, the interface standards were changed so that only parts intended to work together actually would.

People stopped calling them androids. They called them Andys. The Andys often did the boring, mundane tasks. Their intelligence had to be limited to prevent them from becoming sentient.

A group of students programmed some to play football. Fun at first, but the results became too predictable. All the 'human' elements were gone. No fouls, no bad language, no inventiveness. The referee became redundant. It became so boring that they eventually gave it up.

We found the Andys handy. They could be sent into unsafe places, or places with little or no air.

Andys were supposed to do whatever they were told to. One manufacturer put this to the test. They told an Andy to walk off a low cliff, whilst juggling a dozen bananas, gargling baked beans and singing 'I do like to be beside the seaside' backwards. It almost did it, but kept veering away from the cliff edge. Maybe it knew more than they thought.

We had someone on board that we called Larry the Limerick. He had a problem with his speech. He didn't talk much. When he did, he often messed up his words, sometimes using Spoonerisms.

Larry frequently wrote limericks. He could say or write them without messing up his words. He'd sometimes pin them on the notice boards to cheer people up. They weren't all that good.

I wasn't convinced that Larry's Spoonerisms were always unintentional. He'd taken a liking to the 1970s music we'd been re-broadcasting. He had his own names for some acts, such as She Tweet, Marry Banilow, Polly Darton, Tuna Tirner and Motherhood of Bran. At least he couldn't get Abba wrong.

Some people (mostly Phil) thought Larry was an Andy with a programming error. Larry sometimes thought it fun to go along with that, just for a laugh. Then came the incident with Phil.

He and Phil had been getting along well. Larry sometimes fixed things for Phil. He would occasionally have to ask Barry for help, usually when he'd taken something apart and couldn't remember how to put it back together. Sometimes Larry would pretend to be an Andy. Phil called him Handy Andy.

Phil had seen Larry lying motionless in a chair, asleep.

Phil wasn't entirely sober, so he wasn't thinking clearly. He'd got it into his head that Larry needed recharging.

He tried to plug him in. Larry shot into the air, cursing and yelling. Phil was very apologetic. At least he'd proved to himself that Larry was a real person. There were no Spoonerisms in Larry's colourful language.

Larry saw the funny side of it in the end and wrote a limerick about it.

It went something like this…

'There once was a person called Larry
Who wasn't as useful as Barry.
He made quite a din
When Phil plugged him in.
Nearly blew him right into the quarry.'

Moving house

One of our older local managers planned to retire soon and move to another part of the UK. We called him Jock. Odd, some thought, as he wasn't Scottish. Something to do with horses, maybe. He and his wife had already bought a large patch of land in England. They intended to build a new house there. Planning permission had already been obtained.

Their existing house had been ideal for them. They liked the location and the local people. Unfortunately, most of their family, including both sets of parents, lived in the south of England, hundreds of miles away. All that travelling to England and back had become tiresome.

Like many people, they had accumulated far too much stuff over the years. Moving it all themselves would have been difficult, as they both had age-related health issues. They asked us if anyone would be prepared to help when the time came. Anyone who volunteered to help would get a generous bonus. They were a nice couple who had always been good to us, so there was no shortage of volunteers.

A few months remained before the planned move, as the new house had yet to be completed. The foundations were in, but little else had been done. Jock liked to prepare for things well in advance. He put up notices about the planned move on our factory noticeboards.

Sue was reading one of them when she had an idea. She'd seen Barry working on something not long before. She thought she knew what it might be, so she went to find him.

It turned out that Barry had been building a spare power unit. He'd been worried that the one in the Bovercraft might fail one day, leaving us stranded light years from home. Building it would give him a better understanding of how they worked.

His spare unit was much smaller than the main one, partly to make it portable. It only used one MPB (Martian Power Bar), which had been kept on board as a spare. The new unit might be just good enough to get us out of trouble in an emergency, he hoped.

Sue suggested to Barry that his spare power unit could power a new force field bubble. The new bubble would surround Jock's existing house and enable it to be physically moved to the new location. That way, there would be no need for Jock to build a new house or package anything up. Perhaps we could move the whole garden as well.

Barry liked the idea. He suggested it to Simon, who spoke to Captain Smythe. The four of them devised a rough plan.

Captain Smythe put the idea to Jock. Jock thought Smythe was joking at first, but quickly realised he wasn't, as Smythe had little sense of humour. Smythe explained that the same technology we used to fly the factory could be used to fly his house. He explained that it could be risky.

Jock seemed surprisingly keen on the idea and considered it worth the risk. The cost savings could be considerable and it would be a lot less hassle. Besides, he and his wife had become quite attached to their house. He eventually managed to talk his wife into accepting the idea (I think she just wanted him to stop going on about it).

When the time for the move arrived, we flew our factory to Jock's house and parked in a nearby field. It seemed unlikely that anyone would see what we were up to in such a remote rural location. Sue and Barry took the spare power unit into the middle of the house and set it up. They created a remotely controlled force field bubble, just big enough to encompass the entire property.

I set up a second, identical bubble, overlapping the first. I powered it from a generator outside the site. This would enable the transfer of the land from the new site into the space left when the property left the old site.

Jock had prepared for the move. He'd had all the services disconnected from the property, as far back as the boundary fences. The new bubble had no independent mechanism for being moved, so we devised a way to tether it to our factory bubble. That meant we could move the whole lot around as one entity.

Even though the existing house was some distance from any towns or villages, we still chose to do the move at night. We switched off our outside factory lights so nobody would see us, then hovered above the house. The site bubble was activated. Then we activated the house bubble and tethered it to our main one. We took off very carefully, taking the house and its garden with us and began our journey. Someone followed us in a company helicopter to check that everything looked OK.

We had to move slowly. It took us several hours to reach the new location. We couldn't risk going faster than the helicopter anyway. When we arrived in the general area of the new site, we couldn't find it. We'd seen pictures of it but had forgotten we would have to find the place at night. We'd literally lost the plot.

Fortunately, Jock had been there a week earlier. He'd marked the four corners of the site with what he thought were just some big useless white sticks he'd found in an old box in his loft. They'd been left there by the previous owners. He described them to me. I realised they were professional fireworks. They were no longer legal for public use.

They could be set off remotely. I found a suitable remote control device in my junk collection and fitted new batteries. We moved well back and tried to set off the fireworks. Three rockets went off, so we soon found the site. The fourth just sparked and fizzled on the ground due to being upside down. We also had to put out a fire in a skip in our factory car park, as Jock had dumped the remaining fireworks in it several days earlier, and other rubbish had been added since.

We slowly descended, lowering the house and garden to their new location. The helicopter landed, and the pilot got out to guide us down. We checked with Jock that it was level and facing the right way.

We separated the two bubbles and moved away. Then we turned off the one in the house. We parked in a nearby field and waited until morning.

When morning came, we went to take a look. Everything looked good. Barry prepared to remove the power unit from the house. Meanwhile, Ned could be seen looking around the site. He'd taken advantage of the chance for more overtime money, as usual.

"I think you've forgotten something," said Ned. Jock looked surprised.

"I think you'll find I haven't," said Jock. He wasn't used to being questioned like that.

"Look where the Sun is."

"Yes..." said Jock.

"Now look where your solar panels are," said Ned.

Jock looked. The Sun was shining, but not on the panels. They were on the north-facing side of the roof.

"So... wotcha gonna do about it, mate?" said Ned.

Jock looked again. He felt sure he'd checked all this, yet the Sun was in the 'wrong' place. He checked the compass app on his phone. According to the phone, the panels were facing south.

Jock shouted at Barry to stop what he was doing and join him outside. I did too. Ned also joined us, looking smug. We all compared compass apps. All but Jock's said the panels were facing north. Jock had a faulty phone.

Barry reconnected everything he'd just disconnected, then we rotated the property to the correct position.

"Good job I was 'ere," said Ned, before walking back to the factory, looking very pleased with himself. Jock said nothing.

After a final check, we removed our power unit from the house and returned it to the factory. We had configured the house bubble and the one at the original site in the same way as our factory bubbles. That meant that the displaced land from the new site exactly filled the hole left where the house and garden had been at the old site. It looked like it had never been there, apart from a driveway that led nowhere and the foundations of an unfinished house.

We returned later to retrieve the generator and equipment from the old site. The bubble had stopped operating, as the generator had run out of fuel. When we arrived, we found a man there from the electricity company, staring at the concrete foundations. He looked confused. He'd been sent to read the meter. Simon told him he was a bit early, as the house hadn't been built yet.

Jock and his wife were pleased with the move. It had all gone perfectly. Unfortunately, the 'new' local council got a bit upset. Planning permission had been obtained for a new house, but not for an old one. They had never encountered this before. The obvious age of the house made it impossible for them to claim it had been built without permission.

Jock persuaded the old and new councils to communicate with each other directly, to sort it out. They decided there had been a 'mix-up with the postcodes', which they agreed to fix.

News of our success soon got around. We carried out several similar house moves after that. We even moved houses and other buildings to other planets. Other spaceships we passed in the drains were amused by what they saw.

We could move many types of houses, but not terraced ones. Someone did ask us to, but we couldn't think of any way to do it without causing considerable damage to the adjoining properties. Smythe had a simple solution to the problem. We just said 'no'. That applied to flats, too.

Some people asked us to move just their gardens. Most were irregular shapes. (The gardens, not the people.) It took our boffins a while to figure out how to create a non-spherical bubble.

At one time, back at my home, I wished I could move my lawn. The people I bought my house from were a rough lot. Their spelling was terrible. Fortunately, they'd employed a reputable solicitor. The sale went through without a hitch.

I don't think they liked me much. I never understood why. I expected problems, but I didn't find any. The house had been well maintained, with a nice garden.

Next spring, the daffodils came up. They were in the middle of my lawn, in an odd pattern. The previous owners must've moved them there. I had to delay cutting that part of my lawn until the daffodils had finished flowering. I called them my daft-odils. I kept meaning to dig them up and move them, but I never quite got around to it.

I flew a drone over my property the following year and noticed that the daffodils in my lawn spelled out the word LUSA. (I said they couldn't spell.) I wasn't pleased.

I remembered Sue's prediction that I would someday marry someone called Lisa. I hadn't taken it too seriously, yet part of me was starting to believe it. Being in a silly mood, I dug up the 'U' bulbs and rearranged them to read 'I'. If I ever married somebody called Lisa, then this might go down well, I thought. Then I forgot about it.

I gained several lady friends the next year, all called Lisa.

Moonpats

Sometimes we were asked to move livestock around the UK. If the animals had to travel hundreds of miles, we could do it much more easily than the usual way. The animals arrived a lot less stressed. Our two androids usually cleared up any mess left behind.

On one occasion, we were asked to move a herd of cattle from a farm in Dorset to another farm in New Zealand. We were more used to transporting sheep or chickens, although we sometimes moved a few cows.

The task proved quite a challenge. More animals were involved than usual and the paperwork wasn't so easy. We had to get permission from the authorities in both countries. Our cars had to be moved well out of the way. We used stronger fencing in our car park than usual.

We landed in the Dorset field next to where the cows were grazing. We switched off the bubble and found the farmer. He delivered a supply of straw and cattle feed to our car park. Amy (who used to be a vet) checked over the animals thoroughly, rejecting two. The remaining cattle were herded into our car park. The farmer signed the paperwork and left, taking the two rejects with him.

We took off and slowly headed for New Zealand. Meanwhile, Barry and the maintenance team wanted to carry out essential maintenance on the artificial gravity system. The boffins also wanted some improvements implemented. Captain Smythe authorised the work, somewhat reluctantly. He'd been assured that nobody would even notice.

Barry's team started working on the artificial gravity system. They weren't supposed to turn it off. Unfortunately, somebody accidentally bumped into the big red 'emergency stop' button. We suddenly had no gravity. At first, we weren't too worried.

Then someone looked through a window and noticed the cows floating around outside. Other stuff could be seen floating around too, from the cows. They were becoming quite vocal. Nobody dared to open a window.

We couldn't take that mess to New Zealand. The people there would've wondered what we'd been up to. We didn't want to land anywhere on Earth until we'd sorted ourselves out, so we landed on the Moon, as the gravity there was (and still is) a lot less than on Earth.

As we slowly descended towards the lunar surface, the Moon's gravity started bringing everything back down. Some of us put on disposable overalls and returned the cows to where they should have been. Some cows landed on the sloping factory roofs and slowly slithered back down.

With so little gravity, it wasn't difficult to get them off flat or uneven surfaces. Some people forgot that although the cows weighed hardly anything, they still had considerable mass. They took some stopping once they got going.

When we landed, the Moon's gravity took full effect. The cows weren't used to the lunar gravity and didn't like it, so we set our main artificial gravity control to Moon normal, switched it back on and then gradually turned it back up to Earth normal. The cows were soon back on their feet. They were encouraged to eat some cattle feed. It wasn't easy. They were distressed and noisy.

We would have to get everything cleaned up before we went to New Zealand. Sue had the idea of using Barry's spare power source to create another force field bubble on the lunar surface, big enough to accommodate the cows.

Barry configured it to merge with our main one at one point. We took some cattle feed into the second bubble and herded the cows into it. Barriers were set up to keep the cows out of the car park while we cleaned up the mess.

Even with both androids working hard, doing the worst tasks, it still took us ages. We found cow dung everywhere, even in the most unexpected places. Our two pressure washers and nearly full tank of water were put to good use.

Then we washed the cows. They didn't like it, but we got it done. We herded the wet, dripping cows back into our car park. Barry collapsed the second bubble and recovered the equipment.

The two androids looked a right mess. I told them to hose each other down, using the pressure washers. That didn't go well. I should have told them to clean each other one after the other. It looked like they were having a pressure washer fight. They squeaked a bit afterwards, so I had to re-lubricate their joints where the grease had been washed out.

There were still a few areas that needed to be washed, mostly in high-up areas. Someone had the daft idea of reducing the artificial gravity again, enough to allow people to jump high enough to reach those areas. They forgot about the recoil of the pressure washers, which sent their operators hurtling backwards. Oops...

We returned home and turned off the bubbles, to let everything dry out and calm the cows down. Then we hurried to New Zealand. We offloaded the cows at their new home, did the paperwork, apologised for the delay and left before anyone could ask any awkward questions.

Future archaeologists could be forgiven for thinking there might have been some truth in that old nursery rhyme about the cow jumping over the Moon. The pats were there. One small step for a man, goodness knows what for a cow.

IDLE MINDS

Things were quiet. We were back home and between contracts. There wasn't much to do, so Barry and his team took the opportunity to get some much-needed maintenance done. The development staff had time to work on their ideas.

Someone had the idea of using one of the rarely used corridors in the factory as a makeshift bowling alley. Simon liked the idea, but we didn't have any bowling balls. We would have to improvise.

We had some footballs left over from a completed contract, so we used those. They were a bit light, so we partly filled them with concrete. Bad idea. They rolled unevenly, so we filled them completely. That made them too heavy. We reduced the gravity in the corridor to compensate. They weren't easy to stop once you got them going. With hindsight, we should've filled them with something else.

We had to put signs along the corridor walls, warning people not to kick the footballs. Joyce put up warning signs on all the corridor access doors. I forget what they used as the ten pins. I think they were inflatable, with weights in the bases. They flew about everywhere when hit.

Captain Smythe heard about it and decided to investigate. He hadn't got all the information. When he opened the door at the 'target' end of the corridor, he saw a football rolling towards him. He'd noticed a sign on the door but hadn't bothered to read it. He was sick of all those signs.

He'd been part of a local football team in his younger days, so he ran towards the ball to kick it. Somebody at the other end of the corridor yelled at him to stop. Too late. A 'crack' could be heard as his foot hit the ball and a 'crunch' as it ran over the toes of his other foot.

He was hopping mad, literally. Someone fetched a wheelchair and rushed him to see Amy. She attended to his injuries, then put his feet in plaster casts. He wanted to complain to the management, but he didn't have a leg to stand on.

One of Larry's dreadful limericks appeared on a nearby wall shortly after that. It read...

'The trouble with Smythe and the ball
Was he'd taken no notice at all.
We thought he was thick,
When he gave it a kick.
Should've heeded the signs on the wall.'

Larry told me later he'd planned to pin up a different limerick, which went something like this...

'The trouble with concrete-filled balls
Is they don't bounce well off the walls.
They soon make you greet
When they land on your feet,

Causing all sorts of trips and falls.'

...but he'd thought better of it. Besides, not everyone there understood Scottish words (greet = cry).

Smythe seemed a bit down after that. He spent less time on the bridge than usual. Simon often had to cover for him when he wasn't there.

I'd been looking for Smythe, as I wanted to discuss something with him. I found him in the cinema, in his wheelchair, watching an old western. I said what I needed to say. Smythe just nodded, quietly. He didn't seem to be in any mood for talking.

Smythe liked westerns. Before his accident, I'd seen him walking down the corridor, practicing his quickdraw. He once called himself 'Quickdraw Smythe'. I gave him a pencil.

Smythe didn't like being in a wheelchair, so Barry made him a hoverchair. It could get him around much more quickly. It had a seatbelt from a car, which he'd been advised to use. He didn't bother, of course.

The chair had a joystick controller and several pushbutton switches in the armrests. Each button would take him to a particular destination. The harder he pushed on the button, the faster the chair went.

Smythe sat on the bridge in his hoverchair. The boffins were doing one of their experiments, so cables were lying across the floor. Someone approached Smythe, carrying something. He tripped over a cable and dropped the heavy object.

It fell onto the button marked 'Toilets'. Smythe's chair whirled around and took him rapidly in that direction. He tried to cancel the shattered button, but he couldn't. He approached the toilets alarmingly fast. The chair had a big red emergency stop button, which he thumped hard with his fist.

The chair stopped sharply, just outside the ladies toilets. He flew out of his chair, collided with the door and fell through it. There were the inevitable screams. He crawled out of there quickly, quite red-faced. After that, he used the seatbelt until he got back on his feet, which didn't take long.

Meanwhile, Sue had been thinking about the original purpose of the Bovercraft. It had never been intended to be flown without leaving the factory. Sooner or later, we would have to move the Bovercraft out. Several people had realised that trying to fly the Bovercraft out through the huge doors without wrecking something would have been almost impossible.

She brought the matter up with Smythe. He agreed. He instructed her and Barry, who were getting along quite well by then (too well, some thought), to devise a better plan.

Existing plans meant manually disconnecting several connectors around the Bovercraft, prior to it departing. Barry had the idea of fitting all the connectors to the craft's rear. When the Bovercraft moved towards the doors, all the connections would automatically disconnect. Automatic valves would be installed where needed. Everything would reconnect automatically when the Bovercraft returned.

The new plan would involve moving the Bovercraft out of the main building on a specially built structure. We called it the Megatrolley. It would run on two strong steel rails, bolted to the floor. The Megatrolley would include three strong cone-shaped supports, pointing upwards. One would be at the front and the other two at the rear. The craft would have three matching hollow cones underneath. When the Bovercraft returned and landed, the three cones on the Bovercraft underside would engage with the ones on the Megatrolley.

Then the whole lot could be moved back into the building. The big connectors would automatically reconnect when the Megatrolley reached the back of the building.

Smythe approved, so Barry and his team got to work. They had it done in a few weeks. The two rails originally planned were replaced by two sections of railway line that I'd had moved from the sidings where Ivor lived. The wheels and bogies also came from there. Barry didn't know where I'd got them from, or how I'd got them there so quickly.

We were ready to test the system. We picked a sunny day, and then fully opened the huge doors. A large motor had been fitted to the Megatrolley, to drive two of the wheels. We slowly drove the huge structure clear of the building, on its rails. The Bovercraft's gravity drive system was powered up, and the craft slowly took off. It hovered about a hundred feet above the ground. Then it descended back onto its locating cones. We drove the whole lot back into the building. We repeated the entire test several times, with no issues.

With that done, we were back to our earlier boredom. Simon persuaded Smythe to let us take the Bovercraft, on its own, on a sightseeing tour of our solar system. That kept us busy for a little while. Our amateur astronomers took lots of pictures. They'd never expected to get so close to the planets they'd been observing through telescopes for so many years.

Even that became dull after a while. We returned home and reconnected with the factory, much to the relief of those left behind. They'd had no power, as we'd taken it with us. We arranged to have the outside mains electricity connected to a large waterproof connector on a post just outside the factory grounds. A heavy-duty cable would connect it to our factory if needed, although that would be a temporary measure.

Our management decided that we should keep taking the factory with us for the time being, until the power issues were properly sorted out.

The time came for us to say goodbye to Zoddoff, as he had completed his time with us. He was due to be moved to another site within the company as part of his apprenticeship agreement. Penny and Joyce were required to do his exit interview and ensure that he returned any company property he had.

The interview went well, except for the last bit. Zoddoff looked nervous. Many had long suspected that he fancied Joyce, although he had never said anything about it to anyone. He eventually handed Joyce a bit of paper with something written on it. I think he'd seen some of Larry's limericks and fancied having a go.

Joyce read it.

"Oh, Zoddoff!" she said. He did, quietly leaving the room, head down, looking quite upset.

"What did I do?" said Joyce quietly, to Penny.

"We don't actually call him Zoddoff. It's just a name we use for him behind his back, as we can't all pronounce his real name. I think he's taken it personally. We'd better go after him," said Penny.

They found him in the corridor outside, muttering and cursing to himself. Fixing this wouldn't be easy, so they told him the truth. Zoddoff seemed to understand. We gave him a good apprenticeship report.

Joyce wouldn't tell me what words were on that bit of paper, or what order they were in. She told Simon, but he wouldn't tell me either.

Fortunes

We were good at setting up space drains. Since we were considered experts in interplanetary plumbing, we were asked to investigate an odd one. It should have been set up years ago, but its use wasn't yet authorised. Rumour had it that the people tasked with setting up the far end had never returned. We were offered good money, so we took on the contract.

We headed off down the drain to investigate. We had a long way to go, so Barry decided to do a little routine maintenance on the drive system MPBs. He would do just one at a time. He assured us it wouldn't affect the system's operation in any noticeable way.

Meanwhile, I was playing with Muttley. Being a young dog, he needed plenty of exercise. I would throw a tennis ball along the corridor. Muttley would chase after it at great speed. He'd catch the ball, come to a slithering halt as his nails clattered on the smooth floor, and then he'd bring the ball back to me. He'd drop it at my feet, tail wagging wildly, waiting for me to throw it again. I got on well with Muttley.

We were near what we called the Engine Room. I threw the ball again. It bounced through the open door and into the room. Barry was working there. He had removed one of the MPBs and had started cleaning it. They attracted dust, which affected their performance. He'd done this on several previous occasions, with no issues. He'd told me earlier that it wasn't a problem, provided he returned the MPB to its place within half an hour of it being removed.

Like most people, Barry liked Muttley. He made a great fuss of him when he rushed in. I called Muttley away and talked to Barry. Barry couldn't talk for long, as he needed to refit the MPB. After we'd finished talking, I noticed Muttley wasn't there. I went after him, leaving Barry to get on with his work.

Barry looked around for the MPB he'd been working on. He felt certain he'd put it on the floor when Muttley arrived. Only the tennis ball remained. Muttley must've gone off with the MPB. Barry chased after me and caught up with me. He told me he needed that MPB back urgently.

Just then, alarms started going off. Unusual vibrations could be felt throughout the Bovercraft. I tried to find Muttley, while Barry rushed to the bridge to find out what had happened.

He found Smythe in the captain's chair, looking annoyed and slightly worried. The bridge staff informed him we had broken through the drain wall and were in normal space. Smythe demanded that we stop immediately, even though we already had.

We had no idea where we were. A sun could be seen close by, so we looked for a planet where we could land and assess our situation. We found one unusually close to the space drain, so we picked a quiet spot on the planet and landed there.

The planet was deemed safe for humans. A group of people went outside onto the planet surface. They found it a strange place, unlike anything they'd seen before. The atmosphere was breathable, but a little thin. The planet had lower gravity than Earth. Several active volcanoes could be seen in the far distance. The sky looked purple. Strange, creeping plant life grew almost everywhere.

The sun seemed bluer than ours and brighter, yet further away. The planet had two moons, one bigger than the other. One looked as lifeless as our Moon. The other looked more habitable. Many unusual rocks and stones were lying around, including transparent crystals of varying shapes, sizes and colours. There were some quite nice ones. They seemed to be just waiting for someone to pick them up.

Meanwhile, I continued looking for Muttley. I found him in a grassy area within our factory grounds, with muddy paws. He'd been burying something. I found the newly dug hole and recovered the MPB. I returned it to a very relieved Barry. He cleaned it thoroughly and then refitted it. Then he reported to Captain Smythe that the (assumed) power problem had been fixed. He left the bridge before Smythe could ask any awkward questions.

Smythe wanted to get back underway, but nobody else did. Our equipment could detect the space drain, so we could see it hadn't gone anywhere. We had no urgent reason to return to it. Most of us wanted to explore this new planet.

I joined the others who had gone outside. I took a small oxygen mask with me, just in case. It took my eyes a while to adjust to the colour of the sunlight. Once they did, things looked a little more normal.

Some of us picked up a few of the coloured crystals. Scuffed traces of pairs of tracks were visible on the ground. It looked like someone had been pushing a trolley and had tried to hide the tracks afterwards.

After a while, a few of the planet's inhabitants approached us. We hadn't seen them coming, as they seemed to blend in with the environment. We could tell they were intelligent. How we knew, we didn't know.

They looked strange. Do you remember that old kids' TV programme, 'The Magic Roundabout'? Well, they looked like Dougal, only green. They were roughly the size of a very large dog. They had oscillating tails, which swept the ground behind them.

They tried to speak to us, making strange bubbling and gurgling noises. Somehow, we understood what they were saying, and they understood us.

I asked them about the crystals. I wanted to know what they were. The aliens didn't know. Some crystals had quite sharp edges and were sore on the feet if trodden on with soft shoes. I found out the hard way. I asked if we could take some away with us. They were happy to be rid of them.

I picked up a large crystal and hurried (limping slightly) to Barry's workshop. I wanted to find out what it was, as I thought they might be useful to us. My attempts to drill into it wrecked several drill bits. I tried to crush it in a vice. That failed miserably. I nearly broke the vice. I put the crystal on top of the vice and hit it hard, with a large hammer. The crystal shot off and got stuck in the wall, still undamaged. I tried scratching a piece of glass with it, which it did easily.

I told Barry. We collected as many buckets as we could find, filled them with the crystals and quietly hid them in the Bovercraft, being careful not to be seen. Then we advised everyone else to take some from the planet as souvenirs.

I went back outside. The creatures were still talking to some of our staff. I asked the creatures if they had ever seen humans before. They paused for a moment, then changed the subject. Something didn't seem right.

We knew Smythe wanted to get underway again, so we prepared to say goodbye to the friendly aliens. Mind you, strictly speaking, we were the aliens.

Before we left, the green Dougals said they wanted to show us something. They produced an old photograph. It showed a human spaceship, with three old humans standing near it. I thought the image didn't look quite right, as though it had been altered. We were told that the spaceship had arrived some time ago. The occupants had aged rapidly and died.

I recognised the name of the spaceship. It was the one that had failed to return after being sent to set up the far end of a new space drain, several years earlier.

Their spaceship must've been pulled through the drain wall by the planet, the same way we had been. That meant Muttley's burial of one of our MPBs wasn't the only reason we were there. Their spaceship must've had insufficient power to get back into the drain. They couldn't see it anyway, so they'd given up trying. We had far more power than them, so we were confident we'd manage it easily.

We said our goodbyes and left. Many were quite sad to leave. It seemed like quite a nice place. Our engines had to work harder than usual to get back into the drain, but we managed it. We found and secured the far end of the drain, close to the planet that we assumed to be its intended destination. We made a careful note of where we were, took photos and returned to Earth.

Barry noticed that Sue appeared to be upset about something. Her face had turned quite white as we went back aboard the Bovercraft. He tried to find out what was wrong.

"Didn't you see them?" said Sue.

"See what?"

"Those... umm... oh, never mind," she replied and walked off, leaving Barry puzzled. He thought it best to let her tell him in her own time. She said nothing more about it and soon returned to her usual self.

Several of us had our suspicions about the crystals. Both Barry and I thought they might be diamonds. We would let the experts investigate. We kept the crystals away from Muttley. He'd have wrecked his teeth if he'd tried to chew one up.

Time of the Signs

Nowadays, health and safety regulations are more sensible than they used to be. Lawyers no longer have the power to become involved in H&S disputes. Such matters are dealt with separately.

However, back in the days of F&S, health and safety could be a nightmare, especially for small companies. A common (and cheap) way to get around safety issues was to put up signs. If someone had an accident due to not following the instructions on a clearly visible sign, the employer almost always got away with it. CCTV usually backed them up. The injured person often got the blame. Many people thought this was unfair.

Unfortunately, too many signs in a small area often became a problem. Some walls supported so many health and safety signs that you could hardly see the wall itself. Few people bothered to read them.

Signs often got ignored. In other factories, some injured workers argued in court that it wasn't reasonable for employers to expect people to read so many signs. Some won their cases.

Simon asked Joyce to keep the signs to a minimum. She simplified or removed many of them, but there were still too many.

At our UK base, new fences had been erected around the F&S site. The fencing looked slightly odd, being mostly round, with four corners. Many signs were attached to the fences. There were the usual ones, telling people to keep out, that CCTV was in operation (it wasn't) and so on.

We had some silly individuals (mostly Simon and Joyce) who had put up extra ones, such as 'Beware of the badger', 'Danger – unexploded porcupines' and 'Warning – juggling with washing machines can be hazardous to your health'. Being in a remote location, they didn't think anyone would notice. For a long time, nobody did (at least, nobody of any importance).

Simon was about to add another sign. It was a huge barcode, about six feet long. When decoded using a smartphone, it was supposed to read 'Welcome to F & S'. Simon had changed it, so it read 'Push off, you nosey wazzock'. He hesitated, as he wasn't sure if he could get away with it.

Then he noticed several new signs he didn't recognise. I think someone had mentioned the site on social media and people had started adding their own signs. It had got a bit out of hand. We soon had 'Trespassers will be fed to the squirrels', 'Danger – sign hanging on fence', 'Do not read this sign', 'If you read this sign, your legs will fall off' and 'I had baked beans for breakfast'.

There were many more, but I can't remember them all. More were appearing daily. Most used the proper HSE colours and formats, so they didn't look out of place from a distance. Maybe his new sign wouldn't be so out of place after all.

For any other site, the extra signs would have been quite harmless. There remained plenty of fence space to put signs on. Unfortunately, the signs attracted unwanted attention to our site. People wondered what we were trying to hide.

The area inside the fence was protected by a force field bubble while we were away. Nobody could get through it. Some people threw stones at it, which bounced off, sometimes causing injuries. We had to put up a sign warning people not to throw stones at the bubble.

It wasn't long before somebody cut through the fence. People tried to break into the bubble. Many tried and most failed, but someone did eventually get through. What he found inside wasn't what he expected.

He found the ground inside the bubble hot and dry. The trees and bushes were not native to the UK. He thought he could see a kangaroo watching him. His weak mobile phone signal couldn't penetrate the bubble. Shouting to his friends didn't help, as they couldn't hear him. He couldn't get out again.

His friends panicked. They didn't want to admit they'd done anything wrong, but they had to do something. They found our mobile phone number on one of the signs and called it. Fortunately, we were on Earth at the time.

We were in Australia when we got the call. We took off, returned to the UK, arrived at the site and landed in a clearing nearby. Smythe, Barry and I went to investigate. The young man's friends told us their friend had vanished and the bubble's interior had changed.

We made the unusual decision to switch off both bubbles, as we could see both. A few minutes later, we received a call from the young missing person. He was calling from Queensland and sounded quite confused. We told him to leave the area and stay away.

We restarted both bubbles and then fetched him back from Australia. We warned him and his friends not to put this incident on social media, or any other form of media. Nobody would have believed them anyway.

We took down the silly signs and added a few serious ones, warning people to keep away. Barry added several obvious CCTV cameras, plus a few dummy ones. He attached remotely controlled hidden cameras to nearby trees. We also got onto social media and created fake stories about the site. We deliberately made them strange to keep the conspiracy theorists busy.

We weren't sure how that one individual had got through the bubble. It worried us. Maybe there had been a glitch in the bubble controls, a brief power cut, or some other reason. We never did find out.

Dreams

We were flexible with our working hours. In the early days of F&S, we used an old, unreliable system for clocking in and out. Nobody liked it. It often refused to connect to our computer network properly.

After our first trip into space, we had less staff, so we adopted a less formal system. Everyone had to write their in or out times in a book instead, watched by a CCTV camera. We eventually converted this to flexitime.

Captain Smythe noticed Sue repeatedly beginning her shifts later than usual. He suspected that something wasn't right. She always kept within the allowed limits, so he couldn't officially do anything about it. She often seemed tired and distracted. Smythe asked Barry to try to find out why.

Barry had a long talk with her. She said she'd been sleeping more than usual, yet still felt tired. Barry also felt more tired than usual, although he didn't admit it to Sue. He took her to see Amy. I think he secretly hoped to discover why he also felt tired.

Amy asked Sue lots of questions, but couldn't figure out what was wrong. She suggested that Sue should spend a night sleeping in the medical department. The medical equipment could monitor her sleep and record everything for analysis in the morning. Sue agreed, so Amy got everything set up, and Sue slept there that night.

The following morning, Sue got up early, like she used to, feeling refreshed. Amy's equipment had recorded nothing unusual, so the problem had to be in Sue's room. Maybe the ventilation system was faulty. She asked Barry to check the filters. They were fine.

Amy planned to spend the next night in Sue's room to watch her there. Sue wasn't entirely happy about that, but when Amy suggested (jokingly) that the alternative was Barry, she quickly complied. (They were getting along well, but not *that* well.)

Sue went to bed early that evening, as she'd been doing for several weeks. Amy settled down in a comfy chair nearby, with plenty of reading material. It wasn't long before they both nodded off.

Amy's watch alarm went off, waking her up sharply. She'd set it to go off every two hours unless cancelled. She got up to check on Sue. Sue was asleep and glowing slightly. The glow looked the same as the light emanating from the small MPB on the table beside her, but not as bright. A dull beam of light could be seen linking Sue and the MPB, which flickered slightly.

Amy called Barry on the radio. I overheard the call and replied too. Amy called us both to Sue's room. Once our eyes had adjusted to the dark, we could see the light between Sue and the MPB. We both thought that the flickering looked like some form of data transfer. I was about to suggest that Sue should sleep without the MPB so close to her in future when something odd happened.

Sue started to talk in her sleep. It started in English, but that slowly changed. She started talking in an unknown language and occasionally made odd noises (verbally). Amy recorded it.

I found it quite alarming. Barry looked even more alarmed, as he could understand most of it. He couldn't understand why.

Amy had had enough. She picked up the MPB and took it back to her medical facility. That broke the link. Sue reverted to normal sleep. When she returned, Amy asked Barry and me to leave the room. She didn't want Sue to wake up and find us there.

Amy stayed with Sue for the rest of the night. She was ready to record any new speech, but there wasn't any more to record. In the morning, she told Sue what had happened.

I talked to Barry about his ability to understand the strange language. He still seemed slightly shaken up. Barry had worked with the MPBs in our drive system on several occasions, so that could have affected him. He'd been sleeping more and having strange dreams, mostly about Mars.

We informed Smythe, as he wanted to know what was going on. He directed that Sue should not be allowed to keep the MPB in her room. She could still study it in the laboratory if she wished.

Weeks passed. (They tend to do that.) We were all curious about the MPBs. Sue tried looking at the small one she had previously borrowed using a high-powered microscope. What she saw startled her. She saw a habitable environment inside it, with alien creatures walking around within it.

I was nearby, so I too had a look. I saw nothing but the semi-transparent MPB. Maybe Sue's unusual psychic abilities were helping her to see things I couldn't. I called Barry. He had a look too, but he saw nothing more than I did.

Barry's eldest son was studying at an English university. He and his young colleagues had been working on equipment that could monitor and record a person's dreams. Barry thought this might be right up their street, so he called his son and explained our situation. They rang him back later, very keen to help, so Sue, Amy, Barry and I took a few days off and travelled to the university. We took the small MPB with us.

Several enthusiastic students greeted us. They showed us to their laboratory. Much of the equipment looked experimental, with wires and cables everywhere. They assured us that it all worked, most of the time. I got them to agree, in writing, that anything they saw during the following few days would not be disclosed to anyone.

Later in the day, we got set up. Sue would be the test subject. They got her 'wired up' to their equipment. She held onto the MPB and fell asleep within minutes. The recorders were started. A few minutes later, images of Sue's dreams appeared on the monitors. They were fuzzy at first, then quite sharp.

The students weren't accustomed to getting such clear images. Sue was their best test subject so far. The images were fascinating. There were alien landscapes, trees, modern-looking buildings and floating vehicles. Humanoid creatures were walking around everywhere.

One creature came into close view. It appeared to be speaking to us. Just then, Sue started speaking. She seemed to be speaking for the alien. Amy had set up a video recording device on a tripod nearby, so she recorded everything.

Barry commented that the scenes looked familiar to him. He could understand the language, so he tried talking to the creature. He found he could talk to it via Sue.

We discovered that Mars had once been a planet full of life, many millions of years ago. The people we had assumed to be Martians weren't originally from Mars. They were explorers. They had found the planet and tried to land there, but had miscalculated and crashed. The smaller MPBs, as we called them, were meant to be a 'last resort', to preserve their life energies (and digitally stored physical forms) in the event of a disaster. They knew they were unlikely to be rescued so far from home. There were far fewer intelligent races in our galaxy back then.

The smaller MPBs contained virtual environments for them to live in. The larger ones were originally the power source for their spacecraft. The aliens hoped that an intelligent race like ours would detect the larger MPBs, discover their life energies in the smaller ones and restore them to physical form.

They told us there wasn't any urgency, but if we couldn't (or wouldn't) help, then they would like all the MPBs returned to Mars. Something unusual in the Martian sunlight helped to recharge them.

We talked for hours. Several more aliens got involved in our conversation. We were keen to help them if we could. They clearly had no hostile intent. We said we'd see what we could do. Hopefully, Sue would be our means of communication with them in the future.

They told us that the MPBs had been intended to always be visible on the surface of Mars, in the hope that a race like ours would eventually find them. They knew that such a race might just use the MPBs as a power source. They were prepared to take that risk. They gave us some useful technical advice, which would enable us to drastically reduce the amount of energy we needed to take from the MPBs.

The students were scared silly. They didn't know what we knew. I assured them they were at absolutely no risk. I even put it in writing for them. We thanked them and then returned (with the MPB and our recordings) to our factory.

We 'forgot' to tell Smythe everything. He didn't have to know. We implemented the improvements to our drive systems suggested by the aliens and tried to keep the use of the MPBs to a minimum.

BLAKEY

I hated mowing my lawn. I found it boring and time-consuming. If the grass was wet, I'd have to wash it off the undersides of my shoes (or wellies) before going indoors. I used to cut my grass with a conventional lawnmower.

I fancied one of those robotic ones, so I bought a cheap one. It seemed to work, although it struggled with long grass. I still had to deal with the cuttings. I wanted a better solution.

Some years earlier, I'd been involved in experiments with teleportation. My employers back then had put much time and money into its development. They had hoped to transport people around the world quickly, without the need for aircraft.

They had limited success. It proved impossible to do what the company wanted. Transporting fruit and vegetables could be done easily, but more solid substances were more challenging. Teleporting over great distances was possible, but it took a lot of power. Anything living always died during the process. At least it killed off any bugs.

They tested the system by teleporting produce from a farm directly to a local supermarket. People were wary of it. Nobody would eat the stuff. Some thought it might be contaminated or radioactive. A false rumour went around that the food could disappear after being eaten. The idea had to be abandoned.

I wondered if I could use the same technology to cut my grass. I removed the cutting assembly from my robotic mower. Then I fitted a thin, square transport plate under the mower instead. I set it up to only transport material from up to about two inches below the plate. I fitted the receiver plate to a wooden structure above my compost heap, facing downwards.

When I pressed the 'Test' button on the mower, it buzzed briefly, and then a few blades of grass fell onto the compost heap. When I moved the mower away, I found a neat, square patch of grass had been cut where the mower had been. It looked hopeful, better than I expected. I set up the teleport system to operate every half second, and then let the mower loose on the garden.

At first, the system worked well. The results looked very neat. The mower's sensors helped it to keep within the bounds of my lawn and avoid obstacles. Unfortunately, the cheap mower had a rather primitive position-sensing system.

A local seagull didn't like it. It attacked the mower, damaging two sensors. The mower didn't know where it was after that. Being cheap, it continued anyway.

Meanwhile, I went indoors, feeling pleased with myself. I started filling in some patent application forms. I should've known something would go wrong.

I heard odd noises from outside. I looked at the compost heap. Some of my flowers were on it. At least, I thought they were my flowers. They could've been somebody else's. The mower had escaped and had headed off down the street.

Some grass verges had been cut, and the mower had been into people's gardens. They weren't pleased. I retrieved the mower and apologised profusely to its victims.

Later that day, the local policewoman came to see me. I got along well with her. She knew I wasn't a troublemaker. She was Welsh, so I sometimes called her Plodwyn. She advised me not to let this happen again. I thought she might have me nicked for 'mowing without due care and attention'.

Before she could finish speaking, a loud explosion could be heard from my garden. The mower had blown up, leaving a large, black hole in my lawn. I told her there wasn't much chance of it happening again after that. She agreed and left.

Talking of black holes... that reminds me of a serious incident we had to deal with shortly afterwards.

Have you ever heard of the Large Hadron Collider? Most people these days haven't. It's been disused for years. However, in the days of F&S, it was still very active. It had been created by CERN, in Europe, at great expense. Several important scientific discoveries were made there.

People used to worry about them somehow creating a dangerous black hole that could swallow the Earth. Nonsense, of course. At least, that's what we thought.

A big experiment was taking place at the LHC. The biggest yet. The collider was deep underground, so nobody worried about the weather above. Unfortunately, at the critical moment, the power lines were struck by lightning. The experiment itself must've attracted it somehow. Something odd came into permanent existence at that moment.

The 'something' could only just be seen with the naked eye. The scientists there didn't know what to make of it. It seemed quite unstable. They had other experiments to get on with, so they moved it into a small, sealed container. They erected a battery-powered force field around it, stored it in a briefcase and put it on a shelf, to analyse later. Then they forgot about it.

A few weeks later, one of the scientists was working late. He was tired. He picked up what he thought was his briefcase and took it home. When he opened it to remove his lunch box, he noticed the strange object inside. The small force field had failed, as the batteries had run down.

The container had disintegrated, and the object had grown. It flashed and spluttered, sometimes appearing pitch black, sometimes brilliant white. He didn't know what to do about it.

One of our boffins received a panicky call from the CERN scientist, as he'd worked with him at university. He needed advice. Our boffin consulted the rest of his group. It was an emergency, so they told Smythe. Smythe told our local management. Nobody would make a decision, so I recommended we get the object off the planet and into space as soon as possible.

By the time we got to see it, the object no longer flashed. It looked completely black. Its size had increased. It had become a small black hole. It took several days for anyone to agree on what to do about it or decide how to move it.

I've never liked black holes. I don't suppose anybody does, now that I think about it. The whole idea has always scared me. This incident started giving me nightmares. I dreamt I was in a supermarket, being chased by a black hole. It pulled things into itself off the shelves as it chased me down the aisles, shouting, "I'll get you, Alan!". I would wake up out of breath, sweating profusely.

The black hole was still growing, at an increasing rate. There was no obvious way to move it, to get it outside. We had to do something about it quickly. We needed to get it away from Earth. No time to bother telling the authorities about it. We had to act immediately.

We had more than one propulsion system. The one we used when we were close to (or on) planets used gravity to repel us from or attract us to things, usually planets. We had become much better at controlling our gravity drive. We could make it highly directional.

We assembled all the senior staff (except Joyce, who was on leave for a week) to decide what to do about this black hole. Rumours were spreading around the factory. They had to stop.

I wanted to give it a name. Smythe glared at me disapprovingly at first but then realised I was right. It would stop us from saying 'black hole' in conversation, hopefully limiting the rumours. Someone suggested calling it Blackie, but I suggested Blakey, so we used that.

That left the problem of what to do about it. Some said we should take it as far away from Earth as possible and leave it there. Others thought that irresponsible, as it could still be a problem for somebody.

The immediate problem was how to get Blakey off the planet. Normally, we would use our gravity drive to move around close to planets. We couldn't do that this time, as we needed it to lock onto Blakey.

We would have to use our main drive to manoeuvre. That wasn't easy. It would require some skilful piloting. We hovered about a mile above the CERN scientist's house, located Blakey and locked onto it with our gravity drive. Then we pulled on it, hard. Blakey shot through the roof of the house, making a big hole.

Blakey was carefully pulled into space, with us keeping well clear of it. We started towing it away from Earth, holding onto it using the gravity drive. Next, we had to decide what to do with it.

We held another senior staff meeting. Sue suggested that if we could find a solar system with no inhabited planets, we could somehow throw Blakey at the star. Hopefully, Blakey would be overwhelmed by it, thus solving our problem. Nobody had any better ideas, so we tried it.

We knew of only one star with no inhabited planets, so we headed there. It was a large one, some distance away. We would have to travel through a dangerous region of space where there were known to be space pirates. They were nasty people. Their spaceships were fast and well-armed. Almost nobody survived an encounter with them.

We had no choice. We didn't have time to look for somewhere better to dump Blakey. Hopefully, our bubble would protect us, but we couldn't be sure. We headed directly towards the star.

It wasn't long before we encountered the pirates. They demanded that we stop and be boarded. Blakey was still growing and would have swallowed us up if we'd stopped, so we kept going. That annoyed the pirates, who pursued us. We told them to leave us alone or face the consequences. They just laughed at us and soon caught us up. They were behind us, so they were pulled into Blakey and destroyed. That made Blakey bigger.

The remaining pirates were furious. They weren't accustomed to losing, so they all came after us. They fired all the weapons they had at us. Most projectiles just bounced off our bubble. Blakey dealt with the rest. They chased us, like the others, still failing to realise what they were dealing with. They perished too, consumed by Blakey. I thought it served them right, but I still felt guilty about the loss of lives.

As we approached our destination, we devised a plan. We would head directly towards the star. As we got close, we would veer off sharply, and then switch off the gravity drive.

We tried it. The first attempt failed. Blakey continued to follow us, although it was noticeably further behind us. We went around in a huge arc and then tried again. This time, we went much closer to the star. When we pulled away, we used maximum power. This time it worked, just. Blakey seemed more interested in the star than us.

We retreated to a safe distance and watched as the star swallowed Blakey. The star seemed to shrink briefly and bulge a little in places. It took several hours to settle down. There were lots of extreme solar flares. As we watched, someone belched loudly, which seemed strangely appropriate.

We moved further away and monitored the star. The boffins took careful measurements at regular intervals. When they were satisfied that the star had returned to normal, we returned home. We informed the authorities on Earth that the part of space where the pirates had been should no longer be a problem. We refused to tell them why.

It seemed unlikely that the CERN scientist's house insurance would have covered him for black hole damage, so our company paid for the repairs to his house roof, on the strict understanding that he tell nobody about what had just happened, ever.

Break time

Shortly after the black hole incident, I happened to be talking to Sue.

"I'm glad that's over," said Sue.

"Me too. I don't want to go through that again," I said. I think we were both still quite shaken up.

"I think we all need a good holiday," said Sue. I agreed.

Simon appeared.

"Did somebody say holiday?"

"Yes. I did," said Sue. "I don't just mean for individuals. I mean for the entire factory. I think we've earned it."

"Sounds good to me," said Simon. "Where should we go? Any ideas?"

"That planet we were on a couple of weeks ago seemed nice. Only I don't fancy having to wear an oxygen mask all the time," I said.

We talked for a while. Every place we came up with had a problem. Many planets could accommodate tourists, but not an entire factory.

The alien races we encountered were often very different from what we'd seen in old science fiction. There were very few 'humanoid' races other than us. Every habitable (for us) planet had a slightly different atmosphere and different gravity. We found some rather smelly. The inhabitants often looked strange to us. We probably looked strange to them.

All the intelligent races we met had several things in common. They all had a sense of humour. They also had most of the other feelings that humans have. When we met a new race, we usually found it effective to make them laugh as soon as possible. It often made our first meetings much easier. It wasn't always easy to tell when they were laughing, so we had to be careful. But I digress.

"We'll have to go somewhere on Earth," said Simon. We agreed.

"How about a desert island?" said Sue.

"I don't think any are deserted anymore," I said. "They've all become tourist destinations. There might be another solution, though."

"What?" said Sue.

"Time travel. Maybe we could go back in time, to when those islands were unoccupied, and have our holiday then."

"We'd better talk to the boffins," said Simon.

Our boffins understood time travel, but we all knew it could be problematic. There were well-documented cases of people going back in time to try to change major events. They always failed to make any noticeable difference. Our timeline seemed to be self-correcting, like a wound healing itself. Many people had learnt the hard way, so few tried.

It could be dangerous, too. One time traveller went back in time and accidentally killed someone in the past. On his way back to the present, he died. Nobody understood why. His death somehow resulted in his victim not dying after all.

Time travel also requires a lot of power. Transporting our entire factory several centuries back in time would have been almost impossible. We didn't have that much power available. Shifting ourselves slightly through time was possible, though. We did that occasionally to avoid radar sweeps when we didn't want to be noticed.

That reminds me... the local police used to make good use of time travel. They had a machine that could lock onto an item of litter and follow it back through time by up to a month. That allowed them to record the litterer in the act. The culprits were located and fined. Word soon got around and the littering almost stopped. But I digress (again).

Barry was with us when we spoke to the boffins about the time travel holiday idea. He suggested that if we couldn't take our entire factory back in time, perhaps we could take just the Bovercraft.

The boffins said it could be done, but we'd still need a lot of power. We could only travel back in time a limited amount. Dinosaur hunting wasn't an option. We would have to build up and store power for several days before making the jump through time.

We spoke to Smythe about it. He agreed to the idea, on the understanding that after our holiday, we would return to the same point in time and space we had left from.

Simon consulted his maps and picked an island. Smythe made a Tannoy announcement about it. He said that if anyone didn't want to go, they should tell Simon in good time.

We started getting ready. Joyce had returned from her own holiday by then. She didn't raise any objections to the plan, or to having a second holiday.

I was discussing something with Simon when Phil appeared.

"Simon, I'm worried about visiting that desert island," said Phil.

"Why?" said Simon.

"I don't want to get eaten."

"Eh? Eaten by what?"

"The cannonballs."

"Cannonballs are round balls of iron," I said. "They can't eat you."

"Yes, they can," said Phil. "Didn't you ever see Robinson Crusoe?"

"I think you mean cannibals," said Simon.

"Yeah, them."

"I can assure you there won't be any cannibals on that island," said Simon. "Don't worry about it."

Phil didn't look convinced, although he seemed to take Simon's word for it. We continued with our preparations.

Some people wanted to tell families and friends they would be away for a while. I pointed out that we would be returning to just after we had left, so it would be pointless. Some still didn't understand.

The time for our departure arrived. Everyone got on board the Bovercraft. We moved it out of the building and took off. We rose about fifty feet, then vanished in a green flash.

From our point of view, little had changed, apart from the trees and other plant life. Also, the factory couldn't be seen. Barry reminded everyone we had only moved in time, not space. We were still above where our factory would be in the future.

From there, we travelled to the tropical island. We didn't use the Bovercraft bubble on that occasion. There wasn't any need to. We left the one around the factory switched on for security reasons while we were away, just in case something went wrong. We could activate or deactivate it remotely.

When we arrived at the island, we parked the Bovercraft in a clearing close to the beach. Smythe intended to make an announcement over the Tannoy system, but he wasn't quick enough. Most people were already heading for the beach, many in swimsuits, carrying towels and other paraphernalia.

The water in a nearby stream was very pure, so Phil topped up the Bovercraft's main onboard water tank from it. He usually filled the huge water tank in the factory grounds when he could. It was *his* task. He was determined to do it well. He had become known as 'Phil the tank', partly because he did.

We had a good holiday. Most people acquired a suntan. We originally only intended to be there for a week. We actually stayed for nearly a month. We were time travellers. There was no reason to hurry back.

Eventually, many of us became bored. We'd used up all the food we'd brought for barbecues, gathered far too many shells and had run out of things to do. It was time to return to our own time.

We agreed on a time for our return. Simon announced it over the Tannoy system several times. Notices about it were pinned on the noticeboards. We did our best to ensure that everyone knew our intended departure time.

During the evening before our planned departure time, we had a big party. Someone found several crates of alien booze that we'd forgotten about. We had intended to test it before drinking it, but we forgot.

Many people got a little drunk. Some got a big drunk and locked him in the food store to sober up. The words 'kettle', 'pot' and 'black' came to mind. Whose mind, I don't know. Most people were out of theirs, including Captain Smythe. We found him outside, trying to dance with a tree. He couldn't understand why it had so many feet.

Simon wasn't sober either. I spotted him in the sea, trying to swim through time. I waded in and fetched him out, as the water was only about three feet deep. Barry had also succumbed to the drink. He'd injured both his wrists, trying to juggle with our improvised bowling balls.

Amy knew she had to keep sober. She was the only medically qualified person we had. She bandaged Barry's wrists and warned him it would hurt later, when the effects of the drink wore off. She also rescued our big drunk from the food store. She'd heard him banging on the door as she walked past. She brought him to her medical facility to warm up, while she kept an eye on him.

The next morning, most of us regretted what we had done the previous evening. Some turned up at Amy's medical facility wanting a cure for a hangover.

Joyce was there. She whispered something to Amy. Amy grinned, then went off to fetch something. She came back with a large wooden mallet. Then she said she could fix a hangover by hitting the patient on the head with the mallet. That should cancel out the headache. She might have to do it several times to find the right spot. She couldn't guarantee it would work. Nobody accepted her kind offer.

We delayed several days before trying to return home. None of us were in a fit state to pilot anything, let alone a spaceship through time.

Once we had all recovered, we got aboard. We flew back to our original location above where our factory would be and went forward in time to a point about twenty minutes after we had left.

We deactivated the factory bubble, descended onto the Megatrolley, moved the Bovercraft back into the factory and reconnected with it.

Someone came rushing into the Bovercraft.

"I thought you'd gone without me," she said.

"We did," said Simon. "Where were you?"

"I had a doctor's appointment. I got held up in traffic on the way back."

"Oh. Umm. Sorry, but we've had our holiday. We've just got back," said Simon. He reached into his pocket and handed her some cowries.

Several days later, someone noticed that Phil, the former zookeeper, wasn't with us. He'd probably wandered off somewhere on the island and couldn't (or wouldn't) find his way back. Maybe he didn't want to. He had tended to keep himself to himself since he'd been with us. He didn't talk to people much unless he had to. Some people joked that the cannonballs might have got him.

We considered going back for him but decided against it. There was plenty of food and water on the island. Our departure time had been well publicised (twice). He had little excuse for being left behind. We thought he was probably happier there.

Somebody else would have to fill our water tank.

HAIRBRAINED SCHEMES

Most of the time, our staff behaved well. Some got slightly drunk occasionally, but problems were rare. The one time it did become a problem, Captain Smythe, of all people, was the culprit.

We were back at our UK base. One evening, Smythe used Ivor to travel to the local town. He'd planned to meet up with some ex-army friends of his for an evening out. Using Ivor would be safer, he thought. He didn't want to risk being caught driving his road sweeper while slightly drunk.

They'd met at the local pub, as planned. They got completely sloshed, not as planned. Smythe had managed to stagger back to Ivor and return to the factory. (I later found Ivor crashed into the buffers, with a flat battery.)

At about 2 AM, we heard loud 'singing'. Smythe was staggering about, singing 'I belong tae Glasgow' at the top of his voice (his friends were Scottish) and occasionally bouncing off the walls. Easier than singing 'I belong to Stow on the Wold', I suppose, especially when you're drunk. The noise woke several of us up, so we went to investigate. Simon, Joyce and I found him propping up a corridor wall. We helped him back to his quarters.

We removed his shoes (odd, as we weren't wearing them) and got him to bed. Simon noticed that both of Smythe's eyebrows had been shaved off. Rough replacements had been drawn on at strange angles. Smythe dozed off. We left him to sleep.

The next morning, Smythe woke up with a terrible headache. He got up and washed his face. Then he noticed he had no eyebrows. He wasn't happy. (Sleepy or Grumpy, more like.) He couldn't do anything about it as he was due on the bridge soon. He got dressed, had his breakfast and went to start his shift.

He walked onto the bridge. People looked oddly at him but didn't dare say anything. He sat down heavily in his chair and started giving orders, as usual. After a couple of hours, things seemed normal, at least to him.

Simon and Joyce were there, working at one of the control desks. They looked at him, turned away and spoke quietly to each other. Then they started staring at one of the displays. Smythe spotted them.

"What are you two staring at?" shouted Smythe. They said nothing, so he got up to look for himself. The display looked odd, mainly because they'd been tinkering with it.

Joyce raised one eyebrow. She looked at Simon, who raised both eyebrows. Smythe was jealous. He didn't have any eyebrows. People in the background were sniggering, so he stormed off.

Simon and Joyce felt guilty. They waited about ten minutes, then went after him. Joyce had an eyebrow pencil handy, so she offered to draw his back on. He wouldn't let her, so she just lent him the pencil.

Smythe returned to his quarters. He tried to draw his eyebrows back on, in front of the mirror. He still wasn't feeling right, so he overdid it somewhat.

A short while later, he reappeared on the bridge.

"Oh look! It's Captain Caveman!" said someone, who quickly ducked out of sight behind a desk. Joyce felt sorry for Smythe and insisted on sorting him out.

Later, someone told Smythe about some powerful, quick-acting hair restorer he'd discovered. Smythe bought some. He put it in his bathroom. The next morning, Smythe got up as usual to wash his face. He reached for the liquid soap, applied some to his hands and washed his face with it. Then he noticed it smelled of peppermint. That didn't seem right.

He looked for the soap dispenser. He didn't find it. He'd run out of soap the previous day. He'd just applied hair restorer to his face and hands. He tried to wash it off, but by then it was too late.

He had to get up early for several weeks after that, as shaving took him much longer than usual. He didn't want to look like a Neanderthal. He got a local barber to trim his eyebrows to look more normal. Luckily for him, the effects were only temporary.

Smythe had been tempted in the past to outlaw being drunk on the Bovercraft. After his own episode, he reduced that to just 'friendly advice', using his own example to show what can happen.

Another hairbrained idea someone had was to start dealing in waste disposal. We were short of contracts, so it seemed like a good idea. We could shift huge amounts of stuff at once and dump it somewhere off the planet if we had to.

Local councils hated dealing with asbestos. Many just stored it, intending to deal with it later. Few ever did. We contacted several local councils and agreed to take it away for a good price. We had to agree in writing to dispose of it legally and responsibly.

We bought several skips and positioned them around the factory wherever we could find space. We filled them with asbestos, collected from the council sites. We only accepted double-bagged stuff. It wasn't long before the skips were full.

We had originally planned to bury it on the Moon. I had other ideas. I had stored the Asbestorot gas cylinder, used several years earlier, in a Portakabin. I retrieved it. It was empty. I'd not closed the valve properly after dealing with the factory's asbestos problem.

I contacted our American headquarters to see if they could get us any more. They couldn't. It had been discontinued. They didn't know why. I tried to find out but found it mentioned almost nowhere. Odd, I thought. Oh well.

Before we could dispose of the skip-fulls of asbestos, we were asked to carry out several other tasks. The asbestos would have to wait. Several weeks later, we turned our attention back to the asbestos issue.

One day, as I walked past one of the skips, I realised that something didn't look right. I felt sure we'd filled them all to the top, yet this one appeared half empty. I fetched a stepladder and looked inside. All the bags were still there, but some were empty. I fetched one out, to examine it properly.

I put on a suitable dust mask, gloves and overalls. Then I cut open the outer and inner bags. All I could find inside was a small amount of fine dust. As I watched, the dust disappeared completely. It wasn't windy, so this made no sense to me.

The bags were already slightly damaged when I took them out of the skip. That had allowed air inside. It probably happened when they were thrown in. I examined another bag, which still contained asbestos. It still looked properly sealed. Using a small screwdriver, I made a small hole in the inner and outer bags. I left it leaning against the skip.

A week later, the asbestos in the bag I'd put aside only contained what I recognised as Asbestorot goo. A few days later, the goo had vanished.

I told Barry. We and his team went around puncturing the bags in all the skips. Not wise perhaps, but we argued that we were unlikely to get asbestosis with Asbestorot in the air. It wasn't long before all the asbestos had disappeared.

We thought that was the end of it. No such luck. We started hearing reports on the local news that some old factory buildings in the nearby town were losing their roofs. They were falling apart, then vanishing. Smythe told us to say nothing about it to anyone.

Ghosts

Few of us believed in ghosts, even after the incident with Ned. However, some wondered if we might be wrong. Strange things were happening. Usually just silly things, but they were becoming annoying. Small objects were being moved around for no obvious reason. Food had been taken. Environmental settings were being changed.

It continued for weeks. Arguments broke out. That wasn't normal for us. Smythe thought we might have stowaways hiding somewhere. Muttley usually sniffed them out, so Smythe talked to Penny. She insisted Muttley was behaving normally.

He announced that everyone should keep an eye on anything of any value. We were to let him know if anything important went missing. That made things worse.

I spoke to Barry about it. He remembered that Sue had been upset about something when we left the planet where we'd found the crystals. Our problems started shortly afterwards. She clearly knew something we didn't.

We found her in the development lab. Barry approached her cautiously.

"Sue, do you remember that planet we went to, with the nice crystals?" he said.

"Yes..."

"You seemed concerned about something, just before we left."

"Erm, yes..." Sue looked uncomfortable.

"Would you mind telling us what happened? It could be important."

"I don't want to talk about it," said Sue. I intervened.

"You know, strange things have been happening since we left that planet. We might have invisible stowaways on board. Is it possible you can see them and we can't?" I said. She paused.

"Promise me you won't laugh," said Sue. We did. (Promise, I mean, not laugh.)

"OK. I'll trust you. Just don't tell anyone else." She paused again, then continued.

"When we boarded the Bovercraft, I saw strange alien creatures boarding with us. Nobody else but me seemed bothered by them. I thought I must be going crazy. I realise now they're probably real, due to the strange things that have happened recently."

"Do you still see them?" I asked.

"Just occasionally. I think they know I can see them, so they try to keep out of my way."

"Perhaps we could make a special scanner. Something that will allow the rest of us to see them," suggested Barry.

"I'm way ahead of you. I've been working on such a device for about two weeks now. It's about ready for testing," she replied.

We set a trap for the aliens, leaving out types of food that were known to have gone missing. We set up hidden cameras and motion sensors nearby. Then we waited.

It wasn't long before the sensors were triggered. We rushed in, to find Muttley helping himself to the bait. Barry took him back to Penny's quarters and asked her to keep him in for a while.

We cleaned up Muttley's mess and set up the trap again with more food. About an hour later, the cameras recorded the bait vanishing. We hurried there with Sue's detector.

It revealed two strange alien creatures eating the food. We locked ourselves and the aliens in. They hid in the far corner of the room, clearly scared of us. One of them squeaked, "No shoot," so they clearly understood us. I think they mistook Sue's detector for a weapon.

They were strange-looking creatures, being nearly three feet high and almost spherical. Two curved horns stuck up from the tops of their heads. They could walk, but they usually bounced along instead. (Larry later called them Hopspacers).

We told them we didn't want to harm them, however we needed to know why they were on board. It took us a while to calm them down. At first, they told us a lot of nonsense. Maybe they were hoping we'd believe them. We didn't. Sue pushed some buttons on the detector. That scared them into telling us the truth.

They were explorers from a distant planet. They had been on a peaceful mission. As they tried to land on the planet where we'd found the crystals, they'd been forced off course by a new space tunnel, which had suddenly appeared out of nowhere.

Their craft's artificial intelligence predicted a 95% probability of a crash, so they abandoned ship and landed on the planet using life pods.

Meanwhile, their now unmanned craft had tried desperately to avoid the crash. Its engines couldn't take the strain. The craft exploded high in the planet's atmosphere. Bits were scattered over a wide area.

Diamonds were common on their home planet and easy to grow there. They were frequently used for spaceship construction. The crystals we had found on the planet were the remains of their spacecraft.

The aliens had no way home. They'd seen us as a chance to escape the planet, so they'd sneaked aboard the Bovercraft, hoping we'd be going their way. Unfortunately for them, we were taking them even further from their home planet.

They'd tried to keep out of sight. However, they still needed to eat, hence the food thefts. They apologised for the trouble they'd caused us.

I asked how they had learnt to speak our language. They said they had learnt it from the other humans on the planet, who couldn't see them.

I felt awkward. I could see Barry did, too. A human space tunnel had caused the destruction of their craft. We had bucketfuls of the bits. We thought it only fair that we should try to return them to their home planet. Barry said as much to Smythe and Simon.

Smythe didn't like it. He couldn't see why we should go out of our way to return those thieving little aliens to their planet. Simon persuaded him it was the right thing to do.

We turned around and took them back to their home planet. It was well away from any space drains. They were grateful and asked if they could do anything for us.

Smythe suggested setting up a trade deal with them. I think he thought it would make him look good. Barry talked him out of it. We weren't authorised to do it ourselves anyway.

Barry didn't want people to know about a cheap source of diamonds. Neither did I. Ours would have been seriously devalued. We both felt guilty.

Nafwyres

Our contracts seem to come in fits and starts. Sometimes we were rushed off our feet trying to meet almost impossible deadlines. At other times, things were quiet. It seemed like an odd way of working, to me. I suspected poor management.

We were in one of the quiet times. There were a few small orders to get through, but not enough to keep us busy for long. We tried looking for work on more remote planets. That got us a little business, but it wasn't easy. Misunderstandings were all too common, resulting in little profit for us.

Simon had an idea. If we couldn't get much business in the present, why not go looking for it in the past? If we were careful not to upset history as we knew it, it might work. Our holiday in the past had been a great success. He felt confident we could get away with it.

Captain Smythe hated the idea. I too had my reservations. After a big meeting, we agreed to try a short visit into the past. We'd start with a small project and see how it went.

We planned to manufacture radios and televisions, using components available in the 1960s. We created a new brand, called Nafwyres. The initial circuit designs were based on the best, most reliable models of the time. Several old publications listed common faults in those designs, so we improved on them.

Modern computers allowed us to design and test things with ease. Production methods unavailable in the 1960s would be used. All models would be easy to service and very reliable.

All the designs were completed and tested in record time. The styling appeared quite advanced, more like early 1970s equipment. The prototypes all worked perfectly. We expected reliability to be good.

We took the factory back to 1968 and hid ourselves well. Then we set up an outlet in a nearby TV and radio shop. Our prices were lower than most. The TVs and radios sold well. The Nafwyres brand soon gained a good reputation. We set up more outlets in other parts of the UK.

The factory was busy for weeks. We were enjoying what we were doing. We took great care to avoid telling anyone about the 'future'. Those who did slip up and say something were just laughed at.

The Nafwyres name started to get recognised by the major technical news outlets. Articles about our designs appeared in Television magazine. That worried us. We hadn't intended to cause such a stir. We were concerned that we might upset history. That concern soon became irrelevant.

I was working in my workshop in one of the outer factory buildings. I happened to look through the window. I thought nothing of what I saw. Just the usual pine trees. I carried on with my work.

Then I realised something. Those trees were the ones at our home base. We were back home, and I hadn't noticed! I rushed outside to check properly. The factory had indeed returned to our base, in our own time. I ran to the Bovercraft and talked to the Boffins.

They hadn't noticed either. We alerted Smythe, who made a Tannoy announcement. He told everyone to assemble in the car park. We did a roll call. Smythe had not authorised our return. He looked quite annoyed. Nobody knew why we were back.

Around two dozen people couldn't be accounted for. They included Barry, Sue, Joyce and Simon. We looked everywhere, but we couldn't find them. They were assumed to be still in 1968.

Back in 1968, our missing people were in the local town, making the most of the time. Barry had been to a local record shop. He'd bought a full set of the top thirty singles of the time, plus several Beatles LPs. He walked back to where our factory had been. It wasn't there.

Barry was shocked. The factory had left without him. Then he noticed a few others from the factory wandering about nearby, looking for clues. He got everyone together to discuss what to do. Some people were known to be still in the town, so they waited for them to return.

By late evening, everyone had returned to the site. No clues were found that could explain what had happened. They argued for ages about what to do. Simon assured everyone that our boffins would almost certainly be looking for a way to retrieve them. In any case, it wasn't a bad time to be marooned in. They would just have to wait.

Sue became quite upset. She clung to Barry. A few seconds later, they both flickered and disappeared. That intrigued Simon. He guessed that Barry and Sue being so close together might have caused them to vanish. Perhaps they'd returned to the factory.

He suggested that he and Joyce should try it. If it worked, then everyone else should huddle together and, hopefully, get home. Simon picked up Barry's records, and then he and Joyce held onto each other. They vanished. The remaining people huddled together and also vanished.

With everyone back at our base, in our own time, we tried to figure out what had happened. The triplet boffins eventually figured it out. They suggested that travelling back in time was like stretching a piece of elastic. One end was in the present and the other in the past. The further back one went, and the greater the mass, the greater the return force.

The time between our present and the fixed point in time we had originally gone back to had been increasing all the time. Our time in the past added to this. The pull had been increasing continually. Sooner or later, the 'elastic' would suddenly pull us back to the present. They also suggested that just one person alone would be unable to return, as the elastic would be thin enough to snap. It would explain why Phil had never returned from the desert island.

We'd narrowly avoided a disaster with our holiday earlier. The boffins worked out that if we had stayed there just a week longer, many of us could have been stuck there when the Bovercraft suddenly returned. When it did, it would have dropped rapidly after its return and crashed, as its drive systems would not have been powered up.

Barry wanted to find out if any record of Nafwyres's existence existed. He found nothing. He had brought back a copy of the Television magazine that featured the brand. He compared it with an original copy, the same month and year, that he found being advertised for sale. They were different. He found no trace of Nafwyres in the older, original version. No old Nafwyres TVs or radios were on sale anywhere. It was as though we had never been back to 1968 at all.

However, we did have a few coins from the time, plus some other objects. They were in excellent condition. Our profits had been converted into gold. We still had it, so it hadn't been a complete waste of time. We kept a close eye on it for a couple of weeks. Some were concerned that things we'd brought back might suddenly disappear, but they never did.

Ron had been unusually quiet during the entire Nafwyres venture. He'd played his part in the work we had done but had said little. I decided to talk to him about it, while we were in the canteen. He didn't want to say much at first but then changed his mind.

He still had his grandfather's old radio, which had been taken from the past. He showed me a photo of it. It looked almost exactly like the radios we'd been making under the Nafwyres brand, but not quite. There were several minor differences, mostly in the styling. It still worked, so the design was good. The manufacturer's name was Nifwires.

We made several more trips into the past when we weren't too busy. We created a strict rule. Nobody should leave the factory alone when in the past. Each time, when we got back, we found we had made no difference at all to history. It was as though our activities in the past were in a parallel universe. Perhaps they were.

On one occasion, we had got hold of a load of old out-of-date fire extinguishers. We were to take them away for disposal. We took them back to London in early September 1666. We gave them to a baker in Pudding Lane, in exchange for some nice bread. We even showed him how to use them.

It didn't help. Some were worried that we might have caused the fire in the first place with one of our demonstrations. Oops...

BORING TIMES

I'd heard that a former colleague of mine was visiting the area, so I met up with him. We talked for quite a while. He had been involved with several major civil engineering projects. He'd heard about some of our achievements and seemed quite impressed.

I happened to mention that we had no planned space trips due for weeks, so he asked me if I could help him with boring tunnels. I suggested hanging pictures on the walls. What he meant was, did I know anything about tunnel construction? His company had won an expensive contract to construct a road tunnel through a mountain.

We both knew such projects were extremely costly, so I said I'd see if our clever people could design some equipment that might help. He left me his contact details, then I went home.

The next day, I talked to our local management about it. They could see an opportunity for profit, so they allowed me to work with our staff and my former colleague to see what could be done.

I talked to the triplets about it. They had some ideas, so I left them to come up with a solution. They devised a plan that would, in some ways, be similar to what we did when we split the asteroid (apart from the big explosion). Meanwhile, I contacted my former colleague to let him know what we planned to do.

The plan was to buy and modify an existing electric road sweeper (no, not Smythe's). Unnecessary parts would be removed. That would leave space for other equipment, such as a spacecraft-standard power supply.

We would add a force field generator. It would create a spherical bubble around the machine, similar to our factory one, but much smaller. The machine would also have its own artificial gravity inside the force field bubble.

It would be able to fly around in the same way our factory could. The original drive system (driving the wheels) would be retained. That would allow the machine to be driven as a normal vehicle when it wasn't being used for tunnelling.

We planned to drive the machine into the mountain, cutting a round tunnel into it, in much the same way as we had cut into the asteroid. Displaced material would be compacted tightly into the tunnel walls. That would make the walls incredibly strong and remove the need to dispose of the displaced materials.

Ron became involved with the machine's construction, as it interested him. He asked if he could borrow some of my tools, as his had gone missing. He'd searched everywhere for them. He suspected that someone might have taken them. I lent him some of mine.

After a few months, the machine was ready for its first test. It looked strange, particularly the back part. We drove it to a clearing in the woods close to our factory, to carry out initial testing.

A brave volunteer got into the driving seat and switched on the system. The machine rose several feet into the air and then rotated to point downward. Then it slowly moved into the ground. It soon disappeared from view. It went down about forty feet and then came back out again. It rotated back to horizontal and landed. We inspected the result.

It looked good at first glance. Then we noticed cracks in the ground leading away from the hole. There were deep rumbling noises. The sides of the hole started to fall in. Oops. All we'd done was push the soil aside without compacting it properly.

The boffins looked into the problem, quite literally. The machine had performed well, but the test result wasn't quite what they had expected. Barry and Sue were there, watching. Barry stood rubbing his chin, thinking. It wasn't doing any good, so I spoke to them.

I suggested that instead of simply pushing the soil aside, it could be transported in layers from the inside to just outside the bubble. Each new layer would be superimposed on top of the others. That would create an incredibly strong wall. I wasn't sure if it could be done that way, so I discussed my idea with the boffins.

They said it could be done, so the modifications were carried out. The force field was elongated, making it more cylindrical.

We added a navigation system, to make it possible to cut a straight tunnel directly from one predetermined point to another. We had to redesign it after Barry pointed out that you can't receive satellite signals inside a mountain.

When the redesigned machine was ready, we tried another vertical test hole. The new hole looked a lot better. Then someone noticed water in the bottom, slowly getting deeper. We'd cut through an underground stream. The system didn't know how to cope with the water, so it hadn't tried.

The boffins redesigned the system so that it could deal with such problems in the future. They also added an experimental scanner so the operator could 'see' ahead of the machine and make any necessary adjustments.

We did yet another test. This time, the hole looked perfect. The walls were extremely tough. We tried drilling into them. It wasn't easy. The drill bits didn't last long.

Smythe insisted on one final test before we delivered the machine to the customer. He wanted this hole tested to destruction. I sometimes thought that Smythe, being ex-military, just liked to blow things up. Oh well. It would be interesting, if nothing else.

We lowered lots of explosives into the bottom of the hole and wired in the detonator. Then we threw in lots of building rubble, old breeze blocks, bricks, rocks, bits of wood and any other solid rubbish we could find.

We hid well away and put on our hard hats, ear defenders and eye protection. Smythe set off the explosives. The resulting massive explosion was quite alarming. A huge column of smoke, rubbish and flames shot out of the hole. It looked impressive, not to mention dangerous.

We went back to investigate the damage. Then we ran away again. Bits of brick and rubble were raining down around us. We should've known better. Everyone rushed back under cover and waited until the bits stopped falling. Then we crept back to the hot, smoking hole.

There wasn't much left in it, other than the bits that had fallen back in after the explosion. The walls were black and pitted in some places, but no cracks were visible. Smythe declared the experiment a success.

Pictures had been taken before we set off the explosion. The explosion itself had been recorded, from several angles. We took detailed pictures of the results, to convince the customer that the tunnels would be strong enough. We also had to apologise to some of the locals for the noise. We assured them we hadn't restarted quarrying activities at the site.

I contacted my former colleague. I told him the machine was ready. It surprised him to hear from me so soon. I invited him to come and see the results of the explosion test. He seemed impressed.

We got all the necessary legal stuff done, brought the machine to the tunnel start site, set it up and started the work. The machine slowly disappeared into the mountain, producing a nice, neat tunnel.

About an hour later, we got a radio call from deep inside the tunnel. The machine had stopped.

It had run out of power. Everyone had assumed it was somebody else's responsibility to charge it up, so it hadn't been. The machine had to be reversed out the conventional way. That proved tricky, as the tunnel bottom wasn't flat. The machine tended to weave about as the driver reversed it out. We recharged it and then fitted a 'Low power' warning light before it went back in again.

We completed the tunnelling within a week. We made three tunnels. Two were for traffic, with one smaller one between the other two for services and maintenance purposes. Other contractors dealt with the remaining details. We were well paid by our happy customer.

Ron returned my tools, as he'd bought some more. He told me his entire toolbox had vanished. As soon as he said 'toolbox', something seemed familiar.

I asked if he'd left anything unusual in it. He said he hadn't, other than a few coins and a strange black ball. He'd found it hidden at the back of a shelf in the main workshop, covered with dust. He'd taken the ball away to study it.

I asked Ron about the black ball. He said he'd not seen anything like it before. It looked like an electronic device, so he'd charged it up. It didn't seem to do anything, so he'd dropped it into the bottom of his toolbox. Then he'd gone off to do something else. When he came back, the toolbox wasn't there.

I told him about what had happened to me years earlier, when I worked with the Asbestorot. I explained about the black 'time bomb' and told him where I'd hidden his toolbox at the time. I found it still there. I returned it to Ron. I got the feeling he didn't quite believe me, although he had to admit that it had become much more rusty.

CHANGES

Those diamonds we found on that alien planet (where the Dougaloids, as I called them, lived) had been on my mind for some time. Barry and I both had bucketfuls of them. It sounds odd now, but we didn't know what to do with them. Some people had heard what they were but refused to believe it.

I was more inclined to believe it. The aliens had told us what the crystals were, but I wanted to know for certain, as they hadn't told us the truth initially.

I took a small one to be professionally analysed, at my own expense. They were indeed diamonds. Good quality ones, at that. People noticed that I appeared more cheerful than usual. Some wanted to know why, so I deliberately tried to look miserable. I hardly said a word to anyone about the diamonds.

The months that followed were scary. Things were about to change. Captain Smythe wasn't certain what those crystals were, but he had his suspicions. He issued a stern warning. Under no circumstances should anyone outside our group be told about those crystals.

People took little notice. They appeared throughout the factory as decorations. Some people wanted me to make them into pendants, but I refused. It would only be a matter of time before visitors noticed them.

I took two small diamonds to a company that could cut diamonds. I asked them to cut one good quality diamond from the biggest one. They could have the much smaller one as payment. They were happy to oblige.

They cut a very impressive diamond for me. I wanted to keep it, but I eventually sold it for a considerable sum of money. Greed soon got the better of me. I had many more cut. I sold them too.

Uncut diamonds were lying around everywhere. Most people were unaware of what the crystals were. They thought they were just common alien stones. It worried me that a fortune in diamonds lay scattered around the factory.

I wondered if people would notice if the crystals were replaced with glass replicas. I had some high-quality cut-glass replicas made, using several different manufacturers. Each had the date and the manufacturer's name engraved on the underside. They looked impressive. Most looked better than the originals. I took them to the factory and showed them off.

I asked for a large pinkish one to be made. I provided a name for it. Unfortunately, the company got it wrong. They engraved the name underneath as instructed, but they called it 'The Pink Leopard'. Oh well. At least it would avoid copyright issues.

As expected, people liked the glass replicas. Hardly anyone believed the rumours that the alien crystals were diamonds. There were so many of them. Most were happy to swap the crystals they had for my better-looking glass replicas. I kept assuring people that the replacements were only glass, as I felt rather guilty. It made no difference.

It wasn't long before I'd acquired almost all the alien diamonds, other than Barry's. I hid them in a secret location in the Bovercraft, which only I knew about. I'd had it included in the spaceship's design, originally intending to store my tools and other stuff there.

Barry also had many diamonds. I didn't know what he'd done with his. He wouldn't tell me. He always managed to evade the question. I wasn't worried, though. We both had plenty.

Even though Smythe had directed people not to talk about the crystals, word still got out. We were pretty sure who it was. I probably shouldn't tell you the culprit, but I'll give you a clue.

It was Phil. There wasn't anything we could do about it. He'd been left on that island hundreds of years in the past. Posthumously telling him off would have been pointless.

One of our upper management people (from America) turned up unexpectedly at our factory. He demanded to be told about the crystals. He'd heard they were diamonds. He insisted they were company property and should be handed over to him immediately. Smythe sent him to me.

I fetched one of the glass replicas and showed it to him. I assured him it was just glass. I showed him the engraved text on the underside. He still didn't believe me, so I got him to follow me to Barry's workshop. I put the replica on top of the vice. Using a large hammer, I smashed the glass crystal to smithereens with one blow. That convinced him. I handed him some more glass replicas. We heard no more about it after he left.

Something had to be done about those diamonds. I needed to act quickly. I had many more cut into good-quality diamonds, using several different companies. I sold the diamonds using a variety of outlets and channels.

I opened bank accounts in several countries. Using different names, I put large amounts of money into each. It wasn't long before I lost count of how much money I had in total. I found the whole business quite scary, but tried my best to act normally. I fooled most people. Barry could tell I'd been up to something, but he said nothing. He also seemed to be acting a little oddly.

A few months later, we discovered that a large multinational company was trying to take us over. We didn't like them. They'd been buying up shares in our parent company and were getting close to owning 50% of the total shares available. That worried us.

We had to do something. I wondered if shares were available in the hostile company. I checked. Sure enough, there were. I had become very rich by then, so I quietly bought some. That went well, so I bought a lot more, using the names on the bank accounts I'd created. It wasn't long before I'd acquired about 25% of the total shares in the hostile company.

I checked to see how much money I had left. I had enough to buy another 23% of the shares. When they became available, I did. Some of those shares were hard to get hold of, but more money almost always did the trick. I sold more diamonds to replenish my money reserves.

Our upper management knew something was happening, but they weren't sure what. I overheard several quite frantic calls between our local managers and the Americans. The pressure was getting to me. I needed to confide in someone.

I knew I could trust Barry, so I told him what I'd been up to. To my surprise, he seemed relieved. He admitted that he'd been doing something similar with his diamonds. We both felt better.

Between us, we acquired well over 80% of the hostile company's shares. Then we announced that *we* were taking *them* over. We had paperwork ready to prove it if necessary.

Things got a bit heated. There were angry 'discussions' between ourselves, our management and the hostile company. All we had wanted to do in the first place was to stop our factory from being taken over. We liked what we were doing. We were having fun. If we were taken over, that would probably have been the end of it.

Eventually, everyone involved agreed that Barry and I would own our factory, the UK site and all F&S assets. There would be no shares in our company. We employed expensive solicitors to help us sort out the legal stuff. Barry left me to sort out the fine details with the solicitors while he dealt with the local management.

Our former employers (the American parent company) and the other company did well out of the new arrangement. Barry and I didn't care. We still had plenty of diamonds left. We never told anyone how we had acquired so much money. We started a few false rumours.

After things had calmed down, we held a general meeting with all our factory staff, to decide what to do. We agreed to continue as usual, helping out where and when needed. We liked doing that. It was a good lifestyle. If we were asked to do anything we didn't want to, then we wouldn't. Everyone would get a pay rise. We called our company Spacemakers.

Anyone who wanted to leave could do so, but nobody did.

SMYTHE AND WESTERNS

Captain Smythe wasn't happy. Barry and I had become 'The Management'. He didn't like it. I think he felt demoted. We started wearing green army surplus jumpers (Simon's idea), but we didn't keep that up for long. We told Smythe to continue as before, but he still seemed rather down. He would often sit alone in the cinema, watching old Westerns.

He calmed down after a few weeks. Smythe-wise, things seemed back to normal, although his obsession with the American Wild West continued. He had a distorted impression of what life back then had been like. That was about to change.

Smythe's walk had changed, too. He appeared to be walking slightly like John Wayne. Some thought he'd been watching too many Westerns. It could also have been due to Simon's tinkering with the captain's chair settings. He'd adjusted them manually, as one of his practical jokes. People noticed Smythe wriggling and moving about in his chair. He couldn't complain, as he'd been very complimentary about it when he first sat on it.

Smythe clearly wanted to live in the Wild West. I disapproved. So did Barry. We planned to let him see what things were really like for himself. Hopefully, he'd drop the idea.

With help from the boffins, we set up a time window in the laboratory. It looked into the past, into a small town somewhere in the Wild West. We intended to show Smythe that things weren't as easy back then as he thought.

We ran the system for about half an hour. Smythe watched intently. Most of us were soon bored with it. We stopped watching Smythe and chatted amongst ourselves.

Smythe glanced around. Nobody seemed to be looking at him. He threw a pencil through the time window. It landed on the dry ground on the other side. He paused briefly, before jumping through the time window himself. That caused a sudden drain on the laboratory power. The overload trips operated, shutting down the time window abruptly.

The boffins hadn't noted the exact time and place the window had been looking into. We thought we'd lost Smythe for good. Good riddance, someone said. We eventually agreed that we couldn't just leave him stranded in the past. We would have to find and retrieve him somehow.

Barry reset the laboratory power trips. Then the boffins restarted the time window equipment. It hadn't been shut down correctly, so the system was frozen. A still image appeared, showing the last displayed image before Smythe's escape. I took photos of it.

The boffins reloaded the system software. They started the system normally and then began looking for Smythe. It took them a day or so to find the same location again. They adjusted the time and place to match my photos as closely as possible. Smythe's pencil provided a useful clue.

We located him in the nearby sheriff's building. Before he escaped from us, Smythe had often daydreamed of being a sheriff. His attempts to achieve that in the real world had failed miserably. We found him locked up in the cells. He looked thin, unwashed and depressed. His clothing looked similar to what others of the time were wearing.

We weren't sure how to rescue him. Simply taking him from his cell would've been unwise. We needed a better plan. One of our staff had a similar accent to the local people of the time. It seemed sensible to ask him to help.

He was an American, called Wilbur. When we asked him to help, he wasn't keen. He didn't like Smythe. Eventually, Wilber decided to be 'professional' about it and put his personal feelings about Smythe aside.

We got him dressed up in suitable clothing. He had almost no hair, so we gave him a wig and a false moustache. Hopefully, that would stop Smythe from recognising him. We also gave him some suitable coins, plus some gold, just in case.

We sent Wilbur back to a well-hidden location behind the sheriff's office. He walked around to the front and then into the building. The sheriff was there. Wilbur introduced himself as Wilbur Smythe. Then he asked about the man in the cells. He told the sheriff he was a relative who had come to take him back home, if possible. The sheriff told him there would be a price to pay for getting him out. Wilbur produced the coins we'd given him.

"Will this be enough?" he asked.

"Hmm..." said the sheriff. "I'll need more than that."

Wilbur produced the gold.

"Where in tarnation did you get that?" asked the sheriff.

"Does it matter?"

"Err... Nope!"

Wilbur sat down with the sheriff. They talked about Captain Smythe. Wilbur asked how Smythe had ended up behind bars. The sheriff told him that when Smythe first arrived, he'd behaved very strangely. He wore odd-looking clothes and spoke with a peculiar accent. Someone had taken pity on him and given him some old clothes.

He'd been in all sorts of trouble. He'd walked into the saloon, made some strange announcements and got completely drunk. They threw him out because he had no money. The locals had dragged him out of town and dumped him there. Then he'd tried to steal a horse but found he couldn't ride it. He got arrested for stealing the horse.

After talking his way out of that one, he'd nearly got shot. He'd been seen pretending to draw a gun at speed, from force of habit. Not having a gun probably saved his life. Then he got arrested for stealing food. He'd been in trouble with the law in one way or another ever since. Being in the cells kept him from being shot. The sheriff had become sick of Smythe and his constant complaining.

Wilbur and the sheriff had a small drink together. They talked more about Smythe (and various other things) and then went to fetch him. Smythe didn't believe that a relative had come to rescue him. He didn't say anything, though. He just wanted to get out of that dreadful town. Smythe thought Wilbur seemed strangely familiar.

Wilbur took him out of sight around the back of the building. We retrieved them both. Captain Smythe was surprised and relieved to be back. He'd almost given up hope of seeing any of us again. That place had been his home for over a year.

Wilbur removed his wig and moustache, so Smythe could see who had rescued him. They got along well after that.

Simon had been standing in for Smythe during his absence. He continued to do so for a few weeks, while Smythe recovered. Smythe had become a very different man. He hated the Wild West. He no longer watched Westerns on his own. If he did watch one, he could often be heard muttering quietly to himself.

Silence preferred

Space is quiet. Very quiet. There's no sound in space. No unwanted noise from traffic, roadworks, aircraft or weather. Some people found it too quiet, especially those who normally lived in noisy towns or cities.

Barry tried to resolve the problem. He set up weatherproof loudspeakers in the car park, to make quiet sounds during the night, at random. Those sounds included traffic noise, distant sounds of a dog barking, heavy rain and occasionally an owl hooting. He even recorded the sounds from the forests near our home base and played them at night.

This proved too much for Simon and Joyce to resist. They added extra sounds. We soon heard an elephant trumpeting, thunderstorms, windows breaking and chains rattling. Sometimes an occasional blood-curdling scream could be heard during the night. Many sound effects were copied from old horror films.

Smythe was awakened one night by a whistling sound followed by a loud explosion. It came from a loudspeaker close to his quarters. He put a stop to the sound effects immediately.

Oh well. It was fun while it lasted, unless you were trying to sleep.

I recall one occasion when silence might have been a better option. Simon had found an old film at a car boot sale. The seller claimed it was a rare musical. It wasn't expensive, so he bought it anyway. He thought he could resell it if it was no good.

We planned to watch it in our cinema. The label was faded and partly missing. We could just about make out the words 'Winnie-the-Pooh'. We hadn't watched a new film for ages, so we all crowded into the cinema to watch it.

Barry normally set everything up and ran the films. We couldn't find him, or Sue. I eventually found them alone in the kitchen, making Whoopee.

Whoopee was an ice cream that Sue had invented. We used to eat it in the cinema while we watched the films. It was absolutely delicious. Muttley liked it too.

Barry and Sue had finished what they were doing, so we took the ice cream to the cinema and handed it out. Barry loaded the film and started it running. When I say 'film', it was actually a data cartridge, but we still called them films. Old habits die hard, I suppose.

It wasn't the version of Winnie-the-Pooh we expected. We wished it had been. It was a little-known rock opera version. I found it dreadful, yet funny for all the wrong reasons. I usually liked old rock music, but this wasn't good. It had songs like 'My Roo Ca Choo', 'Eye of the Tigger' and 'Tigger Feet'. Oh well.

The plot was no better. The central (human) characters had taken on the names of characters from the books when they were kids, as nicknames. They were on a mission to 'rescue' Eeyore from a donkey sanctuary. Pig (formerly Piglet) worked in a sewage plant. Pooh got arrested for stealing honey from a supermarket. Odd, because he hated the stuff. Christopher Robin went down with measles. Alice was a traffic warden. She gave him a ticket.

I later discovered that the film had been taken off the market. There had been numerous complaints and copyright infringements. Simon had a rare copy. I don't think he'd have been allowed to sell it.

We needed something to take our minds off what we'd just seen and heard. We weren't all that busy, so Sue suggested something that had been on her mind for weeks. She wanted us to return to Planet Dee. There were some things that she wanted to investigate further. Most of us wanted to explore the place more, so we returned to the planet.

As we had cleared the mines around the planet on our first visit, we weren't expecting problems. When we arrived, we found that most of the mines were back. Some were incomplete and appeared to be reforming themselves.

When we had cleaned up the area before, we had dumped all the material we had collected somewhere on the planet, in a big heap. We could see a thin stream of material coming from there, somehow recreating the mines.

Now we understood how the mines had survived there for so long. Every time one blew up, it would reform sometime later. Captain Smythe respectfully suggested we abandon our planned visit to the planet, but Sue wasn't happy. She and Barry had an alternative suggestion.

She proposed that we blow up one of the mines as before. Then we would collect all the fragments of explosive material and remove them from the area. When the mine reformed, it wouldn't be able to blow up again. That way, we could capture it safely and examine the technology.

Smythe wasn't happy with that idea. Simon wasn't either. Barry suggested that we take the bits of explosives to a distant part of the galaxy. If we left them there, the mine wouldn't be able to reintegrate them.

I outranked Smythe, so we implemented Barry's plan. We blew up a mine, collected all the explosive material we could find and dumped it several light-years away.

By the time we got back, the mine had reassembled itself. There appeared to be a bit missing. We fired sausages at it, hitting it several times. It shuddered slightly but remained intact. We brought it into the factory, de-sausaged it thoroughly and deactivated it.

We landed on the planet, to allow Sue to get on with her investigations. Most people took the chance to explore the place at their leisure. Some of us went grape-hunting. We failed to find any more, partly because it was the wrong time of year for them.

Sue, Barry and the boffins spent months examining that mine. The technology was very different from what we were used to. They had hoped to find a reader for the glass data cylinders, but there wasn't one. The boffins learnt quite a lot from that mine.

Reunions

Remember the manager I told you about, who survived the space potato crash? His name was Engelbert. He didn't like that name. Being short and fat, he didn't mind being called Big E. Some people referred to him as Uncle Bert. He wasn't amused.

After the accident, he spent many weeks in hospital. He soon recovered from his physical injuries. Recovering his memory took longer. The doctors eventually allowed him to go home, so his wife collected him from the hospital. With her help, his remaining missing memory eventually returned.

He had been unusually quiet since the accident. That slowly changed as his memory improved. He had been an outspoken man before the accident.

The accident and the events of the weeks preceding it had been on his mind a great deal. He had been present at the meeting where the idea to build the Bovercraft had first been discussed.

When he was well enough, he contacted the original parent company's senior management. He wanted to know what progress had been made with the planned spacecraft while he'd been away. They wouldn't tell him anything and refused to say why.

That both puzzled and annoyed him. He would have to find out for himself. Big E made an unannounced visit to our UK site. He'd done that several times in the past, to find out what we were really up to. Some people had been caught doing 'homers'.

Nobody liked him. His intelligence wasn't in doubt, but he could be quite intimidating, despite his short stature. He would glare at people over the tops of his glasses. People tried to keep well out of his way.

Fortunately, we were back at our base when Big E turned up. He strode in and demanded to see one of the managers. Spotty Herbert sent him to see Smythe, who sent for Angry Charlie.

Charlie was his son, which Smythe knew. Charlie had become well used to his father's outbursts. To him, it was like water off his Teflon-coated false teeth. (Ducks had become extinct.) Smythe told Charlie to show his father around and explain what we'd been doing since the accident.

Charlie did his best but could hardly get a word in edgeways. Eventually, his father got all the senior staff together, so he could 'speak' to us.

"Will somebody please tell me what the yellow tepid zonkelworts you lot have been up to since I was here last?" he said, loudly. We didn't use traditional swear words in those days. The government had banned most of them several years earlier. People had devised alternatives.

"I'll go take some measurements," said Simon, with a straight face. "Would you like imperial or metric?" Big E's face went red. I half expected to see steam coming from his ears. Charlie managed to calm him down.

I felt sorry for Charlie, so I took over from him. I outranked Big E, so I wasn't bothered. I briefly explained most of our achievements since his previous visit, not stopping to listen when he tried to interrupt me. By the time I'd finished, he'd calmed down somewhat. We were able to have a more civilised conversation.

He seemed impressed with what we'd done. Then Charlie reappeared, wearing stuff that his father disapproved of. Big E insisted that Charlie get changed immediately. Charlie told him where to go. He said he had more right to be there than his father. Big E looked confused.

At that point, I thought it best to let Big E know about the new management structure. I explained that Barry and I were the new factory owners. Strictly speaking, he had no business being there.

His face went red (again). He clearly didn't believe me. I took him to our canteen area, where framed copies of the formal ownership documents hung on the walls. He read them carefully, trying to find fault with them. He failed. I hardly heard a sound from him. His face went pale, and then he apologised. I'd never heard him do that before.

He spoke little after that. I showed him around a little more, and then he left. I don't recall seeing him again after that. Charlie told me later that he and his father still talked regularly. I got the impression that Big E was actually quite proud of Charlie.

We had another small reunion after that. Ned's son had been gold prospecting in Australia. He turned up unexpectedly one day at the factory to see his father. They talked for ages. It wasn't long before they started talking about gold.

In the factory, we needed gold. Some of the high-tech stuff we were making depended on it. It had become increasingly difficult to get hold of. Prices were high and rising fast.

"Listen, son, did you find any gold on that lease of yours?" said Ned.

"I found a little, but not much. Hardly enough to cover my costs," said his son. "It's also bloody hot out there. Too much for me. I'm considering selling the lease."

Ned started thinking.

"Could we borrow a part of your lease for a while?"

"Borrow it? Yeah, sure. As long as you put it back afterwards." Ned's son didn't realise what Ned had in mind.

"If we find some gold, how about we give you half and we keep the other half?" said Ned.

"Sounds good to me."

They found Barry and me in the canteen. Ned's idea was to swap land between part of our property at Spacemakers and his son's lease in Australia, in much the same way as we had done with Jock's house. With the bit of Australian land hidden in our nice cool forest, we would search it for gold and then return it to Australia.

I liked the idea. Barry did too. We gathered together all the equipment we would need, set things up at Spacemakers and then went to Australia. We didn't bother telling the authorities in either country. There weren't any procedures for importing or exporting areas of land.

Once we were back, with part of Australia on our land, we went to have a look at it. It felt weird, being able to step from UK soil straight onto a part of Australia. The ground still felt quite hot. Too hot. We went back to the factory while it cooled down.

The next morning, Ned and his son went straight onto the Australian soil with metal detectors. Anyone amongst our staff with a metal detector joined them. I think a lot of small bits of gold got pocketed.

Then I had a better idea. We still had the tunnel boring machine. It had a scanner that allowed the operator to see what was ahead. I borrowed the scanner and put it on a large trolley, along with a portable power unit.

We used it to detect gold. There were some quite large nuggets, a few feet underground. We hired a small digger and dug them up. It wasn't long before we had enough gold to last us years. Our staff were told that if they found any small bits of gold on the surface, they could keep them. I don't think anyone did any proper factory work for a while.

A few weeks later, we swapped the patches of land back. We gave Ned's son half the gold, as agreed. Our original patch of land, which had been in Australia for weeks, looked a bit cooked.

THE MOONBASE

We often brought back souvenirs and other junk from other planets. The factory frequently became cluttered with unnecessary stuff. From time to time, we would have a good clear-out. We stored anything we weren't using in locked Portakabins, hidden in the forests. Not an ideal solution. Those Portakabins became filled almost to the ceilings. They were often damp. We needed somewhere else to put things.

Barry suggested we build an underground Moonbase and store our junk in it. As the Moon had remained mostly unexplored, it was unlikely anyone would find a hidden base there.

Most of the time, the only visitors to the Moon were rich 'lunar loonies'. They did odd things there, such as trying to play table tennis, racing electric vehicles and bouncing around on Spacehoppers. One idiot tried drilling for oil. He swore he'd found some in the lunar dust. It turned out to be gear oil, from an electric vehicle.

I agreed with Barry's plan. He wanted our Moonbase to be on the dark side of the Moon so we couldn't be seen from

Earth. I wasn't so sure. Too obvious. I argued that it would be the first place people would look. I suggested hiding in plain sight.

We chose a site right in the middle of the side facing the Earth. Barry planned to use the equipment we had built for boring tunnels on Earth. We could use it to construct a base under the lunar surface. Unfortunately, when we tried to land at our chosen location, we had a problem.

Our past contracts had required us to land at a variety of locations on Earth. Some of our early landings had caused problems at our landing sites. Our force field bubble had cut through underground cables and pipework. Since then, Barry's team had set up equipment and alarms to warn us of such issues before we landed.

When we tried to land on the lunar surface at our chosen location, those alarms went off. Smythe wanted us to land anyway. He argued loudly that there couldn't be any cables, pipes or anything like that on the Moon. I wasn't entirely convinced. There had to be a reason for those alarms going off. We moved a short distance from our original chosen site and landed without problems.

Barry and I got into our space suits. We drove an electric vehicle onto the lunar surface, through a specially weakened point in the bubble. Then we went to where we had originally planned to land and looked around.

At first, we found nothing unusual. Then we noticed footprints.

They were the wrong size and shape to have been made by humans.

Several trails of footprints converged at one point. We brushed aside the dust to reveal a circular metal hatch on the ground, about six feet wide. We couldn't get it open.

Barry found a small control panel nearby. It looked dead. We pressed the buttons. Nothing happened. There wasn't any more we could do, as we hadn't brought any tools, so we returned to the factory. We talked to the boffins (and Sue) about it.

A short while later, we returned to the hatch with more equipment. Smythe accompanied us. He wanted to see everything for himself. I think he was sick of sitting on that bridge.

Smythe wanted to force the hatch open. I wouldn't let him. Like many in the factory, Sue had been watching via our helmet cameras. She contacted us via our helmet radios and advised us to take the control panel apart first.

It wasn't easy to remove the screws. None of our screwdrivers fitted. We had to improvise. We eventually got the panel off. The technology looked alien to us, yet not too unfamiliar. Electrical wiring had been used rather than fibre optics. I guessed that if we could apply a little power to the two thickest wires, we might get something to work.

We had brought a small portable variable power supply with us. Barry made temporary connections using crocodile clips. We tried just a few volts at first. Nothing happened, so we wound the voltage up slowly until one of the lights on the panel glowed dimly.

We kept the power at that level for several minutes. Then we tried to check for evidence of overheating. That's not so easy in the coldness of space, with thick space suit gloves on. It all seemed fine, so we increased the power until the panel lights reached a sensible brightness.

I pressed the red button. I could feel a slight 'thump' through the perimeter of the hatch. Nothing else happened, so I pressed the green button. We felt another thump. The hatch depressed slightly and slid open. I nearly fell in.

Looking inside, we could see a ladder descending into the darkness. Smythe wanted to go in and look around. I stopped him, as I didn't want the hatch to close behind him and lock him in. Sue advised us to disconnect the power, which we did. The panel lights slowly dimmed and went out. I tried pressing all the buttons. One caused a slight 'clonk' as the remaining power drained away. Nothing worked after that.

We allowed Smythe to go in. Barry followed. The small torches on the sides of their helmets enabled them to see where they were going. Meanwhile, I fetched some proper lighting equipment and a better power source from the factory.

I returned to the opening and went in. Smythe and Barry were exploring what had once been a complex alien Moonbase. The aliens must've been watching humanity long ago, hiding under the lunar surface.

The technology appeared fascinating. It wasn't as advanced as what we had found on Planet Dee, but it still looked more advanced than ours.

Barry looked around for the Moonbase power source. He feared it might have been removed when the aliens left. Eventually, he found it hidden behind a panel at the far end of a long corridor. It looked like it had been disconnected by the aliens just before they abandoned the place.

He carefully reconnected it, expecting lots of sparks. Nothing happened, other than a small green light coming on. He followed the power cables back to a large isolator and switched it on.

The corridor lights came on. Barry walked back to the now well-lit control room. The equipment appeared to be working. There were control desks around the room, fitted with advanced-looking displays. The chairs were uncomfortable for humans and the controls looked odd.

With the better lighting, we could see evidence that there had once been an airlock at the entrance from the lunar surface. The old bolt holes were still there. Faded patches could be seen where something had once been. The original airlock must've been fitted as a self-contained module. We would have to make and fit our own.

We examined the air systems. The gas cylinders were almost empty. The remaining gas traces were different from our air. We would have to adapt the systems to suit human requirements.

Barry and his team constructed an airlock module. It was based on a similar existing design intended for something else, so it didn't take them long. They fitted it to the Moonbase entrance. The air systems were adapted to suit our needs. We (mostly Barry and Sue) spent weeks exploring and adapting the Moonbase.

The equipment seemed designed to last. We found plenty of space, including some strange living quarters. Barry found a well-organised storeroom with plenty of spares. He and his team put them to good use, fixing anything that didn't work. We found cameras and various receiving antennas hidden on the lunar surface, linked to displays and recording devices.

Like us, the aliens had used artificial gravity. They must've come from a planet with much stronger gravity than on Earth. We couldn't cope with it for long and had to turn it down. Their system was better than ours and consumed less power. We copied their design and installed it in the Bovercraft as a backup system.

The aliens had taken it a step further. They had left several portable antigravity devices for moving heavy objects around. Our boffins had been trying to do that for some time but hadn't quite got the hang of it. We took a couple back to the factory.

Out of curiosity, we tried using the receiving equipment to monitor transmissions from Earth. We picked up all sorts of transmissions. We were probably the first beings to receive anything using that equipment. The aliens must've abandoned the base thousands of years earlier when they found no signs of advanced technology on Earth.

I fitted a strong combination lock to the entrance hatch. We were careful to hide our footprints and the hatchway every time we left the place. Most of our junk ended up there.

We left the remaining (less valuable) stuff in the Portakabins. Most of it had little value. There was no point in taking it to the Moon. Local rumours that we kept valuable equipment in the Portakabins were no longer true.

I visited the Portakabins one day to create a list of items for disposal. I found that a door had been forced open, and the lock was damaged. We had good factory security but little to protect the Portakabins.

We found it hard to believe that any of our staff could have been responsible. It had to have been done by somebody else. The culprits were likely to try again, so we set up traps. We fitted hidden cameras inside and around the Portakabins. Motion detectors inside each Portakabin would set off the traps, locking the doors and activating the alarm.

Several days later, the alarm went off. Barry, myself and two police officers went to the affected Portakabin. When we opened the door, we found Wide Bertha and Big Con inside. They tried to get away but didn't get far. Both had been under observation by the local police for months. They were soon off to the local nick.

Superdog

Over a year had passed since our last official holiday, on that desert island. Most people wanted another holiday. We weren't particularly busy, so Barry and I agreed to see what could be done.

Most of us didn't want to travel that far through time again. Several people had been uneasy about it during the last holiday. They were worried that we might upset things in our present, although we hadn't spotted any such effects since our return. We probably wouldn't have known anyway.

Several Earth-like planets had been discovered since our previous holiday. We held a vote to decide which one to visit. We chose a planet not too far from us. We'd been there before and everyone seemed to like it.

Other friendly races we knew had misgivings about our chosen holiday destination. They wouldn't explain why. They seemed embarrassed about something. We were told that it wasn't dangerous.

Few people lived there, so we chose to go there anyway. Nobody from the other races tried to stop us.

We scanned the planet extensively before landing. The planet had slightly lower gravity than Earth. Everything else looked good. We landed at a warm location, near a deserted beach.

The location had everything we could have wanted. There were long sandy beaches and interesting shells. The trees looked similar to palm trees. The widespread, varied vegetation looked interesting. A small river ran down to the beach, with very clear-looking water.

We tested the river water first. We found it clean and pure, so we refilled our main water tank. Everything else we tested seemed fine. Smythe announced over the Tannoy system that we could all go out and enjoy ourselves.

Some of our staff took an interest in the native fruits and vegetables. There were many varieties. They thought it would be nice to have something new that we could eat. A few volunteers collected buckets of whatever fruits and vegetables they could find.

The buckets were left in the laboratory, on the floor, for later investigation. Amongst them were bunches of what looked like bananas, only longer. We called them bananananananas.

In all the excitement, someone forgot to close the laboratory door. We'd also forgotten about Muttley. He'd escaped from Penny's quarters, as she hadn't closed the door properly.

Muttley could smell something unusual. He tracked it down to the laboratory. Muttley sniffed at each bucket, avoiding most of them. However, one bucket contained fruit that had a strong, cheesy smell.

Muttley wasn't scientifically minded. He just helped himself. He ate most of the contents, then decided he'd had enough and walked off. About half an hour later, he started acting strangely.

Someone noticed him and paid him some attention. She took him by the collar, intending to lead him back to Penny's quarters. He seemed to be lighter than air. Muttley was breaking wind frequently, and she couldn't stop laughing. She had to let him go.

Muttley was emitting nitrous oxide gas from his rear end, at an alarming rate. He also seemed unnaturally happy. He could hardly keep his feet on the ground. Somehow, he found his way outside. Nobody could catch him. He could leap tall people with a single bound. People started calling him Superdog.

We stayed on the planet for several weeks. People were worried about Muttley at first. He seemed happy enough, though, leaping from tree to tree, grazing on the smelly fruit. We left him to it and got on with our holiday.

When the time came for us to leave, we had to try to catch Muttley. Easier said than done. Muttley had gained a little weight, but that wasn't enough to keep him on the ground. We'd see him high up in the trees, tail wagging furiously, barking at us.

Getting him back down would be difficult. Several people tried and failed. To Muttley, it was just a game. Simon suggested that someone should eat a little of the smelly fruit so that he or she could catch Muttley. Nobody dared.

I returned to the Bovercraft and fetched one of his favourite tennis balls. I threw it along the beach. Muttley could never resist chasing a tennis ball. He came down after the ball (too fast) and ploughed into the sand. I grabbed his collar, then led him back to the Bovercraft, still almost floating in the air. I left him with his owner, Penny. Her dog, her problem.

By then, the other types of fruit had been analysed. They were found to be harmless, but useless to us. They tasted bland and had little nutritional value. On the other hand, we found

Muttley's cheesy fruit interesting. It had many unusual properties. We collected and stored some of it. We also gathered some of the seeds, hoping to grow them ourselves. Barry called it Flying Fruit.

When we returned to Earth, we analysed the smelly fruit in more detail. We discovered that it had remarkable healing properties. We carried out safety tests on it, which it passed. Then we made it into a daily supplement for people with ailments that were difficult to treat. Some people improved considerably.

Muttley's weight soon returned to normal. He seemed no worse for his experience. He actually seemed better than before, other than the increased flatulence, which we no longer found funny. It had become absolutely foul.

Only Penny would take him for walks, wearing a gas mask. It had to be done at a fixed time each day so people could be elsewhere in good time. Muttley returned to normal after a few (smelly) weeks.

We had noticed several grey hairs on his muzzle previously, but they were gone. He looked younger than before. We considered supplying the Flying Fruit supplements to the general public. That idea was abandoned when we discovered how much testing would have been needed before we could legally sell any of it. We also realised we could never have kept up with the demand.

We tried to grow the Flying Fruit ourselves. We had little success. It didn't seem to grow well on Earth. We planted some seeds at the edge of one of our forests. Planting them about fifty years in the past helped. We found the fruit as tasteless as the other alien fruit. We assumed that something on the other planet was changing it somehow.

When we returned from the Flying Fruit planet, we encountered Foodies. They were waiting for us as we exited the drain. As usual, they wanted food. They usually left us alone, but this time they made a right nuisance of themselves. They refused to get out of our way unless we gave them food.

Ron hadn't been with us when we sorted out the Custard Zone, as he'd been away on a course at the time. He'd heard about Sue's custard-busting invention. He wondered if it could be adapted to work in reverse. Ron had some unusual ideas sometimes. He'd tell us he could think sideways.

He spoke to Sue about it. She hadn't considered the idea before. Ron seemed to be up to something, and Sue wanted to know what. He planned to fire food from the sausage gun and then enlarge it considerably before it reached its target. That amused Sue, so they modified the original machine to work both ways.

The next part of Ron's plan was to deal with the Foodies. They wanted food, so we'd give them some. We'd fire it at them, enlarging it before it reached them. It was much the same idea as had been happening in the Custard Zone. Sue told Barry, who told Smythe. We were determined to give it a try. Smythe didn't like the idea, but we overruled him.

We had to decide what food projectiles to use. Ideally, it would make as much mess as possible. We chose treacle pudding and made loads of it. Whenever a Foodie spacecraft approached us, we hit it with a massive treacle pudding. There was often more pudding than spacecraft. It looked quite silly, with the spacecraft's engines sticking out of a giant treacle pudding. The Foodies had to return home slowly to get unpuddinged. At least they'd have something to eat on the way.

The Bobberts

Barry had been away for a week, visiting a friend of his, who worked for a large, well-known car maker. Its UK manufacturing plant had become uneconomical to operate, so its owners were closing it down.

It always saddened me to see a place like that closing. However, it often provided opportunities to acquire interesting second-hand equipment. Such chances were rare, so Barry had made some enquiries.

Important assets had been transferred overseas. Valuable items were due to be auctioned. Many tools and other small items had already been relocated into people's garages.

However, a line of scruffy-looking industrial robots remained, used for car assembly. Such robots, especially worn-out examples, were hard to sell. They didn't go for much. Many were scrapped. Barry had worked with similar machines in earlier employment. So had I. We knew what they could do.

Barry got permission to go to the site and inspect them. Two of the site's technical staff accompanied him as he inspected the machines. He walked around with a clipboard, inspecting each machine and taking notes. He would occasionally point out defects. Someone asked if he had ever been a used car salesman.

The machines looked in a very sorry state. Barry asked if they had been properly maintained. They hadn't been. He was told that the maintenance team had been asking for downtime for years, to do proper repairs and servicing of the machines. Their requests had been repeatedly refused by management. Spares had been bought but never used. To Barry, it was a familiar story. He'd experienced it himself in former employment.

The robots had become worn and unreliable. Several showed evidence of improvised repairs. Two had been making unhealthy noises. They were a good make, which explained why any still worked at all. Car production had often been halted due to robot failures.

Barry paused, pretending to do various calculations, while muttering quietly. Then he asked how much the company wanted for them. A figure was suggested. Barry said he thought it was a little high, considering the state of the machines.

The site manager joined them. Barry commented on the poor condition of the machines. He pointed out that if they were of much value, they would have been long gone by then.

The site manager paused. He admitted that the company had been unable to find anyone to buy them. They would even consider paying someone to take them away. They needed to have the buildings cleared as soon as possible so that the site could be sold.

Barry rang me up to talk about it. We were both keen to take them. The car manufacturer had bought a considerable quantity of spare parts for them. I recommended that we take all eleven robot systems, as long as they were complete and included all the spare parts. We would be responsible for disconnecting and removing them from the site. They were happy to accept our offer.

The next day, we landed our factory in a field close to the car manufacturing site. Barry, Ron and I walked to the site, bringing two antigravity devices recovered from the Moonbase. We started work. It turned out to be easier than we thought.

We picked a robot, moved and locked each axis to make the robot (the moving part) as small as possible and attached an antigravity device to it. Then we disconnected the cabling and removed the floor bolts. The antigravity device made it possible to float the robot just above the floor, horizontally.

We used the other antigravity device to support the control cabinet and cabling after we disconnected them. Then we moved the system out through the main doors and off the site. It was a calm sunny day, so pushing the entire system to our factory was easy. We stored it in a disused building.

We did the same for all eleven robots. It took less time than we'd expected. We collected all the spares and other parts too, including the service manuals. Ron asked for the service history, but he was told there wasn't any. Everyone seemed happy. We did the paperwork and left.

Some people (including Captain Smythe) thought we were barmy. However, we could think of all sorts of possible uses for the machines.

Barry and his team got to work with some enthusiasm. They started by bolting two of the robots securely to the floor of one of the buildings. Then they replaced all the worn or damaged parts. It wasn't long before they had both systems restored to good working order. Each machine had an identity plate, marked B1 to B11.

Barry proudly showed them to Sue. She wasn't sure what to make of them. She knew what they were, but she knew little about how to use them. We already had two android robots, so she suggested we call them something other than robots, to avoid confusion.

Barry suggested Roberts. She reminded him we already had somebody with that name, so we called them Bobberts. We planned to call them Bobbert 1, Bobbert 2 and so on. They already had 'B' numbers.

Then came the matter of what to do with them. Once B1 and B2 had been refurbished, we agreed that the boffins would be allowed to experiment with one, while the maintenance team would see what they could do with the other. There would be a bit of friendly rivalry to see who could find the best use for the Bobberts.

The boffins had many crazy ideas. Most were quite clever, but none were practical. However, they did write some excellent software for controlling the machines.

Our maintenance team came up with a good practical idea. Building companies had been building houses using giant 3D printing machines for years. The idea worked well, but the results were sometimes rough, especially if the printing machine wasn't well maintained or had been poorly assembled. The machines were often huge.

Our maintenance team wanted to use the Bobberts, with their considerable accuracy, to build small sections of buildings, using the machines as 3D printers. The printed sections would be designed to interlock on-site. Each part would be designed and printed in great detail. They would include built-in conduits for wiring and other services, with wall cut-outs for fitting electrical sockets, etc. Even the mountings for window and door frames could be included in the designs.

We all liked the idea, so the boffins got busy with the software. They ditched the original firmware and wrote better code to replace it. They and Barry's team created a unique system. The Bobberts would work together in pairs. They could interact and avoid collisions.

Each pair would be controlled by a powerful central computer. Each Bobbert would also have an Andy 'brain' and at least two cameras. Battery technology had improved considerably since the Bobberts were first designed, so they were adapted to run from large batteries.

They could move around the factory. That enabled them to return and charge themselves up when necessary. They could change their own tools and fittings. There were fixed points on the floor that they could attach themselves to when operating.

It was a clever, flexible system. It just needed the design for the required part. The computers and the Bobberts would do the rest.

It wasn't long before we'd made all the parts for a small prototype building. We assembled it in a clearing in the woods.

We were quite pleased with it. That was until Smythe blew it up. Typical of Smythe. He liked blowing things up. He asked us first, of course. We were horrified at first, but then we thought about it. It would reveal any weaknesses in our designs, so we let him do it.

Smythe positioned the explosives in the middle of the building and then detonated them remotely. He appeared to be in his element. Most of the roof blew off and two windows blew out. There were cracks in some walls. One of the section junctions had come apart.

We took down the remains of the building, carefully documented the damage and then redesigned the damaged sections. We made a new kit of parts and built a new, stronger building.

The next explosion test proved more successful, with much less damage. We repeated this until we were sure we had a strong enough design. I remember the last test making me laugh. The whole building just jumped a few inches into the air when the explosives went off.

Then we set about getting our designs approved by the relevant authorities. They passed all the tests easily. We started selling DIY house kits.

They were relatively cheap to make, and the basic design was very flexible. If a customer wanted something we didn't have parts for, we just designed new parts to suit and added them to our catalogue of options.

The Bobberts were kept very busy. High and increasing demand meant that Barry's team had to work hard to get all the remaining Bobberts repaired, serviced and adapted.

FLICKERING FLICKS

We were all (I thought) in the Bovercraft's cinema. I forget which film we were watching. It had almost completed, and we (or Muttley) had eaten all the ice cream.

The light from the projector had been flickering oddly. It wasn't enough to annoy anyone, so we'd ignored it. Then it suddenly stopped altogether, plunging us into darkness. All we could see were the Exit signs above the doorways, and Barry's teeth.

Barry had false teeth. The front ones had tiny LED lights installed in them. He could switch them on or off with his tongue. He did a quick investigation, while everyone else remained in their seats. After a few minutes, he announced that there had been a general power failure. He advised everyone not to leave the Bovercraft. Meanwhile, he would investigate further.

Several months earlier, I'd installed an emergency backup power source using conventional technology. At the time, Captain Smythe thought I'd been making a lot of fuss about nothing. I'd just proved him wrong. I activated it.

Barry discovered the cause of the trouble. The MPBs that had been powering the Bovercraft all that time were hardly glowing at all. They were producing almost no power. He removed them to prevent further damage.

I had hoped that my improvised power system would never be used. It wouldn't last long, but at least it could power our artificial gravity and several other vital systems for a while.

We still had Barry's portable backup supply. Unfortunately, it wasn't compatible with our main systems, as he'd modified it for other purposes. Oops. Barry had never had a chance to fit and test it properly. There had always been something more urgent to do.

We fitted its MPB into our main power unit. That helped, but just one couldn't provide enough power to run everything normally. Ideally, we would need replacement MPBs. That could mean returning to Mars, which wasn't possible with the small amount of power we had. In any case, there might not be any more to find. We didn't want to risk being marooned on Mars, so Smythe advised us not to try.

Smythe asked for an assessment of our situation. We were in a space drain, heading for Earth. Our momentum would get us there, but the drain exit pointed straight at the Earth. The bubble that should have protected us had collapsed, exposing the factory to space.

Simon did a roll call. Everyone but Sue was aboard the Bovercraft, as we'd been watching the film. Sue had been working in one of the factory buildings. Simon called her by radio. She sounded fine but said she could hear air escaping from the building. She tried to plug the small hole in the wall. That slowed the leak, but not completely.

Joyce had insisted we had systems in place to try to preserve life in that sort of situation. Practice exercises had shown that getting into spacesuits could take too long, so every building had several small, horizontal chambers lying on the floor against the walls. Each could accommodate one person and had a built-in 2-way radio. Anyone in danger could climb into a chamber, close the clear polycarbonate cover and call for help. Joyce made sure they were tested at regular intervals.

I'd still had misgivings, so I'd gone to see Joyce.

"Those rescue chambers... I'm a bit concerned about them," I'd said.

"Why?" asked Joyce. "They do work."

"Yes, but what if help doesn't arrive in time?"

"That's not very likely," she'd replied. "Do you have something in mind?"

"Yes. How about we add wheels, so the occupant can move around if necessary?"

Joyce giggled slightly. Goodness knows what she was thinking of.

"We could make them motorised," I'd continued.

"Why don't we just leave electric cars in there?" said Joyce.

"They're not spaceproof. My Korteener certainly isn't."

"OK, I'll give you that. I don't want them motorised, though."

"Why?" I'd asked.

"KISS."

"Err... what...?" I went a bit red.

"It stands for 'Keep It Simple, Stupid'," she'd said, laughing at me. "Motors and batteries can fail. If the wheels are turned manually from inside the chamber, they'll be much more reliable."

I agreed and got on with the modifications.

But back to our problem. We would have to rescue Sue. Unfortunately, all the spacesuits were in the factory buildings.

We were legally required to carry out urgent safety modifications due to a recent accident. There were no spacesuits in the Bovercraft and none at Sue's location.

There should have been two left in the Bovercraft, but Smythe had overridden Joyce's concerns. He had insisted that all the spacesuits should be done in one go, as the modifications were urgent.

Sue was alone, so she had climbed into one of the chambers. We couldn't think of any way to rescue her before her oxygen supply ran out.

Barry had an idea. The smaller access doors for the building containing the Bovercraft were missing (removed for repair). All the air had rushed out. If Sue could turn the chamber wheels, she might be able to get her chamber out of her building and to the Bovercraft.

The doors of Sue's building would have to be opened somehow. Our two androids could have done it, but they couldn't be contacted. Both were working out of sight somewhere, outside of any buildings. Androids have to be given instructions verbally. Calling them on the Tannoy system wouldn't have worked. There's no sound in a vacuum.

Being an ex-military man, Captain Smythe came up with a military solution. Blow the doors off. Simon pointed out that the sudden decompression would cause considerable damage. Sue's chamber might be blown out into space. We'd have to wait until the air in Sue's building leaked out.

Sue said she could see the atmospheric pressure gauge on the wall. The pressure had dropped slightly, but enough air still remained for someone to breathe. She climbed out of the capsule, removed her temporary wall repair, climbed back in and waited.

It took about an hour for enough air to escape. Smythe told her to position the capsule as far from the doors as possible. She did. The main building doors were opened remotely.

Nobody wanted to be the one to fire at the doors, so Smythe did it himself. The doors on Sue's building were destroyed, along with much of one wall. I resisted the temptation to quote from a well-known film.

The explosion attracted the attention of the two androids. They went to investigate. They found Sue and pushed her capsule around the rubble, out of the building and up to the Bovercraft. A low-level loading platform had been installed in the Bovercraft, which could be raised or lowered. The system included an airlock. The androids pushed her chamber up the small ramp and onto the loading platform so we could get her on board.

With Sue safe, we turned our attention to getting home without crashing. Going to Mars wasn't an option. Barry had fitted the single MPB into our main power unit, but he had intentionally limited the power output to avoid overheating it.

When we left the drain, we had just enough energy to arrest our forward motion. Then we paused, to allow Barry time to check on the condition of the MPB. It had survived but had become too hot to touch.

We could store energy up to a point. We stored as much as possible before attempting to return to our base. With some skilful piloting, we limped home. We came down quite slowly at first, then faster than we would have liked, like trying to stop a heavy car with poor brakes. The bubble was restored just before we landed to ensure an accurate landing. We landed heavily, but intact and on target.

Once down, we slowly allowed the air into bubble, then collapsed it. We had stored some spare MPBs in a Portakabin in the woods. There were more than we realised. Barry fitted them into our main power unit. That restored normal power. All the others were put back in the Portakabin.

I returned to the Portakabin a week later to check on the MPBs. A slight pale orange glow surrounded them. The worn ones seemed to have recovered slightly by draining power from the others. I felt that we needed to find a way to recharge the drained MPBs.

THE VISITOR

We had few visitors when we were at home. Under the previous management, special arrangements had been set up with delivery firms. We collected from them when we could. Some didn't like having to store stuff for us, sometimes for weeks. After Barry and I took over, I persuaded a small, local company to act as a delivery address for us for a small fee. That made things much easier, as we only had to collect from one site.

We had a welcome visitor from time to time. It was a friendly black-and-white cat. It belonged to one of the local farmers. It used to walk in as though it owned the place. Everyone made a great fuss of it. We weren't supposed to feed it, but some still did. It would usually stay for a day or two, then leave.

Penny tried to keep Muttley out of the way when our feline visitor appeared. Muttley was used to cats, as Penny used to have two, but he would chase any he didn't know. Usually, he was taken for long walks in the woods by Penny, Joyce, Barry, or sometimes myself. Muttley could detect the cat's presence, as he could smell it. We usually distracted him with a tennis ball when we thought he could smell the cat.

Inevitably, the time came when Muttley spotted it. I was taking him for a walk at the time, in the woods, off the lead. Muttley suddenly raced off, ignoring my calls, barking. So much for Penny's obedience training, I thought.

I couldn't see Muttley, so throwing the tennis ball wasn't an option. I eventually caught up with him, a bit out of breath, to find him at the bottom of a tree. He was barking up at the cat, with his tail wagging wildly. The cat looked down on him from high in the branches, hissing at him occasionally.

Muttley became bored with it after a while. He wasn't barking as much and his tail had slowed down. I threw the tennis ball. Muttley seemed torn between the ball and the cat. He started walking towards the ball, then noticed the cat had come down. He ran up to it. He seemed surprised when the cat just stood there, still hissing at him. Muttley backed off when the cat moved towards him.

If Muttley had run away, the cat would probably have chased him. They approached each other cautiously and sniffed each other. The cat was used to dogs. It knew how to deal with them. After that, they got along just fine. I sometimes wondered which would have been better at guarding the place... Muttley or the cat.

Cats and dogs play differently, but after a while, they found a way to play together. I thought it quite unusual.

On one of those dog walks, Barry noticed a small, single-track road leading away from the factory. He didn't know where it went, so he asked me. I told him it led to the old quarry site. I'd forgotten to tell him about it. I'd ensured that the railway line and associated stuff were included in our purchase when we bought the site. Nobody had told him about the railway. I suppose it wasn't too surprising, as very few people knew about it.

This fascinated Barry. He liked railways. He walked there when he next got the chance and found Ivor (the engine). He spent much of his spare time during the following weeks tinkering with it. He made it go somewhat faster than normal. (Joyce didn't know about that bit. Just as well, I thought.)

He nearly lost it on one corner. Those engines weren't designed for speed. You don't need speed for shunting. He got Sue involved, too. She helped him with the work. She quietly fitted a speed limiter without Barry knowing. She couldn't see any need to go so fast. It wasn't as though he could race with anybody. It was only a single-track line anyway.

One day, Barry and Sue were walking towards the railway line. Sue suddenly saw something and screamed. She nearly deafened Barry.

"Good grief," said Barry. "What was that about?"

"I saw something," said Sue.

"What? Another ghost?" said Barry.

"No. I think I saw a snake. A big one."

"We don't have big snakes around here."

"We do now!" Sue insisted.

As they watched, a four-foot snake crossed the path ahead of them.

"Let's get out of here!" shouted Sue.

"Hang on a minute... I need evidence," said Barry. He chased after the snake and photographed it.

"OK, let's go," said Barry.

They hurried back to the factory. Barry showed me his photo. We looked it up. It was native to Australia. It must've got onto our patch of land when it was in Australia.

Muttley got no more walks for a few days, while we checked the whole area for foreign wildlife. Ned's knowledge came in handy. We found several snakes, which we took to a local zoo. Several small nasties had died, due to our colder climate. Ned thought he'd spotted kangaroo footprints, but we never found one.

Re-homing

We were home, and things were quiet. The last major contract had just been completed. There wasn't much to do other than tidying up. We no longer needed to make a huge profit, as long as we made enough to pay our wages. We did what we did because we liked doing it. We took time to pause and relax when we could.

Simon's piano playing had improved, with help from Joyce. He'd been learning to play 'The Banks of the Ohio', but had become bored with the original lyrics, so had written his own. They went something like this...

> 'I had a dream the other night
> That my left foot did not feel right.
> I picked it up to take a look
> And then I dropped it in the brook.
>
> It didn't hurt just like it should
> Because my foot was made of wood.
> It floated off and then got stuck.

'At last,' I thought, 'a bit of luck'.

I had with me a length of string.
Maybe I'd catch the blinking thing.
I tied it to my new false teeth
And threw them in to assist me.

But in my haste to get them back
I slipped and fell, then heard a crack.
The length of string caught in the wind
And I let go the other end.

My new false teeth chased down my foot.
The homing teeth worked as they should.
They caught instead, a rubber duck.
Then wet got in and blew them up.

I thought I'd build myself a raft,
Even though it sounded daft.
I didn't know where to begin.
I lost my grip, and I fell in.

I thought I'd drown, but I was wrong.
I'd have to end this dreadful song.
When I stood up, about to weep,
I found the brook just one foot deep.

I sploshed along as best I could
Then I retrieved my missing foot.
I hopped back home, knowing what to do.
I'd fix it on with superglue.

I stood back up and then fell down.
My foot was on the wrong way round.
A cuckoo clock had injured me.
Sometimes I wished that I could see.'

Simon said it was a 'work in progress'. Hmmm.

A huge flat-panel TV had been fitted on a wall in the factory. Comfy chairs were nearby, close to where the Bobberts were quietly charging. Many of us were sitting there, watching the international news.

We saw some distressing scenes. A tornado had torn through dozens of houses. Such things didn't normally happen there. The weather forecasters had given plenty of warnings. There had been no loss of life, but many buildings in a large residential area had been destroyed.

We felt sorry for the victims. Winter wasn't far off, so we decided to help. Our 3D-printed building kits were ideal for the job. We had many ready-made sections already in storage.

We contacted the insurance companies that had insured the wrecked houses. They were happy to let us construct the new buildings. Our replacements would cost them much less than usual.

We got to work. The original plans were available for some properties. We often ignored them, as most people wanted to improve on what they had before. We reused the original foundations where possible. In some cases, we only had photos of the houses, taken before they were destroyed.

The considerable computing power of our Bobbert systems made it easy to design replacement buildings quickly. They were usually to much higher standards than the originals. Integrated solar panels were built into all the roofs as standard.

The Bobberts were busy for weeks. Building kits were shipped and put up in record time. We were doing well, we thought. The orders kept coming in.

Then we noticed that production had suddenly stopped. Much work still had to be done, yet the Bobberts were missing. We found them outside in the car park. They were playing five-a-side Bobbertball. The eleventh one acted as a referee.

Someone had left the big TV on, as usual. Unknown to us, the Bobberts had been watching it. They'd watched quite a lot of football matches.

I think Bill and Ted might have been the ringleaders. They were the first pair of Bobberts to be used for 3D printing. They'd been given those names because we thought the work they'd done was 'excellent'. I think that gave them a sense of superiority.

We named others too. One pair had accidentally knocked somebody over. We called them Assault and Battery. We called another pair ACDC and Motorhead, for obvious reasons, plus the 'heavy metal' used in their construction.

The Bobberts refused to return to the construction area. We couldn't do much about it. They were bigger and stronger than us. We knew they would run low on power sooner or later, so Barry disconnected the power to the charging area. That stopped them.

We modified the software so it couldn't happen again. Then we took the TV away. I suppose it was our fault for making the Bobberts too intelligent. Production soon resumed.

Our car park hadn't been constructed with Bobbertball in mind. We had to get it resurfaced. Some cars had also been damaged, as the Bobberts had used one of the concrete-filled footballs. The company had to pay for the car damage, as we weren't insured for that sort of thing. The ball looked pretty shredded by the time the Bobberts had finished with it.

We built dozens of new houses. The owners were pleased with them. Most were much better than what they'd had before. They cost much less to heat and complied with the latest standards.

Some dishonest people at the edges of the destruction area destroyed their own houses. They wanted better ones. Those houses were usually in a poor state anyway. The insurance companies soon got wise to it and refused to pay up. Some people became homeless. Served them right, I thought. They had to pay for our replacements themselves.

After that, we got several house building contracts worldwide.

Beachcombing

Making all those house parts required huge amounts of plastic, amongst other things. In those days, many manufacturers still used it. Environmental concerns resulted in several countries introducing laws to limit its use.

The Bobbert 3D printing setups used special 'filament' to make the parts. It looked like cable on a drum. It consisted of mostly plastic, with several other ingredients added for strength. What we needed wasn't commercially available, so we made our own.

The boffins called our special filament 'scratch'. They argued that many worthwhile things had been made from scratch. It was clearly good stuff.

Making the huge reels of scratch required more plastic than we could easily get hold of. We usually used bags of plastic pellets, intended for use in industrial injection moulding machines. Recycled plastics were cheaper than the new stuff, but not so easy to find.

Sue suggested that we use locally sourced scrap plastic. Barry agreed. Mind you, Barry tended to agree with Sue anyway. I agreed with them.

Two of our boffins were experts in working with polymers. They'd worked with injection moulding machines in previous employment. They reckoned it should be possible to separate the different types of scrap plastic automatically, clean and shred them, and then make them into scratch.

That just left the problem of where to get the scrap plastic from. We tried several local sources, but their prices were prohibitive. We approached several local councils, hoping they'd let us take away scrap plastic, but that didn't work either. They already had contracts with other companies and didn't want to change.

As our main site wasn't far from the beach, I suggested beachcombing. It used to annoy me to see so much rubbish on the local beaches. Most had been left by tourists, or by shipping throwing stuff overboard. In decades past, well-meaning groups of people had tried to clean up the local beaches. I couldn't recall anyone doing that for years.

Picking up large quantities of rubbish by hand wasn't practical, although a few volunteers did collect some in bin bags for experimental use. We needed a better way.

The boffins suggested flying the factory slowly over the coast to collect the plastic. We would pull it off the beaches below us, directly into a special skip in our factory car park. A computer-controlled system would automatically identify plastic items, lock onto them using fine gravity beams and pull them into the skip. The system would be able to deal with dozens of items simultaneously.

We built the system. We tested it during the night, flying over a local beach upside down, with our artificial gravity switched on. Then we looked in the skip. It had worked well. Most of the sand and seaweed had fallen away as the plastic rose from the beach. Our people got busy separating it, manually at first, then using machines.

We completed several successful night-time test runs over local beaches. Barry and I handed over responsibility for the beach cleaning to Captain Smythe. Both of us told Smythe not to do it during the day.

Barry and I had to go away for two days to attend a meeting. We left Smythe in temporary charge. Smythe didn't like doing the beach cleaning at night. Nobody did. He eventually chose to do a daytime run over a quiet beach. The scientists had devised a way to make us invisible a few weeks earlier, so he thought we'd have no problems.

Simon had more common sense than Smythe. He had a pretty good idea of what would happen. He picked a time when several witnesses were present on the bridge and then advised Smythe not to do it. Smythe ignored him. Simon liked a laugh, so he left Smythe to get on with it.

The daytime beach cleaning went ahead. Plastic stuff appeared in the skip, as usual. Simon noticed people running around on the beach. Many were heading for the sea, obviously distressed. There seemed to be a freak whirlwind below us. The dry sand swirling around made it difficult to see what was happening.

Simon advised Smythe to go and look in the skip. He went and looked, somewhat reluctantly. It contained the usual rubbish. There were plastic bottles, some packaging and a few toys. We also found several current credit cards, three pairs of sunglasses and five towels. Several items of plastic-based beachwear were there too, some still slightly warm.

Barry and I got back earlier than expected. Someone told us what had happened. We found Simon and Smythe at the skip.

"Smythe, I thought we told you not to do the beach cleaning during the daytime," I said.

"Sorry sir. It won't happen again, sir." He'd taken to calling Barry and me 'sir'. I guessed it was his way of coming to terms with us outranking him. Perhaps he regarded us as his 'superior officers'.

"Alright, Smythe. At ease. We'll let it go this time," said Barry.

Simon tried hard not to laugh (much). Smythe looked rather sheepish and very embarrassed.

We knew we'd have to return the personal items, but we weren't sure how. Anyone trying to do it in person risked being arrested. We couldn't just drop them on the beach, as the owners would already have left. We needed a better plan.

One of Sue's ideas saved the day. We went slightly back in time, returning to when we had collected the stuff. We closely followed our earlier selves, while spinning and invisible. That stirred up the air, lifting some of the dry sand.

The small sandstorm would hide what we were doing. We released the things that had to be returned. They dropped onto the beach and were recovered by their owners. Local papers later reported an unusual local whirlwind, but little more.

We knew we'd have to be more careful next time. The boffins reprogrammed the collection system to reject anything of value or within a certain temperature range.

Apart from that, the system worked well. We collected a large quantity of plastic. The beaches were much cleaner afterwards. Any plastics we couldn't use were shredded and sold.

We did more than just beachcombing. It seemed like an ideal opportunity to tidy up parts of the planet plagued by plastic waste. That kept us busy for months. We were well paid for the clean-up work. We acquired much more plastic than we could ever use. We sold much of it. The best stuff got stored in our Moonbase stores if we didn't need it immediately.

It soon became a lot of hassle. We became tired of it. We just concentrated on areas that badly needed to be cleaned up. Even then, we still had more requests for cleanup operations than we could handle. We couldn't do it all. It would've taken us years, maybe decades.

The boffins designed a much smaller system to do the job. We sold several to a few trusted companies and then left them to it.

Earth's plastic pollution problem looked much improved. Some politicians suggested that restrictions on using plastics could be lifted. Others reminded them that we'd only lifted the bigger bits. Much of the problem still remained. Dealing with the small stuff (including microplastics) would be far more difficult. We had intended to devise a system to deal with microplastics, but we never quite got around to it.

Eye in the Sky

Our boffins were quite pleased with themselves when they discovered how to make us invisible. That ability sometimes proved useful, although we didn't do it often. Some of the younger ones wanted to take it further. They wanted us to be able to look like something we weren't.

We talked to Captain Smythe and Simon about it. None of us could see any reason not to let them try. They were permitted to give it a go. We thought it might be amusing.

It wasn't as easy as they'd expected. They didn't realise, at first, that just using a flat image wouldn't be convincing. We had to look three-dimensional if we were to fool anybody.

The tests were quite interesting. We appeared as a light aircraft. Then an airship, a hang glider and several types of clouds. Then it got silly. We appeared as the Starship Enterprise, a London bus, a giant bowl of fruit and a flock of low-flying pigs. As far as I knew, our tests weren't seen by anyone else.

We installed the new equipment properly, tested it again and then forgot about it. There were more important things to do.

A few months later, a local commercial airport contacted us. They'd been having trouble with small drones being flown illegally over or near the runways. The police were contacted. They noted the details but did nothing else. Several aircraft had suffered from drone strikes. We had gained a reputation for coming up with innovative solutions to problems, so we were asked if we could help.

We flew to the airport and landed nearby. We were shown to the Air Traffic Control tower, where some of us talked to the controllers. As we watched, two drones flew over the runways. I thought could see two youngsters in the distance, hiding behind a bush. I think they were trying to make a political point, but I can't remember what. The drones were a hazard to aircraft. Something had to be done.

Sue recommended that we use our camouflage capabilities. Barry agreed. He told our young boffins to make us look like a giant human eyeball in the sky.

They soon had it set up. We hovered just above the ground, not far from the side of the main runway. We thought it looked impressive. By rotating the image, it could appear to look around.

Some said the eyeball looked terrifying. We were getting complaints, so we tried to make it less scary. Sue and Joyce gave it eyelids, makeup and false eyelashes. They also made it blink occasionally.

It scared off the drone pilots for a while, but they eventually got used to it and the trouble restarted. We had to physically intervene. We landed nearby, leaving the eye effect switched on. It looked like half a giant eye peering out at people from the ground.

Then we used fine gravity beams to latch onto the drones and individually crash them into a skip, in a locked compound.

The drone owners wanted them back. Some got arrested when they were caught trying to break into the compound. We could sometimes match the drone serial numbers with the owners, although some had been scratched off.

The ATC staff were happy. They let their colleagues at other airports know. By that time, our efforts had appeared in the local newspapers. We became a deterrent to mischievous drone operators.

A short while later, the government got to hear about it. They congratulated us. Then they asked if we could help with another problem, namely space junk. The problem had existed for decades. Somebody needed to deal with it, so we agreed to try.

We went back to our base and operated from there. The UK Space Agency lent us a mobile tracking system, which we set up in our car park, to locate space items. Every item we found was automatically identified, based on its orbit and the latest ephemeris data.

Any item deemed to be junk was slowly and gently pulled to our site using a fine gravity beam. We had to pay careful attention to the weather forecasts. Badly damaged satellites were left in a big heap until we realised they could still be valuable.

Some satellites were still intact. Some were just out of fuel or had failed to deploy fully after reaching orbit. We had to store them in a specially constructed ultra-clean, gravity-free storage area, while we worked on them.

We got several satellites refuelled and working again. We carefully pushed them back into space, close to their original orbits. From there, their operators took control and returned them to their proper orbits.

Later, we set up a separate system at our site to automatically locate and retrieve orbiting rubbish, bits of paint, discarded boosters, nuts and bolts, etc. and bring them back to our site.

Satellites were expensive to build and deploy back then. We made a small fortune repairing and refurbishing them. Some were damaged as we pushed or pulled them through Earth's atmosphere. One got attacked by an eagle. Sometimes we would collect the bigger satellites from orbit using the Bovercraft and return them to orbit the same way if necessary.

We had one incident where we accidentally retrieved an operational satellite. We soon put it back again, refuelled as a goodwill gesture.

Nuts and Vegetables

It was a sunny day in late summer. Barry and Sue had taken Ivor for a run along the railway line. It was a scenic route in a nice part of the country. The line ran close to the beach in places.

Barry had stopped Ivor near one of the beaches. He and Sue were sitting on the beach, having a picnic. On the way there, they'd stopped several times to gather hazelnuts from the trees alongside the line. They'd got about a bucketful.

We had equipped Ivor with a two-way radio. If anyone had trouble with the locomotive, they could call for help. I used it to call Barry, as one of his staff needed his advice.

"Spacemakers calling Barry," I said into the microphone. Silence. I waited a few minutes, then tried again.

"Spacemakers calling Barry and Sue," I said.

"Nuts to you," came Sue's voice over the speaker. She had a habit of starting to speak before pressing the transmit button.

"Say again?"

"We're bringing some nuts to you. We've been gathering hazelnuts. I know you rather like them," said Sue.

"Ah. Thanks. Could you please tell Barry that he needs to get back here, as someone wants his advice. It's not urgent, though," I said.

"We'll be back in about half an hour," said Barry. A rather long half hour, as it turned out. More like two hours. Typical Barry. We were expecting it. When they got back, Sue handed me the bucket of hazelnuts.

We used to use that beach a lot. We converted one of the old abandoned quarry wagons to make it more suitable for transporting people. Ron added a door and some steps to one side. He also bolted some old car seats to the floor. It allowed several of us to visit the beach at once, pulled by Ivor. Great during the summer.

We occasionally used this arrangement to collect blackberries. As far as we knew, nobody else had access to our private line. Nobody but us had any reason to be there anyway.

One year, we tried planting vegetables along the banks at the sides of the line. We got a good crop of potatoes, carrots and other things. Then I had another daft idea.

We modified another wagon to plant vegetables. Barry and Ron bolted one of the Bobberts securely into it. The boffins programmed it to plant vegetables alongside the line on both sides. It was the one marked B11. It had been the Bobbertball referee.

The other Bobberts usually worked in pairs. This one often got left all by itself. We called it Eric (Simon's idea). Don't ask me why. Eric's wagon was linked to (and pulled by) Ivor so that Eric could remotely control Ivor's speed.

We had several teething problems with the system. Eric tried to plant seeds in the ballast, in the trees or on the floor of the wagon. We soon had the bugs fixed.

We bought bags of seed potatoes and various other seeds. We loaded them into the wagon, set up the system and then left Eric and Ivor to get on with it.

About a day later, they still hadn't returned. We'd been distracted by something else and had forgotten to check if they were back. Something had gone wrong. We still had one of those old 2-man handcars, so we headed down the line to find out what had happened.

We found them about half a mile from the far end of the line. They'd been programmed to stop there. We'd forgotten to tell them to return afterwards. Barry drove Ivor back, using it to push the handcar along. An easy task for Ivor, as it had been designed for shunting larger things.

It occurred to Barry that Eric could also be used to gather the crops when they were ripe. We programmed it to do that, testing everything thoroughly, by pulling up weeds. When the time came, it all worked perfectly, apart from Eric pulling up a couple of fence posts. We got enough fresh food to last us for ages.

Simon suggested that Eric could be used to pick blackberries. We tried it, but many weren't ripe or were squashed. We abandoned that idea. Anyway, I think most people preferred to pick them themselves.

We had hoped to use Eric and Ivor this way in future years, but we didn't get the chance. I blamed our younger boffins.

The youngsters were frustrated by the apparent lack of intelligence of our two androids, so they upgraded one of them. They added huge amounts of extra memory, including long-term memory. They also gave it much more intelligence. I don't think they realised it wasn't legal.

It didn't go well. The android became self-aware. All androids were programmed to protect humans. This one took it too far.

It discovered that Phil had been marooned in the distant past and decided to do something about it. Our attempts to convince it that Phil wasn't in danger fell on deaf microphones. Then it went missing.

Other things disappeared too. Several large solar panels had been taken from one of the Portakabins. The door had been torn off. Ron couldn't find his toolbox (again). Many other bits and pieces couldn't be accounted for.

A few days later, I discovered that Eric was missing too, along with most of its attachments and spares. Nobody had a clue where it had all gone.

DRAINAGE ISSUES

As the years passed, space drain usage increased rapidly. As more planets were discovered, more drains were needed. Several near-misses within the drains had been reported. New rules and restrictions were applied. Some were set up to allow only one spacecraft in the drain at once.

It reminded me of those old films, usually science fiction, where somebody has to crawl through an air duct. There always seemed to be air ducts, just big enough for one person to get through. What would happen if two people met in the middle? In any case, some should have come crashing down, due to the extra weight. People weigh more than air. But I digress.

The older races were concerned about those drains for other reasons. They wouldn't say why. I think they thought we wouldn't believe them. They let us discover the problems the hard way.

After many years of use, strange things started happening with some of the older drains. Transported goods were disappearing. They would reappear later, where they were supposed to be. Some travellers became ill, semi-transparent or invisible. Fortunately, the effects were only temporary. The oldest drains were getting a reputation for odd things happening. Nobody knew why.

We heard of a strange case where a company had delivered a batch of aluminium castings to a remote planet via one of the older drains.

When the castings arrived, they were slightly too small. The customer wasn't happy. They accused the foundry of forgetting to allow for shrinkage when the castings cooled. They demanded replacements.

The foundry made more castings. All were carefully checked before they left the foundry. When they were delivered, they were much too big and slightly rubbery.

Several weeks and many heated arguments later, someone noticed that both batches of castings were back to normal and to specifications. The space drains got the blame, but nobody could prove it.

None of the effects were permanent. They corrected themselves within a few weeks. It had become a serious problem, though. Travellers with fast spacecraft avoided using those drains.

We were immune to those effects. Our force field bubble seemed to be protecting us. Important delivery jobs using those old drains got handed to us. It meant more business for us, so we had no incentive to do anything about it. Several other spacecraft were also unaffected, but that fact wasn't discovered until much later.

Meanwhile, Sue and the boffins had created some decent equipment that could easily read and translate the data on the alien cylinders from Planet Dee. Sue had made it possible to search for things. We searched for information on space tunnels.

We discovered that the Plonkers had also used space tunnels, at first. They had later abandoned the technology. They'd had the same problems as we did. They had also developed faster ways to travel through space.

We were keen to learn more about the 'faster ways'. We found some information about it, but not enough to make a working drive. Luckily, our triplet boffins were smart enough to fill in the gaps.

They worked with Barry and his team to create a new drive system. It included a new power source, much more powerful than our existing MPB-based one.

A few months later, the new system had been installed into the Bovercraft and was ready for testing. Smythe wanted to try it out. He nearly got us blown up, trying things before they were ready. The boffins drew up a detailed plan for testing the system, including what to do if things went wrong.

It took us a couple of weeks to fine-tune the system so that it worked well. We found we could travel much faster that way than by drain, or by using the MPBs. We rarely used the drains after that. There wasn't any point.

The problematic older drains were shut down, and the associated space hardware was removed. Replacement drains were set up, but they suffered from the same side effects as the old ones. Sue discovered the cause in the Plonker documentation. I can't remember the reason for the problems, but I remember it making me laugh.

We didn't think it was fair to keep the information to ourselves, so we eventually let everyone else know what they needed to do to avoid the drain problems.

Alien home

We used the new power system from then on, keeping the old system in reserve. I don't think we used the MPB system at all after that.

I talked to Barry about the MPBs.

"I feel rather guilty about draining those MPBs the way we did," said Barry.

"Me too. Those aliens wanted them returned to Mars. Perhaps we should," I said.

"Yes. If we take them to Mars, maybe we could find a way to recharge them," said Barry. "Let's take them there anyway."

I retrieved all the MPBs from the Portakabin, and then we went to Mars.

After we landed, Barry and I got into our space suits and took the MPBs onto the surface of Mars.

"How about leaving the MPBs in the sunlight for a few days?" asked Barry. "That might recharge them a little."

"We don't know how long it'll take," I replied.

We left them scattered around in the Martian dust and returned to them a week later. I examined one of them.

"This one doesn't look any different," I said.

"Oh rats. Never mind. It was a good idea," said Barry.

"Maybe they just need longer," I said.

"Those things were here for millions of years. I don't think I'll still be around millions of years from now," said Barry.

"Neither will the Bovercraft," I said.

"Or the Human race, for that matter."

I had an idea.

"Wait a minute... why don't we just send them back in time? We could send them back into the past, then collect them in the present."

"Let's go talk to the boffins," said Barry.

We did. They rigged up a portable time window machine for us. It was a smaller version of the one that had sent Smythe back to the Wild West. The boffins warned us to be careful with it.

We put it on a trolley and pushed it out onto the Martian surface. We powered it up.

"We'd better test this thing first," said Barry. "We need to get the hang of it."

"Agreed. How about sending something back just a few minutes, first?"

"I know. I'll send my watch through. When we retrieve it, we can compare it with yours," said Barry.

We did. We set the location to be just a few feet away. The time to go back would be twenty minutes.

"Here goes," said Barry. He took off his watch. We compared the time with mine. Then he carefully threw it through the time window. It reappeared a few feet away.

Barry's watch read nearly thirty minutes ahead of mine.

"Near enough," I said.

"Let's try something bigger," said Barry. He fetched one of his work boots from the Bovercraft, adjusted the machine's controls and threw the boot through the time window.

It reappeared, just as the watch had. Barry picked it up.

"Oh no! Look at it!" I looked at it. It was full of sand. The sides looked very worn. I checked the controls on the machine.

"How far back did you intend to send it?" I asked.

"Sixty minutes."

"This is set to sixty years."

"Oops..."

"Now it's saying 'Low battery'," I said.

"I think we'll need to run a power cable from the Bovercraft," said Barry. "We'll need much more power if we're going to send anything further back in time."

We did. We disconnected the battery and connected a proper power supply. After a few more tests, we were ready to try the MPBs.

"We'll just try one first. I'll set it for one hundred years," said Barry.

We sent one MPB through and then examined it.

"This looks slightly better," I said. Barry looked at it.

"It's less pitted than before. Let's try a thousand years," he said.

We did, several times. By the time we'd finished, the MPB looked perfect. We did the same with the rest of the MPBs. Then we took the equipment and the MPBs back to the Bovercraft.

Barry thought it high time we honoured our promise to the aliens living in the smaller MPBs. We'd greatly benefitted from the power that their MPBs had provided. We returned home.

Barry, Sue, Amy and I met in our medical department, to discuss what to do about the aliens. Amy had recorded everything that had happened when we were at the university. We wanted to replicate what the students had done.

Amy already had much of the required equipment in her medical department. I felt confident that Barry and I either had the remaining equipment needed or could 'borrow' it from somewhere.

Sue could remember some of what had happened at the university, but not everything. She'd been asleep during the experiments. Amy showed her the recordings. Sue agreed to continue to be our means of communication with the aliens.

A week later, we had all the equipment set up in the medical department. Ron had built the special helmet. He'd made a good job of it. I invited him to attend, but he said he had other things to do.

Sue sat in the chair, and Amy wired her up. Everything was switched on. We planned to bypass the sleep stage to allow Sue to communicate with the aliens directly, while conscious. We hoped to see them on the monitors.

Sue held onto the MPB we had used the last time. She closed her eyes and concentrated hard. Nothing. She reclined the chair as much as possible and tried to relax more. Still nothing. I started checking things. I found a cable end lying on the floor, which led to the special helmet.

I plugged it in. Sue jumped. I should have told her what I was about to do. I started to apologise, but she shut me up. She was getting something. Images appeared on the monitors. We were getting sound too, directly this time.

We could see the alien environment on the monitors, but no aliens could be found. It took Sue a while to find an alien to communicate with. He (we assumed it to be a 'he') looked like he'd just been woken up, mainly because he just had been.

He told us that if they detected no external activity with the MPBs, they all went to sleep. No point in being awake for millions of years with nothing to do. He woke up properly when Barry told him why they were being contacted.

We intended to try to restore the aliens to physical form. Since Barry and I were in charge, nobody could tell us we couldn't. We knew it wasn't going to be easy.

Over the following days, with technical advice from the aliens, we put together special equipment to restore their bodies and minds from the digital data. Much of it looked similar to the experimental transporter technology I had once worked on, but more advanced.

Then we had to build a proper interface for the MPB itself, as Sue wasn't a computer. That bit wasn't so easy. It required a greater level of detail and accuracy than we expected. We got there in the end.

We started by recreating a small flower from inside the MPB. It appeared briefly, then fell apart in a pile of dust. We increased the power and tried again. This time we got the scale wrong. A three-foot daisy appeared. It stayed together, though. We kept trying until we got it right.

Next, we tried a small creature. That worked too. It scurried off and hid under a table. Then it started eating the daisy. We watched it for a while. It seemed fine.

We were ready to try it on one of the aliens, who had bravely volunteered. With great caution and attention to detail, we managed to recover him from the MPB. He looked well, albeit shaken up. Not surprising, considering that he hadn't been properly alive for millions of years.

Sue explained that Amy was a doctor. Amy would check him over as best she could. She directed him to lie down on the couch, then showed him the images of his insides on the big displays. Amy couldn't make much sense of the images, but our alien seemed relieved.

Barry and Sue could communicate with him, but I couldn't. That bothered me a bit, but it couldn't be helped. He told them his name was Hu. At least that's what it sounded like.

Hu was keen to recover the rest of his people from the MPBs, so we got busy with that. Hu kept an eye on things, making adjustments as necessary. He had a much better idea of what to do than we did.

The process took us several hours to complete. We recovered nearly a hundred people, plus a few pets and anything else they considered important or valuable, including several data crystals. Most of the aliens were taken to our canteen area, as there wasn't enough room for them all in the medical department. That raised a few eyebrows. Some of them tried to learn a little English from our staff, which kept everyone amused.

We got along well with them. It turned out they were all called Hu. I decided to call the first one Dokta. (Well, I thought it was funny. I don't think anyone else did.) They stayed with us for several weeks. We knew they couldn't stay with us indefinitely, so we asked where they were originally from. Maybe we could take them back there.

They weren't certain if their home planet still existed. If it did, it might not still be habitable. It was on the outer limits of the part of our galaxy that we knew. It took us quite a while to get there.

When we arrived, we looked for signs of life on the planet. We found it still habitable but with no signs of intelligent life. We landed and looked around. We occasionally found evidence of an ancient civilisation, but not much. Most of it had disintegrated long ago.

We prepared to leave. However, a number of the aliens wanted to check something first. Before they left their planet, there had been talk of building a special underground complex. It would store examples of everything they were and knew. They wanted something to survive in the event of a planet-wide catastrophe. Was it ever built, and if so, had any of it survived?

We had to find out. Several such locations had been envisaged, but our aliens could only remember the location of one of them. We relocated to that area. We used the Bovercraft's scanners to search deep underground and eventually found the place.

We found the entrance buried. Much soil and rubble had to be moved to reach it. When we did, we found a sealed door. We had no clue how to open it, but the aliens knew how. We were told that if we'd tried to break in ourselves, we'd have been in trouble. The gas inside would have made us seriously ill.

They pressed a few buttons on a panel nearby. We heard a hissing sound as the normal atmosphere inside was restored. We all went in. The aliens had advised us to bring torches, which we needed.

We found the interior amazing, albeit very dark. Everything seemed perfectly preserved. The aliens told us that the gas that had just been removed was very special. It preserved almost anything indefinitely. We found equipment far more advanced than ours built into the walls. There were short corridors leading off from the main room. They led to storage areas containing huge quantities of seeds and equipment.

Barry noticed several slots in one wall, near the entrance. He asked about them. They were designed to accept those MPBs from Mars. We'd been asked to bring them with us. The aliens inserted them into the slots.

The lights came on dimly. We heard various clonking and whining noises as the place seemed to awaken. The lighting soon improved to normal levels. Various displays became active, showing text and graphics we couldn't understand. We were told that the system had started running a self-check routine. It would take a while.

Everything needed to restore a dead planet was there. The planet wasn't dead, so that was a big bonus. The aliens told us that they would remain there. They would restore as much as they could and try to rebuild their civilisation. They hoped to find more of their race digitally stored there.

We handed over all the remaining MPBs, as they didn't belong to us. We also gave them as much food and other supplies as we could spare. Barry provided them with technical information that they might need if they wanted to contact us in the future. Sue gave them recordings and information on our language.

They thanked us profusely, and then we headed home, feeling quite pleased with ourselves.

Distant Cousins

At the outer limit of the part of the galaxy we knew, is an unusual planet. It's unusual because it's incredibly similar to Earth. The people there look human. They sound human. That's because they *are* human. We had been unaware of the planet's existence.

Around four or five thousand years ago, humans on Earth were being watched by a highly advanced and intelligent race. They weren't happy with Man's progress and decided to interfere. They felt that Man could do better things.

They got involved with the ancient Egyptians. They pushed them into building giant pyramids. The alien race told the Egyptians that the pyramids would last thousands of years.

The Egyptian leaders were given many fancy foods and other incentives to build the pyramids. They would have to find their own 'official' excuses for building them.

Work on the pyramids progressed rapidly. The aliens lent a hand with moving the larger stone pieces and helped with the design work. The locals did most of the building work, using heavy machinery provided by the aliens.

Many people protested about the alien interference. They argued that they were perfectly capable of building such things themselves. They felt insulted. The protests caused severe delays.

The aliens didn't like the criticism, so they relocated thousands of protesters, along with their families, pets, livestock and a good supply of food and seeds, to the distant planet I mentioned earlier. They planned to bring them back when the pyramids were complete. That never happened, as the aliens were in serious trouble at home.

Meanwhile, the humans on the distant planet thrived. Before they met the aliens, they knew nothing about space travel or distant planets. Some realised that later generations were unlikely to believe it. They made careful notes and hid any spare alien technology and information they could find.

Many of the modern descendants of the original group assumed that they had evolved on that planet. Others thought otherwise. Several archaeological digs had turned up alien artefacts. When fossils were found and studied, the path of their human evolution became unclear. Some people believed that humans were not even native to that planet.

By the time Spacemakers came into existence, their technology roughly matched ours. The advanced technology left by the aliens no longer worked. Most artefacts were kept in museums and displayed in glass cases.

Their social development had gone a bit strange. In most ways, they were fine, although excessive humour had become outlawed. Goodness knows why. There were no comedy programmes on their TV or radio. For centuries, people were told that laughing could harm their health. Some even believed their heads would fall off if they laughed too much, although nobody could prove it.

One of the modern inhabitants of that planet had discovered the existence of small natural space tunnels and had started studying them. He realised that every tunnel had to lead somewhere. He set up listening equipment at the ends of several, although he didn't seriously expect to detect anything.

One day, while flying his small spacecraft close to his planet, he started receiving signals from one of the tunnels. He recorded them and took the recordings back to his workshop for analysis. They appeared to be television broadcast signals. He knew about old television broadcast formats, but this one was unknown to him.

The tunnel ends were easy to move, so he moved this one to his workshop on the planet and secured it there. He started analysing the broadcasts. It took him a while to design and build improvised equipment to display the strange TV transmissions.

The images he saw were only in black-and-white, as he hadn't figured out how to decode the colour information. What he saw interested him greatly. He soon found a way to hear the sound as well.

The broadcasts were coming from other humans. There were comedy programmes, something unknown on his planet. They had to have come from somewhere else. He didn't understand the language, but the visual comedy made him laugh. He tried to suppress it, but couldn't.

For the next few months, he studied this alien language. He learnt to speak and understand it quite well. The transmissions came from a place called Earth. The language was English. He didn't tell anyone about it, as he didn't want to get arrested for humour crimes.

The broadcasts fascinated him more and more. He just had to find out where they were coming from. It became an obsession. It occurred to him that it might be possible to travel down the tunnel to the source of the transmissions, but he thought the tunnel might not be wide enough. It seemed quite flexible, though.

His intense curiosity eventually got the better of him. He removed any bits from his small spacecraft that stuck out of the sides and then tried to force the craft down the tunnel. At first, it wouldn't fit. As he pushed his spacecraft's power to its maximum, he suddenly heard a sort of 'plop' and disappeared down the tunnel.

Forcing his way down the tunnel like that put considerable strain on his spacecraft's engines. He kept it up for some time, but the engines were overheating. He would have to stop soon.

As he reached for the control to shut down the engines, he suddenly emerged from the other end of the tunnel, high in a planet's atmosphere. He brought his craft to a stop. At first, he thought he was still above his own planet, but as he descended, he noticed some things didn't look right. He guessed (and hoped) that he'd found Earth. He landed in a field, got out, locked the craft and switched on its invisibility cloak remotely.

By sheer chance, he'd landed near our local town. He walked cautiously to the outskirts, then along a few streets. People looked at him, staring at his unusual clothing. They were speaking in English. He'd wanted to visit Earth for months, but he found actually being there a bit scary. He'd learnt much of the English language but had never had to use it for real.

He wasn't sure if he could return to his own planet. He'd exited the small space tunnel very rapidly, so he wasn't quite sure of its location. Few on his planet were likely to miss him for a while, so he had no need to return any time soon.

He used to be highly sociable. He'd lost contact with most of his friends, due to getting so involved with the small space tunnels. He'd been working alone for months. He decided that getting home would be a task for later. No rush.

He wandered around the outskirts of the town, trying to keep away from people. Eventually, he came across the town end of our railway line. He opened the gate and walked down the line. He'd never seen a railway before. It looked fascinating. The wear on the rail top surfaces suggested to him that some sort of vehicle must run along them. Monorail systems existed on his planet, but they were nothing like this.

As he walked along, stepping from one sleeper to the next, he came across Ivor, stopped partway along the line. He walked up to it, then around it, studying it. Before he could climb aboard, someone shouted at him.

It was Simon. He'd been gathering blackberries at the side of the line.

"Hey! What do you think you're doing?" called Simon.

"I think I stand here talking to you," came the hesitant reply. Simon smiled.

"Where have you come from?" asked Simon.

"There," said the visitor, pointing along the line. Simon suspected he'd found a fellow joker and wanted to learn more about him.

"What is your name?" asked Simon.

"No, my name is not What, it is Jiptu."

"Where do you live?"

"Far away. Very far away," said Jiptu, briefly glancing upwards without realising he was doing it. Simon stared at him. He looked human, yet Jiptu looked different somehow. That fascinated him.

"Would you like some blackberries?" asked Simon, after a pause.

"What is blackbellies?"

"These are blackberries. You can eat them. They grow here." Simon picked some more blackberries and ate them. Jiptu did the same.

"Is good!" he said. To Simon, Jiptu clearly wasn't local. He looked out of place and slightly nervous, although he seemed harmless enough.

"Are you from this planet or a different planet?" asked Simon, cautiously. Jiptu looked worried.

"Different," he said. That puzzled Simon. We'd met a lot of alien races, but none that looked this human.

"You don't need to worry, Jiptu. I work for a company that can travel to other planets. We have met many other races. Would you like to come back with me and meet the rest of us?"

"I like that," said Jiptu. They both climbed aboard Ivor and went back to Spacemakers.

When they arrived, Muttley came rushing out. He jumped up at Jiptu and tried to lick his face. Simon expected Jiptu to run away, but he didn't. Jiptu was clearly used to dogs. He made a great fuss of Muttley. Simon thought that odd, as he didn't know of any other planets with dogs.

Everyone gathered around. Simon introduced Jiptu, who then told us about his planet and how he had arrived on Earth. We were all fascinated by the idea of another Earth, occupied by real humans. We wanted to learn more. We temporarily incorporated him into our staff. He could make friends, and his knowledge could be invaluable to us.

Kebea

Jiptu spent a lot of time with us. We allowed him to use one of the disused factory offices as a temporary home. He looked quite young, probably in his late twenties. It surprised him to see so many variations in human appearance on Earth. Most people on his planet looked like he did.

He was intelligent, outgoing and keen to learn. His English improved dramatically during his time with us. He enjoyed being with us. He could laugh openly without fear of criticism. We reminded him that almost nobody had ever suffered from illness or injury due to laughing. He watched just about every comedy film we had. We occasionally reminded him that what he saw in our films wasn't typical in the real world.

Jiptu seemed quite at home with us. He liked our food, as well as some of our older popular music. We granted him the freedom of the kitchen. I once caught him raiding the fridge in the middle of the night.

"Al, me chew at midnight," he said. I think he'd heard an old song from the 1970s and not quite understood it. (He sometimes called me Al. I resisted the temptation to call him Betty, as he wouldn't have known what I was talking about.)

Jiptu came from a planet called Kebea. The aliens who had taken the humans there had called it something else. The humans had found the name too difficult to pronounce, so they had renamed it.

The oldest human relics found on Kebea were only a few thousand years old. That caused many to suspect that they had not evolved on that planet. Many small glass objects had been discovered at archaeological digs, usually in gold containers. Gold was common on Kebea. It had little value there. (I wished we'd known that earlier.) The artefacts were on display in their museums.

Simon introduced Jiptu to Amy. She wanted to examine him and see if she could help him with any problems.

He climbed onto the examination couch. He wasn't worried, as he'd seen similar things on his own planet. Amy did her examinations. She displayed images of Jiptu's innards on a large screen. He looked completely human. She couldn't find anything even slightly wrong with him. He seemed exceptionally healthy, even for his age.

He thanked her and climbed off the couch. Just then, someone else walked in. It was unusual for Amy to have two visitors in one day. The patient complained about several unexplained aches and pains.

Amy did her usual checks. She failed to find his problem. Jiptu recognised the symptoms and advised Amy on what he believed to be the correct course of action.

Amy didn't have any better ideas. Jiptu's suggestions seemed harmless, so she carried them out. To her amazement, the patient improved within minutes. She suggested that it could be mutually beneficial if their two planets were to compare medical knowledge.

We didn't have much to do at the time, so after talking with Jiptu, we all agreed that we should go to his planet and introduce ourselves to a few people there. Jiptu warned us about using humour. Just as well, as using it was one of our usual tactics in a first-contact situation. Jiptu could translate for us.

Jiptu moved his small spacecraft to our car park, then we took off. We followed the outside of the small space tunnel that Jiptu had used to travel to Earth, as we were much too big to get into it. It took us quite a while. Kebea was further away than we expected. We didn't want to lose sight of the tunnel by going too fast. Nobody we knew had ever been to that part of space before. There were no man-made space drains anywhere near there.

We arrived at Kebea and made our factory invisible. Following Jiptu's guidance, we landed close to the outskirts of a small town near Jiptu's home. We kept our factory invisible. With hindsight, we needn't have bothered. Our factory looked typical of most factories in the area, although the locals might have been surprised to see a new one suddenly appear.

Jiptu showed a small group of us to his home. It looked much like a typical Earth dwelling, with some slight differences. He showed us around. Then he took us to his workshop. He showed us his recordings of our TV transmissions.

The picture quality of the recordings was poor, mainly due to distortions caused by the small space tunnel, but the sound came through fine. They were definitely ours, from several decades earlier. Jiptu had told us a lot about those transmissions before we left Earth. I gave him a small television and a digital recorder so he could receive and record the signals properly, in colour. I also provided him with technical details of the PAL broadcasting standard, plus a few others.

Over the following days, Jiptu introduced us to some of his closest and most trusted friends. We expected them to be alarmed, but they weren't. They had long thought there must be humans elsewhere in the galaxy.

Most of our staff wanted to leave the factory and explore. Tannoy announcements were made, advising people to avoid the locals as much as possible, but that didn't stop some.

We spent the next few weeks trying to learn the local language. It was easier than we expected. We tried it out, buying goods from local shops. People thought we looked strange, but most were more curious than anything else.

Gradually, we became more familiar with their society. We found it very similar to ours. We had to be careful not to laugh or make jokes.

Eventually, we decided to return home. Jiptu returned to Earth with us. He wanted to learn more, and he still had much more to tell us about Kebea.

Connections

Jiptu spent much time exploring the Bovercraft and our factory. He wanted to talk to everyone and learn as much as possible. He seemed to soak up information like a sponge. We occasionally used Ivor to take him to the local town, to let him get used to the people there. Sometimes we'd let him drive Ivor back.

He'd gone to the laboratory. He watched as the boffins studied the data on one of the alien glass cylinders. Jiptu stared at it. He seemed unusually interested in it.

"I know this," he said.

"Eh?"

"I have seen these things before. Some like this on Kebea."

"We found this on a different planet," said one of the boffins.

"I understand. I have seen more like this on Kebea," said Jiptu.

"Where?"

"They in our museums. We think they left by aliens. We think they important. Not know what they are for. We not make them ourselves. Found with alien things."

The word soon got out. Almost everyone wanted to return to Kebea, as it had been several weeks since our previous visit. We held a meeting with our entire staff to discuss the matter. We agreed that we should introduce ourselves to the Kebeans properly.

We headed for Kebea. We went more directly this time. A team of people, including myself, Barry, Charlie, Joyce, Simon and Sue received a crash course in Jiptu's language. Lorna's language skills were good, so we included her, too. She picked up the language quickly.

We landed on Kebea at a carefully chosen location. We didn't try to hide ourselves this time. Jiptu and his friends contacted the local media and several major television stations. Also invited were representatives from several minority groups. They included a group of what translated into 'humourists'. They believed humour to be harmless and should be encouraged.

We and our new friends got everything arranged. The television camera crews set up their equipment within our factory grounds to broadcast live to much of Kebea. One TV crew wanted material for a possible documentary. Simon showed them around our factory.

Large TV displays were put up nearby that everyone could see. Barry's team built a raised stage for us to speak from, with microphones and large loudspeakers. We felt like we were preparing for a pop concert.

When the event started, Jiptu stood on the stage and introduced himself. Then he explained what he had found, how he had travelled to Earth and what he had learnt since. He explained that the entire factory they were standing in and broadcasting from had travelled from Earth. He assured everyone that the people of Earth were just as human as anyone on Kebea. Then he handed the microphone over to me.

I had prepared for this. I had memorised my speech, in their language. I thought I was up to it, but I wasn't. I could talk in front of a few dozen people without problems, but this was something else. I suddenly realised there could be millions of people watching.

I could feel my legs turning to jelly. I did the best I could. Most people could see I was nervous and just as human as they were.

Just then, a young Kebean woman spoke up. She had already caught my eye. She was the leader of the local group of humourists. She asked me about humour on my planet. Was it allowed?

That was just what I needed. I assured everyone it was most definitely allowed on Earth. Humour had clear medical benefits and nobody's head had ever fallen off from laughing. She smiled.

We started showing our video footage. It included carefully selected visual comedy sections from our film and TV archives. People just stared at first, but I could see from the stage that some were grinning. Some had their hands over their mouths. Giggles broke out. We just laughed normally.

The young woman who had spoken to me laughed too, sometimes quite loudly. She kept trying to stop herself, but she couldn't. That just added to the humour. It wasn't long before everyone gave in to it.

When the main clips had finished, Jiptu asked how people felt. Everyone felt fine. People wanted more. The conclusions were obvious. We didn't have to say any more about humour. They'd got the message.

We showed them a lot more of our footage. We made it clear that although we weren't perfect, we were just as human as they were. There shouldn't be any problems with alien infections either way.

After the event, some broadcasters asked if they could have copies of some of our material. We'd expected that. We handed them information packs we'd prepared in advance, including two complete films that Sue had converted to their broadcast standard. Jiptu had added subtitles in their language to one of the films.

The young humourist woman proved to be a real character. She had a very good sense of humour. She told me her name (I had asked). She said it was Shuwiphattymus, or something like that. I thought she might be winding me up. I said I'd call her Shuwi. She gave me a funny look but went along with it.

In the following weeks, we got to know the Kebeans well. We thought it incredible that our two civilisations had such similar levels of technology when we had been separate for thousands of years.

Some speculated that the small space tunnel between our planets had something to do with it. For the tunnel to exist at all couldn't be a coincidence. Some suggested it could be the remnant of a much larger tunnel, created thousands of years ago by the aliens.

Jiptu wanted to show me the data cylinders in a local museum. We went to take a look. They were exactly like ours. I asked the museum curator if we could borrow one. He recognised me from the television broadcast but was still reluctant. He had to get permission from his superiors. We lent them one of ours, which we had already read, to replace the one we were borrowing.

We invited the curator to come to our factory and see what data the cylinder contained for himself. We gathered in the laboratory, where our cylinder-reading machine had been set up, and started the machine.

The cylinder contained information about the construction of the pyramids on Earth and the relocation of some Egyptian people to Kebea.

The information astounded the curator. We told him about the uninhabited planet where we had found our data cylinders. We suspected the aliens from there might be the same ones that had moved his ancestors to Kebea thousands of years ago. We felt that he and his people had a right to know. We also warned the Kebeans about the space mines and told them how to deal with them. That made Shuwi laugh.

Several weeks later, we returned to Earth. Jiptu stayed behind. Lorna stayed too, to learn their language and customs better. Shuwi came back with us to Earth. I got along well with her. She would sometimes play practical jokes on me. I think she was trying to get my attention, which she had anyway.

Shuwi had no known relatives on Kebea. She had been fascinated by the video footage she had seen of Earth. She studied the English language and soon became fluent in it.

Shuwi was very technically minded. She had devised several silly inventions on her home planet. Some had to be abandoned, as they made people laugh. That wasn't allowed. Being on Earth gave her a lot more freedom to invent silly things.

She invented programmable wigs, mainly for women. They could be configured to just about any style, colour or length by pressing buttons on a remote control. Very handy, unless one's kids got hold of the remote. They sold well.

She also created wigs that could change colour depending on the wearer's mood. Red meant angry, blue meant cold, green meant happy, yellow meant afraid and pink meant... um... never mind. I never liked blancmange anyway, ever since that episode when I was a kid. It involved roast potatoes and the neighbour's kid's Spacehopper. (Don't ask.)

It wasn't long before news of Kebea's existence hit the headlines on Earth. A local MP tried to take the credit for finding the planet but soon got caught out. He had to step down, triggering a by-election.

Earth needed a Kebean ambassador. Shuwi volunteered and got the job. Her original name didn't seem to suit her on Earth, so she decided to change it to something less unusual. She seemed fascinated by our old cartoons, so she chose a name from one of them.

She chose the name Lisa.

Ex-Dougals

We were becoming a sort of space ferry, regularly transporting goods and people between Earth and Kebea. There wasn't a proper space drain anywhere near that route. Other spacecraft did the run sometimes, but we, with our recently upgraded drive system, could get there and back much faster.

Kebean technology roughly matched ours. We were more advanced in some areas. Their medical knowledge far exceeded ours, as did their knowledge of ancient artefacts.

We transported many scientists, architects, historians, archaeologists and other such people between the two planets. We occasionally transported rich tourists too, who paid us well. Any loonies, extremists or other undesirable people were usually detected during the journey and not allowed to leave the factory on arrival.

Ambassador Lisa made many trips between Earth and Kebea as part of her duties as ambassador. She also wanted to see the sights on Earth, particularly Egypt and the Great Pyramids. I offered to take her there myself. I didn't seriously expect her to accept, but she did. She brought two of her friends with her. I wasn't expecting that. It made sense, though, as they were experts in ancient languages.

They were fascinated by the Egyptian hieroglyphics. Lisa's two friends could read most of it, as they had studied similar markings found on Kebea. They translated sections that our archaeologists had been struggling with.

We soon became tired of the almost constant trips between Earth and Kebea. We announced that we were taking a break from it. The number of trips required had decreased, and other spacecraft were capable of doing the work. There were plans to set up a new space drain between Earth and Kebea.

We thought we could sit back and relax, but our hopes for a bit of peace and quiet were soon dashed. One of our factory shop floor staff approached Simon about a matter that greatly concerned her. She'd kept it to herself as we'd been busy, but she felt that now would be a good time to speak up.

Her son had become involved with a group of other young people who were determined to travel through every space drain known to exist. They mostly wanted to travel through the rarely used drains. That wasn't normally a problem. Unfortunately, some of the young people had disappeared. She hadn't heard from her son for an unusually long time.

Simon asked her which drain had been next on her son's list when he last contacted her. It turned out to be the one that had taken us to the Dougaloid planet. On our last trip there, we had completed the work on that drain. We had moved it further from the planet, hoping to prevent future travellers from getting pulled there accidentally. The drain had been declared open for use.

Simon spoke to me about it. Ambassador Lisa was with me. She urged us to investigate. Lisa cared about people. She had a way of charming people into doing what she wanted.

We told Captain Smythe and then set off down the aforementioned drain. Barry suspected that small, low-powered spacecraft might still be vulnerable to the Dougaloid planet's gravity.

As we slowly travelled down the drain, we kept our sensors active, looking for anything unusual. We eventually detected a gravitational pull. We headed towards it. We pushed our way through the drain wall and found the planet we were looking for nearby.

We landed on the planet, close to our previous landing site. Many of us took the opportunity to explore the planet for a while. Barry, Lisa and I walked to where we had been before. What we found wasn't what we were expecting.

Not far away, we found the upturned housings of three Dougaloids. They were little more than hollow four-wheeled housings, with enough space inside for one person. There were interior controls for making the outside bits move. That explained the tracks on the ground we had seen on our previous visit.

Lisa had never been to any planets other than Kebea and Earth. All this fascinated her. She seemed puzzled by my reaction to seeing the empty Dougaloid shells.

I owned up. I felt quite embarrassed and told her about them. When I told her about The Magic Roundabout and showed her a picture of Dougal on my phone, she laughed almost uncontrollably. I promised I'd show her some episodes when we got back. I knew she'd like them.

As we examined the scene further, we found trails of human footprints. Something was afoot (several feet). We followed the trails.

After about half a mile, we discovered a spacecraft. I recognised it from the photo we'd been shown on our first visit. We went in, expecting to find nobody, but we were wrong.

The three occupants were in remarkably good health for dead people. They'd been having a laugh at our expense the last time they saw us. No wonder they could understand what we were saying. I asked about the Dougals. They'd been made just for fun. They thought it would be funny to have a planet inhabited by Dougals.

They still didn't know what the crystals scattered around the area were made of. They'd only found them in the local area, not further afield. They clearly weren't scientifically or technically minded. We thought it best to say no more about the matter.

A few other young people appeared. When we looked around, we saw several other small spacecraft on the ground, not far away. They had created a small community and seemed quite happy where they were.

The mother of one of them had followed us. An emotional reunion followed. We didn't think we should hang about for too long, so we offered to return anyone who wanted to come with us to Earth. They all accepted our offer. They liked the planet they were on, but nobody wanted to be stuck there permanently. We moved all the small spacecraft into our car park. Most had been hired and had to be returned.

Lisa noticed the crystals lying around. She liked the look of them. She asked me to tell her more about them. I went a bit quiet. I suggested that if she found any nice ones, she should pick them up but keep them hidden. I said I'd tell her about them when we returned to Earth. She looked puzzled, but she trusted me. She picked up some of the nicer crystals and hid them in her pockets.

We left the planet and moved the drain still further from the planet. Hopefully, nobody else would get pulled off course in the future. We didn't tell our passengers about that, though. Besides, Barry and I didn't want anyone else to discover the source of our wealth.

We returned to Earth.

Seas end

Ambassador Lisa and Jiptu got along well. That sometimes made me a little uncomfortable. I told myself to mind my own business and just got on with my work. They often went on walks together. They talked a lot, sometimes taking Muttley with them. I sometimes felt they were planning something and were intentionally avoiding me. Muttley wasn't complaining, though. He got more walks than usual.

They both returned to Kebea. They said there were important matters they had to attend to. Neither would say what. They just made up some quite weak excuses when I asked.

While they were away, Sue and the boffins revealed more of what they'd found out about the Plonkers, who'd made the glass data cylinders and the space mines.

They'd found some images of them in the cylinder data. They looked remarkably like the two races we'd met earlier, the Bees and the Seas (as we called them). It had to be more than a coincidence. The cylinders revealed why the race had died out.

They'd had major disagreements with the Seas. The Seas didn't like the Plonkers interfering with the people of Earth.

They were determined to stop them. They created a deadly virus, which would only be activated if it came into contact with humans. Humans would be immune to it. They warned the Plonkers that they would release it on Earth if they didn't stop interfering with the humans.

The Plonkers ignored them and carried on. The Seas shipped the virus to an undisclosed location on Earth. They told the Plonkers about it, warning them that if the work on those silly pyramids didn't stop, the virus would be released.

The Plonkers were having enough trouble with the human protesters as it was. They started moving troublesome people from Egypt to the planet that would later become known as Kebea.

In the rush to move people, the virus, in its unmarked container, was accidentally released. The Plonkers caught the disease and infected the population of their own planet. It eventually wiped out the entire population of Planet Dee. By the time they developed a vaccine, it was too late. Space mines were constructed and deployed around the planet to keep people away.

Those events happened thousands of years ago. Some people amongst similar races assumed the virus was gone, so there was talk of re-inhabiting the planet. We thought it was a bad idea. We talked to the Bees and Seas about it, hoping common sense would prevail.

The Bees wanted nothing to do with the planet. They weren't the ones who had caused the problem.

The Seas had other ideas. Their politicians were an arrogant lot. They didn't like being told what to do, and ordered that the mines be deactivated. They planned to colonise the place, as it suited their life form well.

The Seas assumed the virus to be long gone. With hindsight, they should've tested for it, but they didn't bother. Even after all that time, a few traces remained. The Seas had been in contact with us, so they became infected. They unwittingly took the virus to their home planet.

When they heard about it, most people fled the planet. They still died, as they were already infected. Some remained, mainly those who thought it was a hoax. They died too. It sounds harsh to say, but in a way, it served them right. After all, their race had created the virus in the first place.

When we searched the Plonker records further, we found details of how to eliminate and vaccinate against the virus. We passed the information on to the Bees. They hadn't been allowing anyone near their home planet since the Seas had first talked about re-inhabiting planet Dee. They used the information to create an effective vaccine to protect themselves.

Planet Dee was declared quarantined. We set up ground-based transmitters there to warn people, in every known language, to stay away. We left the planet and got well clear. Then, following instructions the Bees had given us, we reactivated the mines.

The Bees became very wary of us after that, even with the vaccine. We thought it best to keep away unless they asked for our help.

Meanwhile, on Kebea, Lisa and Jiptu had attended several events. Some were quite large. They told people about Earth, our technology and customs. Lorna had become fluent in the Kebean language, so she became Earth's ambassador to Kebea.

Lisa returned home, where she hid the crystals she had collected on the Dougaloid planet. She could see I wasn't comfortable talking about them, so she kept quiet about the matter.

The Kebeans seemed to really like us. Many were keen to show us some of their culture. They organised a traditional celebration, which we understood to be in our honour. We all felt very important. They invited everyone in our factory to attend. Lisa and Jiptu had been nagging me for weeks to learn more about their culture and customs. Maybe this was what they had in mind.

Upgrades

As we still had a few weeks to go before the big celebration, we got on with other things. Most of us felt daft flying around in a factory. Time to do something about it, I thought.

We held another general meeting of the entire staff, in the factory car park. Everyone agreed we should stop taking the entire factory with us if we didn't need to. Most of our trips could be done factoryless. People disliked working in the factory buildings while we were in space.

We decided to carry out a major overhaul of the Bovercraft. Equipment that had remained unused since our first flight was removed. Important equipment was given a major service and sometimes upgraded.

We reconfigured our drive and power systems. We no longer had any MPBs, so the power unit that had used them was removed. Barry's team installed a conventional power unit as a backup for our main one. Captain Smythe suggested that we remove the sausage drive. Nobody wanted to, so we kept it. It amused us.

Joyce had been nagging us for ages to improve our safety systems, so we got on with that. We reinforced the Bovercraft's outer skin considerably and tidied it up.

Barry's team gave the bridge a major overhaul. Many changes and additions had been made since our first flight, often done in a hurry. We took the opportunity to tidy things up and make the craft easier to operate.

Considerable improvements were made to the Bovercraft's appearance. At last, it looked like a proper spaceship. We fitted some big things on the back of the Bovercraft that looked like giant rocket motors. They looked powerful and lit up brightly when powered. They didn't do anything useful. They were just there for show.

We redesigned our procedures and systems for takeoff and landing. Several critical functions would happen automatically, but they could be done manually if required. Our protective bubble would automatically adapt to suit our situation. It would shrink to enclose only the Bovercraft if it flew on its own, and revert to full size if we took the factory with us. The bubble would only operate when we were at least two hundred feet off the ground, unless we took the factory with us.

Work on the upgrades didn't involve everyone. Some took the opportunity to take long holidays and visit relatives. Penny would frequently take Muttley for walks in the nearby woods, but she soon found she didn't need to bother. Muttley was allowed to run around as he wanted to, often going to the woods to play with the local farm cat. We were well away from public roads.

Muttley had a small tracking device fitted to his collar so that Penny could monitor his location. I think it had been designed for birds, as it included an altimeter. Simon had configured the device to warn Penny if Muttley started flying again.

That reminds me. We'd forgotten about the alien plants we'd planted near the edge of the woods. When we'd picked the fruit, we'd found it tasteless. Then we forgot about it, as we had other things to do.

Muttley hadn't forgotten. I think he'd always hoped to find more. He didn't understand about travelling to other planets. The trees in our forests looked a little like the ones that the original fruit had come from, so Muttley often tried to find more. He failed, of course, but he kept trying.

He eventually found the alien plants that we'd planted. We'd forgotten about them. The fruit was much riper than before and had started to smell cheesy.

Some had fallen to the ground. Muttley helped himself. It wasn't long before Penny's dog-tracking alarm went off, telling her that Muttley was airborne. She found Simon and asked if it could be a mistake. It wasn't. They both set out in search of Muttley.

They found him in a tree with the local cat. Then they heard a 'Moooo!'. It came from high up, almost directly above Penny. She ran back a few feet. Too late. A pile of cow poo hit the ground hard, about six feet in front of her. She'd avoided a direct hit, but she still got covered in poo splatter. She wasn't pleased.

Penny walked back to the factory to get cleaned up. When she arrived there, I noticed her looking quite annoyed. She smelled bad, too. She told me what had happened. I said I'd deal with it and went to join Simon in the woods.

Muttley hadn't eaten much of the fruit, so he soon floated back down. He must've chased the cat up the tree. The problem was the cow. The fruit trees were near the forest edge, next to the local farmer's field. The cow could easily reach the fallen fruit. It must've kept munching until it floated away. The cow seemed quite intoxicated, high in more ways than one.

We called the farmer. I wanted to try to bring the cow down before he arrived. Simon thought it would be funnier not to. He wanted to watch the farmer's face. Meanwhile, I fetched a length of rope from the factory.

About half an hour later, the farmer turned up on an electric quad bike. Simon was right. The look on his face was priceless. Simon explained about the flying fruit.

I climbed a tree as high as I dared and threw the rope over the cow. We pulled it back down. The farmer tied the rope around the cow, with the other end tied to the tow hitch of his quad bike.

Then he slowly drove off, towing the floating cow, like a child with a helium-filled balloon. He passed two local kids, who mistook it for a real balloon. They said they wanted one. They fled when it released another poo bomb. The farmer couldn't stop laughing all the way home.

After that, we cut down all the flying fruit trees in the forest. They weren't native to Earth anyway. We destroyed the fruit but kept the seeds.

The upgrade work on the Bovercraft was almost complete. Some people referred to it as 'The Ship', so Simon painted a realistic-looking anchor on the side.

We had to give it a proper name, so we called it Spacemaker One and carefully painted the lettering on it. We also fitted navigation lights for use while in Earth's atmosphere.

We conducted several test flights, carried out a few more alterations and adjustments, and then announced that we were ready to resume normal operations. Spacemaker One would do most of the space flights on its own. The factory would remain on Earth unless needed.

Some of us had ideas about building a second spaceship, which we would call Spacemaker Two. It would be smaller than our existing spaceship and much faster. We never got around to building it.

I kept telling myself that I should learn more about Kebea and their traditions, but with all that was going on, I kept forgetting.

DANCES WITH WOOLS

Only a few days remained before the big celebration on Kebea. Lisa and Jiptu had been nagging me for weeks to learn more about Kebean customs and traditions. I felt uncomfortable that I still hadn't.

There was bound to be something in the planned celebration that would go better if I knew what to do. I started urgently looking for information, but I didn't know where to start.

I don't think any of us knew what the event would be about. Most believed it to be a celebration of the reuniting of our two civilisations. Others thought it was just an excuse to have a big party and get drunk.

I didn't have much luck finding out about Kebean customs. We had plenty of information in the Kebean language, but I couldn't use it. I could speak a little Kebean, but I couldn't read or write it. I started asking around to see what I could learn from other people. Nobody knew any more than I did about Kebean customs.

Then I spoke to Barry. He'd seen Sue working on something that might help. I paid her a visit. As luck would have it, she'd been working on a translation device. It could read data in the Kebean language from their storage media and display the results in English. Jiptu had helped her with it before he and Lisa returned to Kebea. She'd been testing it using a Kebean encyclopaedia.

I told her my problem. She let me have a go with the device. She said it was about time someone other than herself tried it. She left me to it while she got on with other work.

I found the device easy to use. Sue always designed things properly. Anything she made was simple to use. She felt it was important that people should be able to use the things she designed easily.

What I found fascinated me. I found the Kebean technology particularly interesting. They had a similar level of technology to ours but had gone about things differently. They had taken far longer to reach their current stage of technological development than we had but had started much earlier. They were driving electric cars while we were still in the dark ages. They'd not had the wars that had caused so much trouble on Earth, so had no need for rapid technological development.

Fossil fuels were available on Kebea but were rarely used. They had realised early on that using fossil fuels extensively would harm their planet. Using them for transportation on Kebea was forbidden.

Instead, they'd tried to use renewable energy sources as much as possible, from an early stage. They had several advanced windmill designs. Their solar panels were many times more efficient than ours, gathering energy from light, heat and radio frequencies simultaneously. Many of their public buildings were circular or hexagonal, with roofs that could rotate.

That allowed them to have their solar panels always facing their sun. Solar lighting vents were common, that directed light from the roof directly into the rooms below.

I became so fascinated by their technology that I forgot to research their customs and traditions. By the time I remembered, it was too late. Spacemaker One was heading for Kebea.

Some people were unsure what we were supposed to wear. Captain Smythe said we should use our common sense.

Before we left, the ladies had taken Ivor to the nearby town. They'd been on a shopping spree to buy new clothes. After they returned, Simon just happened to be walking past a group of chatting women. Joyce said something about a fancy new dress. Simon misheard her, thinking she'd said 'Fancy Dress'.

He went to see Barry. They agreed to go as Batman and Robin. Captain Smythe disapproved, but he couldn't do anything about it.

Someone else wanted to go as Tarzan. Smythe put his foot down and refused to allow it. The costume was totally inappropriate for her. Her high-pitched voice wouldn't have worked either. Also, Tarzan didn't have an artificial leg, ginger hair or ponytails. At least, I don't think he did. She was winding him up, of course.

The day of the celebration arrived. We arrived at Kebea and waited in orbit until they were ready for us. When we came down, we were directed to a landing site just outside the village where the event was due to take place.

After we landed, I asked if I could look around the celebration site before the event started. I hoped to pick up a few clues. Nobody objected, so I found the building and walked in.

It looked unusual by Earth standards. It was huge, circular and constructed from a variety of materials. It looked like it had existed for centuries and had been updated occasionally.

Inside, there was just one room. The lighting looked old, yet used energy-efficient technology. There were intricate designs on the ceiling. I saw a circle of tables and chairs positioned around the walls. The chairs were behind the tables, facing into the room, allowing everyone to see each other.

I noticed a hole in the centre of the floor, about three inches in diameter. I could see no obvious reason for it. The wooden flooring looked worn in a large circular area several yards wide, centred on the hole.

On the walls were several dozen of what appeared to be roughly knitted round woollen mats. Each was about three feet in diameter, hanging there like pictures. Under each was a pair of names, written in the Kebean language.

As I watched, two people brought in a circular wooden table. They positioned it directly over the hole in the centre of the floor. It had a ring of holes around the edge and a bigger one in the centre.

Then they brought in a wooden post, lowered it through the centre of the table and located it into the hole in the floor. The top end of the post looked about a foot higher than the table and narrower at the top. It had many small hooks sticking out from it near the top.

I noticed a large wooden box next to the wall. It looked ancient, with intricate carvings. The lid had been left open, so I looked inside. It contained reels of wool. Each reel had a round wooden handle at each end.

I moved aside quickly, as the two people needed access to the box. They removed the reels and located each one into the table edge by dropping a handle into one of the holes. The loose wool ends were tied to hooks at the top of the central wooden pole.

Several people in the room looked at me strangely, but nobody said anything. I felt awkward. I seemed to be getting in the way, so I apologised and left. I started walking back to our factory.

I'd also been getting odd looks from some other local people. Some stared, then looked away as I glanced towards them. Others smiled politely and then walked away from me. They seemed to know something I didn't. I wondered if some kind of elaborate wind-up was about to take place at my expense. I told myself to stop being stupid, as I continued walking back to the factory.

About two hours later, we all arrived at the event. Some were in fancy dress, but most weren't. Batman and Robin looked embarrassed, but I think it cheered everyone up. Goodness knows what the locals thought. Joyce felt sorry for them, so she dressed up as Catwoman and joined them. Someone turned up in a red suit, a red tie, a red shirt and red shoes. He was from India. He thought it was funny, but I don't think anyone else did.

The Kebeans showed us in and directed us to our seats. Jiptu sat on one side of me, Lisa on the other. I felt uneasy. Something was happening, which involved me. I felt sure of it. Lisa was known for her practical jokes. They had always been harmless, yet this worried me.

We were given a nice meal. The Kebeans had gone to the trouble of preparing foods that we would recognise, as well as some of their own traditional delicacies. Much wine was consumed. It was powerful stuff. We were advised to be careful with it.

After the meal, there was traditional Kebean dancing and music. I hadn't seen or heard anything quite like it before.

Then a bell rang. The main event was about to begin, we were told. Several people got up and walked to the centre of the room. Each picked up one of the two-handled reels of wool from the table edge. Lisa and Jiptu were among them. They pulled me into the group and handed me a reel.

I just stared at it. My heart was beating somewhat faster than usual. I wished I'd taken Lisa and Jiptu's advice, as I had no idea what was happening. My wool looked more elaborate than the rest. I looked at Lisa's. It looked elaborate too, albeit in a different colour.

I should've twigged what was happening by then, but I didn't. Maybe I'd had too much wine.

Then the music started. Lisa told me not to worry, and to do what everybody else did. Easier said than done. People were moving about all over the place in a big circle, moving up, down, over and under the woollen strands. It appeared to be some kind of knitting dance. A mat began to form in the centre. It reminded me of an old English Maypole dance.

I kept falling over. I thought I'd get knitted to the floor. Everybody just smiled at me, helping me up when they could. I started to get the hang of it after a while. I found it rather fun.

Then the bell rang again, and the music stopped. Lisa stood right next to me. Everyone else put their wool on the floor and returned to their seats. I was about to do the same, but Lisa stopped me.

"Not you," she said.

"Uh...? What's going on?"

"You didn't read up on our customs, did you?" said Lisa, with a grin. She knew I wouldn't have.

"Here," said Lisa, handing me her wool. She looked me straight in the eyes, grinning. I took it. People started clapping. That scared me.

"Now give me yours," she said.

"Why?"

"I'm asking you to marry me, you fool! If you hand me your wool, then you accept my proposal." I gazed at her for what seemed like ages, and then slowly handed her the wool.

Everyone clapped and cheered. We were led back to our seats. I couldn't believe it. I was apparently married to Lisa. I had always liked her, but I had thought her beyond my reach. She told me she and Jiptu had been planning this for some time. That was why she had spent so much time with him in the weeks leading up to the event.

Two people removed the woollen mat, created during the knitting dance, from the pole. They tidied up the ends and then hung the mat on the wall. Our names were put up just below the mat, like the others. It was a sort of record of the marriage dance. I could clearly see the bits where I'd fallen over.

The rest of the evening was a bit of a blur. Suffice it to say, I was happy. Very happy. I think I had too much wine.

Lisa and I spent the next few weeks just enjoying ourselves. We also had a formal ceremony on Earth. I didn't want to go back to work at Spacemakers. We were very well off, so we agreed that I would leave the place. I formally handed over control to Barry so that Lisa and I could settle down properly.

After our wedding, Lisa and I lived on Kebea for about two years. Our son, John, was born there. I rented my house out during that time to keep the place lived in. A substantial basement existed under the house, so before we moved to Kebea, I hid anything of value in there. I locked and concealed the trapdoor.

When we eventually returned to Earth to live in my house, I uncovered the basement trapdoor. I found everything still in there, undisturbed. After that, I used the basement as a 'man cave' workshop.

We lived happily there for about twenty years. John grew up there.

Thursday

While John was growing up, Lisa, John and I would take annual holidays. We often had unusual holidays, exploring foreign countries. One year, we did something slightly different.

Lisa hadn't been with us when we had our first factory holiday, on an island hundreds of years in the past. I told her all about it and about Phil. She seemed upset that we had left him there. I told her he'd passed a survival course in Australia, so he would have been fine.

She suggested we take a holiday on that island and see if we could find any evidence of Phil. I told her his body had already been found, and that he had lived to a great age. Nevertheless, she still wanted to go.

We expected the island to be well populated, but it wasn't. There were a few people there, mostly doing scientific research, but hardly anyone else. We brought a large tent and enough provisions to last us for a couple of weeks. We both had mobile phones, so we could call for help if necessary.

John, being an energetic teenager, insisted on putting up our tent. I showed him where the factory and I had been previously and told him to put it up there. I don't think he believed my story about Phil. He said it was a bit far-fetched, even for me.

We started exploring. I wanted to prove to John that I wasn't making it all up. I looked around for evidence that we had been there before. I found none at first but then noticed three slight depressions in the ground, equally spaced. I wouldn't have spotted them if I hadn't been looking for them.

I told John and Lisa that Phil often used to stick smiley faces on things he had worked on. If we found one, it would be a clue that he'd been there.

For two days, we found nothing. The only unusual thing we noticed was a small hill, not far away. It looked out of place. You don't normally expect to find something like that on a small desert island.

John was getting bored and wandered off. Then Lisa called me over to something. It looked like a gravestone that had fallen flat. We brushed off the weeds and dirt. We found an inscription on it, carefully carved in English. It read,

'Here lies Phil. 2071-1799'.

We noticed a precisely carved smiley symbol under it. The ground nearby had been dug up, presumably when Phil's body had been found. The presence of the gravestone hadn't been mentioned in any articles about Phil's discovery.

As we searched for more evidence, I heard a shout from John. We looked around but couldn't find him. Then we discovered a hole in the ground. John had fallen into it. He seemed unharmed, apart from a few scratches. He shouted up at us.

John had fallen into a large underground space. There had been a wooden covering over it, which had rotted away over the centuries. Lisa and I found a concealed entrance and carefully made our way down there to join him.

I had a small torch on my keyring, so I used it to look around. The space didn't look natural. It looked man-made. We found other rooms adjoining the main space. It looked like somebody had built an underground dwelling area. It seemed hard to believe that Phil could have done all that himself.

In one of the rooms, we found equipment that I recognised. It had disappeared when the modified android had gone missing from the factory. I couldn't see much in the darkness, as my small torch had little power left.

From force of habit, I reached for a light switch near the doorway. To my surprise, I found one. I switched it on.

Dim lighting came on, flickering occasionally. As we looked around, we found the missing android. We also found Eric, in a corner of the main room. I walked up to the android to see if there was any life in it.

"Hello... anybody there?" I asked, tapping the android on the head, not really expecting a response. Its eyes opened slightly.

"Power... panels... clear..." it said quietly.

"What?"

"Please... clear the panels," it said. It had been plugged into a socket on the wall, presumably to charge itself up. Then I realised what it meant.

I followed the power cables outside. They led into the undergrowth. I found several large solar panels, mostly covered by weeds, leaves and other debris. I cleared them as much as possible. Two were broken, so I bypassed them. Then I returned to the underground cavern.

John and Lisa had been talking to the android, which had recovered slightly. The lighting looked a little brighter. The android had been named Thursday, by Phil. Phil could never remember which day of the week it was, so he'd called every day Thursday. Needless to say, the android had appeared on a Thursday.

Lisa was curious about the Bobbert, which we'd called Eric. There wasn't much left of it. Most of the casing metalwork had corroded away. Thursday's condition looked improved, but it couldn't move much.

"Thank you. I feel a little better now," said Thursday.

"How long did you look after Phil for?" I asked.

"Until he died. How long ago, I forget. My memory is slow these days. Eric and I buried him not far from here."

"What did you do after that?" asked John.

"There wasn't much we could do. I felt I had served my purpose well and needed someone to switch me off."

"Did you find anyone?" asked Lisa, looking concerned.

"No. I searched the entire island and found nobody. Even if I had, they wouldn't have known what to do. I probably wouldn't have been able to tell them anyway, as they wouldn't have understood modern English."

"How did you get here?" I asked.

"I found several prototypes of what you called 'time bombs'. I made modifications and adjustments, then used them to get Eric, myself and many other things here. I apologise for the thefts, but I felt that Phil's well-being outweighed other considerations."

We talked for quite a while. We learnt a lot about Phil, what he had been like and the daft things he did. Thursday seemed to be enjoying talking to us, after being alone for so long. I spoke briefly to Lisa about Thursday, then I faced the android.

"We could take you back with us and get you fixed up. Would you like that?" I asked.

Thursday paused, thinking.

"All things considered, I think it best if I remain here. This body no longer works properly, and I think it unlikely that you would be able to find enough suitable spares. All I ask is that you switch me off permanently before you leave."

Lisa looked upset. So did John.

"Please remember that I am only a machine. Do not be upset. Machines don't die. I have existed for far longer than any other android. I am satisfied that I have performed well," said Thursday. "I suggest that you take my memory modules. They contain records of what happened here. You might find them interesting."

We agreed. With a slight lump in my throat, I disconnected the android.

"Thank you," said Thursday, as its eyes closed for the last time.

I switched it off properly and removed the memory modules. Then we returned to our makeshift camp. There didn't seem to be any point in continuing our exploration of the island, so we cleared everything up and returned home.

Back at my workshop, we connected the memory modules to my computer and reviewed the video records.

Thursday had arrived on the island roughly a year after Phil. Phil had thought he'd have no trouble surviving alone, but he'd overestimated his abilities. Thursday's arrival probably saved his life. The solar panels were set up to recharge the android and the Bobbert, Eric.

Eric did much of the work of digging out the underground accommodation. Thursday wired in the electrics. The two machines did most of the work required to look after Phil, including planting vegetables and other plants on the island. It was a fascinating record.

We couldn't keep all this information to ourselves. Time travel was known to exist by then, so we didn't need to keep it all secret. Lisa managed to find some of Phil's relatives and passed on much of the video footage to them.

Transitions

Lisa, John and I were happy living at my house. John was educated locally, and later moved to a place of his own with his girlfriend. We made a lot of friends there. Not everyone appreciated Lisa's musical talents, though.

Lisa was quite musical. She tried to learn a few of our Earth instruments. I suggested she play instruments that had headphone sockets, but that's not so easy with a trombone. My stuffing a rag up it didn't help.

Then she spotted a set of old bagpipes at a car boot sale. I tried to steer her away from them, but it was too late. She just had to have them. When we got them home, we found that the bag had disintegrated. Phew.

That didn't stop her, though. She invented compressor-pipes. She fitted a small electric compressor instead of the bag. The noise drove us nuts for days. John eventually put a stop to it by drilling extra holes in the wooden parts.

Then she wanted a horn of some kind. I bought her a shoehorn. She said she wanted a French horn. I bought her a French shoehorn.

"Try drilling holes in it and blowing in one end," shouted John, from his room.

"Just get on with your homework!" Lisa shouted back.

She once told me she wanted to play heavy metal. I suggested a tuba. She seemed to like playing loud instruments.

Then she discovered the foghorn. I took her to a disused lighthouse and showed her what it was. I pointed out that if she'd tried to 'play' that thing in our house, she'd probably have blown the windows out. It only had one note anyway.

Life at my house was fun for many years. Then disaster struck. Lisa and John had been for a night out in the local town. They were on their way back. It had been raining heavily, and Lisa was driving. A car headed towards them at speed. The other driver skidded, losing control. Lisa tried to avoid it by veering into the hedge, but it was too late.

Lisa and John both had serious injuries. John needed a blood transfusion, so he had some of mine, as we both have a rare blood type. Lisa's injuries were far more serious. She couldn't be saved.

Shortly before she passed away, she jokingly said that if I didn't behave myself after she'd gone, she would come back and haunt me. It amazed me that she could still be joking at a time like that. She never lost her sense of humour.

After she passed away, we took Lisa's body back to Kebea to be buried there, according to Kebean tradition. She had told us long before that if anything happened to her, we were to bury her close to where she was born.

John stayed with me for several months after that, to keep an eye on me, while his girlfriend looked after their house. Then he moved back in with her, leaving me alone, although he did visit regularly.

I had lived there alone for many years before I met Lisa, so I tried to return to that way of living. It wasn't as easy as I'd imagined. There were signs of Lisa everywhere. I tried to keep busy with various projects and got involved with local events. Robocat was sometimes good company.

Sometimes people do odd things in such circumstances. My odd thing was to try to build an android version of Lisa. I bought an Andy, in kit form, that looked a bit like her. I changed any parts that didn't look right. Some physical features could be programmed in, so I soon got it to look something like her. I found a way to use photos of her to improve her appearance.

The result was quite startling. It looked just like her. I tried to get it to behave like her but failed miserably. It might have fooled some people, but not anyone who knew her well. It had no sense of humour. It couldn't improvise or do anything unexpected.

Andy Lisa was better than nothing, but very boring. It could do the household chores (which I felt slightly guilty about), but it had no character. No spirit. I felt quite stressed out. I started wishing I'd never built the thing.

Eventually, I'd had enough. I needed a clean break. After much soul searching, I decided to move somewhere else.

I took the Andy and Robocat into the basement, then took the batteries out. I put Robocat's charging plate in there too. Things that had belonged to Lisa, or things that greatly reminded me of her (apart from photos) were put in there, much of it in carefully sealed boxes. I treated the furniture to prevent woodworm, just in case.

A few pipes and cables went through the basement, so I rerouted them. That meant there would never be any need for anyone to go in there. Then I closed and locked the hatch. I re-floored the corridor over it to stop anyone from finding it, even if the carpet was changed.

When I sold the house, I didn't include the basement in the sale. I intentionally didn't mention it in the documents provided to the new owners. In theory, the basement would still be legally mine. I had separate documents created to that effect, carefully written, which the new owners of the house didn't see. An odd thing to do perhaps, but I wasn't thinking all that logically at the time.

Everything else was loaded into a removal lorry. It followed me to my new house, around a hundred and forty miles away. I felt sad to leave the old place. I'd been happy there.

I worked in a variety of jobs over the decades that followed, mostly of a technical nature. There was always somebody who needed my help. The time came when I had more technical experience than most people alive.

I had skills in a variety of fields. I remember Larry once calling me a 'jackal of trades'. He meant 'Jack of all trades', of course.

I made a point of changing jobs and moving roughly every ten years. I needed to make sure nobody noticed that I wasn't physically getting any older.

My actual age caused problems for me. The pension companies became suspicious that I wasn't who I claimed to be. 'Nobody could live that long', they said. I eventually agreed to stop claiming most of my pensions. The companies didn't ask any more awkward questions after that. I also re-took my driving test several times.

John had to do similar things. He had inherited my anti-ageing characteristics, partly due to the blood transfusion. He eventually moved back to the town where we had once lived. By that time, he was living on his own. So did I, most of the time, although I did have girlfriends sometimes. Nothing too serious, though. Getting married again wasn't an option for me.

John contacted me one day, as he'd noticed a 'for sale' sign outside my former home. He wondered if I'd be interested in it. I wasn't keen at first, but then I changed my mind. It had been nearly eighty years since Lisa passed away, and my feelings had changed. I contacted the estate agents and then drove to the house.

It looked the same, but different. Several owners had made changes, mostly to the interior decoration and fittings. The garden had changed too. The place where the daffodils had been had become a flowerbed.

I could find little wrong with the place, so I asked the owners why they were leaving. They came up with several quite minor excuses. Little of what they said made sense to me, so I asked their neighbours.

The neighbours on both sides were nice people. They told me the owners thought the place was haunted by a strange woman. They thought it might be a poltergeist. I wasn't worried. I didn't believe in such things.

I decided to buy the place. My offer was accepted. I moved in soon afterwards. It made it easier for John to visit me, as he lived in the same town. I soon settled in. The place had suited me well before, and I felt it would again.

Then I remembered the basement. I'd forgotten about it. I found it still sealed in. I removed the extra flooring and tried to open the hatch, but I couldn't. The lock and hinges were rusted up. I'd lost the key anyway. I forced it open with a crowbar and went in.

I found everything as I had left it, albeit covered with a thin layer of dirt and spider webs. I noticed Andy Lisa in the corner. I felt rather silly that I'd built it.

I found Robocat, carefully packed in a box. I brought him back upstairs. He looked OK. I bought and fitted new batteries, and then tried him out. He'd become rather stiff after all that time. I switched him back off and gave him a thorough overhaul. He worked fine after that, so I reinstated his charging plate in its original location.

When the daffodils came up, they had spread out quite a bit. It amazed me that they were still there. I thinned them out, so they once again spelled 'LISA'. It amused me. I thought that if her spirit was watching me, she might approve.

SPIRIT HAVING NOT QUITE FLOWN

I'm over a hundred and forty years old now. The effects of the anti-ageing experiments from so long ago are starting to wear off, so I know I'm not immortal.

My son, John, looks older than me. That's because he is. I tried to warn him that messing about with time travel was a bad idea, but he ignored me. On one occasion, he made a blunder. He forgot to set a timer just before travelling back in time. That resulted in his being stuck in the past for sixty years. He had to get back the 'long' way, avoiding me and his younger self. He won't make that mistake again.

About a year ago, something odd happened to me. I'd settled in well into my old home and had resumed my earlier pre-Lisa way of living.

I couldn't be bothered with working much. Sometimes I did small engineering projects for local companies. Repairing things for people often kept me busy. I soon gained a reputation for fixing things cheaply.

Several people who had asked me to fix things were complaining, because I still hadn't. I didn't always feel up to it.

Fixing things for people is something I do out of interest, not for profit. Not everyone is well off, so I try to help when I can.

Unfortunately, a few were taking advantage. I felt sure that some things people had asked me to fix had been rescued from the local dump, to be repaired by me and then sold locally. It was starting to get me down.

I'd made some homemade beer. I sat in my kitchen drinking it, feeling sorry for myself. Not much from that batch was drinkable. Several bottles had exploded in my basement, making quite a mess. Probably too much sugar. I thought I might as well finish it and then make some more. I may have had too much.

I happened to be thinking about Lisa. She had died many decades ago, but I still thought about her sometimes. I stared into my pint glass and noticed my somewhat intoxicated-looking reflection staring back at me.

Then I noticed another blurry face looking back at me too. She looked like Lisa, when she and I were young. I knew I was drunk, but I didn't remember hallucinating before. I looked around sharply but found nobody there. I put it down to my state of mind and carried on drinking.

I looked at the reflection in the glass again. There she was, smiling at me. I'd forgotten what effect that smile used to have on me. Again, I turned around. Still nobody there. I muttered and mumbled, and then finished my drink. It was getting late, so I went to bed.

I woke up the next morning with a headache, resolving not to drink so much in future (as usual). I got up and got dressed. Then I shuffled to the bathroom and started brushing my teeth. I looked at my reflection in the mirror. There was Lisa again, more clearly this time. That scared me. I turned around quickly, splattering toothpaste on the wall. I saw no sign of anyone. Surely I couldn't still be that drunk.

Nervously, I looked back in the mirror. Lisa was still there, grinning, like she'd just played a joke on me. My heart raced, and I felt a bit odd. I tried talking to her. I felt silly, not knowing what to say, yet she seemed to be talking back to me.

I wanted to hear what she was saying, but I couldn't. Seeing her again after so long was a shock, yet I was happy to see her face again, even with my headache. She looked young and well. I finished cleaning my teeth and washed the white toothpaste ring off my mouth. Then I cleaned the toothpaste off the wall. It took me a while to calm down.

In the days that followed, I often saw her in the mirror. I got more used to it. I remembered her joking long ago that she might come back to haunt me, but I never thought she actually would. Maybe she'd seen the daffodils in my garden. Whatever the reason, I was pleased to see her, albeit quite scared.

I gradually accepted her presence, even if she was just an image in the mirror. I couldn't hear her, but that didn't stop me from talking to her. After so many years, I had much to say. She could respond by nodding or shaking her head.

I spent much time telling her about things that had happened to me since she'd passed away. She seemed interested. I tried to ask her what things were like on the 'other side', but I don't think she wanted to tell me. Maybe she wasn't allowed to.

I found that if I asked her a question she could answer, I somehow got the answer in my mind, as though she had put it there. One thing that scared me slightly was when she correctly told me where my keys were when I couldn't find them.

I noticed shortly afterwards that my house appeared tidier than usual. I didn't recall making any more effort to tidy up.

Maybe I had, without realising it, as I knew Lisa might be watching. However, there were times when I knew I hadn't put something away, yet it was back in its proper place the following morning.

I had seriously considered the possibility that I was going nuts. However, things were happening that couldn't be explained unless they were Lisa's doing.

It soon became clear to me that Lisa could move things. She had never liked mess or clutter. She had told me off frequently when she was alive for being untidy. I considered putting up a tiny camera to see if I could capture her moving things, but I thought better of it. She would have seen me putting it up and wouldn't have been too pleased.

Before Lisa's ghost started appearing, a local woman, also called Lisa, had taken an interest in me. She must've heard about the daffodils and thought they were for her. I assured her they weren't and explained the reason for the daffodil lettering. She understood. I called her Lissie after that, which she seemed happy enough with. She would visit me occasionally, as we got along well.

I told nobody about Lisa's ghost for weeks. I didn't want people to think me crazy. That was until Lissie visited one day.

I heard a knock on the door. When I opened it, Lissie was standing there, grinning at me. I invited her in. We sat down in my living room.

"I've just brought your tin opener back. Thanks for lending it to me," she said. I took it and put it aside. She paused and looked around the room. "You've been tidying up, I see."

"That's not my doing," I replied, slightly hesitantly. She paused to think.

"Alan, what are you up to? Have you got a housekeeper?"

"Umm... no, not exactly..."

"I think you're hiding something," she continued.

I could see I wasn't going to get away with it. I decided to tell her the truth, although I felt pretty sure she wouldn't believe me.

"Lissie, do you remember me telling you about my wife?"

"Which one?"

"I've only ever had one, called Lisa."

"Like me?"

"Yes, I do, but..."

"Stop being silly. Anyway, what about her?"

"Well, I think, maybe, just possibly, she's... erm... not quite as dead as I thought," I said slowly.

Lissie looked alarmed. She looked me straight in the eyes.

"Alan, are you telling me your wife is still alive?" she said, loudly.

"Well, not exactly..."

"Then what exactly?" I paused.

"I think she's a ghost. She's the one who's been tidying things up. She can move things, a little bit, so she does what she can. I see her in the mirror sometimes and hear her in my mind," I admitted.

I don't think Lissie knew what to make of it. I think she felt scared and a little threatened.

"There's nothing to worry about, you know," I said. "Lisa's ghost is quite harmless. I can still do whatever I want and there's nothing she can do about it." As soon as I'd finished speaking, I realised my mistake. I could hear Lisa's voice in my head, shouting, "Wanna bet?"

We heard a loud crash from the kitchen, followed by cutlery falling on the floor. Lissie looked scared. We went to the kitchen to investigate.

I picked up the toaster and put the cutlery back in the open drawer. I went to the mirror.

"Sorry, Lisa. I wasn't thinking," I said, as I looked into it.

"What...?" said Lissie.

"I wasn't talking to you."

"Then who... Alan, you're nuts! I'm off." Lissie left. I heard the front door slam, quite loudly.

I could see Lisa in the mirror, laughing and making silly faces at me. I haven't seen Lissie since.

THE THEFT (NEARLY)

As the weeks passed, I found it easier to make out what Lisa was saying to me. No longer just impressions, feelings, or her making faces at me. I could actually hear her voice in my head. She said I needed a guard dog to protect all my stuff. She had always liked dogs.

Robocat isn't good at guarding my property. He's a useless guard cat. He wasn't programmed to do that. However, Lisa has found a way to get into him. She makes him do things he wasn't designed to do.

If he does anything unusual, it's almost always Lisa's doing. She often tries silly things, like trying to make him speak. Sometimes she'll get a word or two out of him, but the noise is usually unintelligible. It's quite funny sometimes.

On one occasion, her use of Robocat came in handy. Lisa doesn't need sleep. She tries to make herself useful during the night, tidying up and putting a few small things away. That requires considerable effort on her part. It's difficult to do much when you're a ghost.

Early one morning, Lisa detected a burglar trying to get into the house. She needed to wake me up. She didn't have enough energy as a ghost to physically shake me. Robocat was on charge and wouldn't respond.

She could tell I was dreaming, so she tried to get into my head that way. I had a very odd dream. I dreamt that Lisa was shouting at me and waving her arms about, but I couldn't hear her.

She got better at controlling my dream. In it, she tried slapping my face, but that didn't work. Then I dreamed that she'd led me into the kitchen and had started destroying the appliances. Blowing up the toaster didn't work, so she melted the washing machine into a puddle. Nope... still asleep. My unconscious mind seemed to be fighting back.

Lisa needed something more dramatic, so, still in my dream, she came crashing through the kitchen wall in a Sherman tank. She aimed directly at me, paused for effect and then fired. That woke me up.

It took me a couple of minutes to calm down. Then I heard unusual noises coming from the front door. Lisa told me it was a burglar. I put on my dressing gown and shoes and then looked for something to defend myself with.

Meanwhile, Lisa got into Robocat and took him over, as he'd finished charging. She got him to pull one of the white sheets off my bed and drag it to the front door. Robocat's teeth tore the sheet quite badly, but it didn't matter under the circumstances. Then she told me to wait before I did anything.

By the time the burglar broke in, she had Robocat hidden under the sheet. Robocat's eyes lit up dimly. He made a quiet, menacing growl. I could see what she was up to, so I switched off the lights. She scared the living daylights out of the burglar, and he fled.

Like most people, I have a small CCTV camera mounted on the outside wall of my house, watching the doorway. It's a small, self-contained unit capable of changing its colour to blend in with its surroundings. It's hard to detect. Some people call them Chamelecams.

I took the video footage to the local police. They soon arrested the burglar. They said he looked shaken. They asked me what happened. I couldn't tell them about Lisa, but I did tell them about Robocat and the sheet. I think they were quite amused.

A little while later, she got up to one of her pranks, using Robocat. He would wake me up every morning, going 'meow... meow... meow...' until I paid some attention to him. It was clearly Lisa's doing, as he'd never done that before. I sometimes thought I could see her in the mirror after I'd been woken up, grinning at me. This was the sort of harmless prank I would expect her to do. She'd always had a great sense of humour.

The first time may have been funny, but it soon became tiresome. I wanted to ask her to stop, but I never knew where she was. She seemed to be pushing me to see how much she could get away with.

One morning, I'd had enough of it. I deactivated Robocat, connected him to a computer and deselected all the sound options. That shut him up, although he still tried to wake me up (silently) the next morning. He seemed a bit frustrated, trying harder than usual. That amused me. I think Lisa got the message. The behaviour stopped shortly after that. I reactivated his sounds later, as he seemed too quiet.

I've built a rockery in my garden. I'm quite pleased with it. I've got water running through it, sourced from a nearby stream and pumped using a solar-powered pump. I found it a handy way to use the otherwise unwanted rocks in my garden.

I've also added some nice-looking alien rocks and stones I'd kept from my adventures on other planets.

Robocat won't go near it unless he's under Lisa's control. Maybe there's something in his programming that keeps him away from water.

I think Lisa approves of the rockery. I sometimes see her face reflected in the water. Occasionally, I can see her, very slightly, without any mirrors, if the lighting conditions are just right.

Someone has made small improvements to the rockery. I had forgotten that Lisa used to like things like that, so this had to be her doing.

HOME AND GARDEN

My house had developed a leaky roof. I wanted to fix it myself but I'm no longer allowed to. Current health and safety regulations no longer permit it. It seems daft to me.

Such regulations used to only apply to businesses. Now they apply to homeowners too. When I bought a new set of ladders recently, I had to fill in an unbelievable number of forms. I had to declare that I wouldn't do any dangerous work unsupervised. Antigravity overalls were banned recently, after a series of accidents caused by poor design. I think I'll write to my local MP. She owes me a favour after I repaired her dog.

Lisa doesn't need ladders. She wanted to help, but she couldn't do much. I was starting to see her directly, without mirrors, so I directed her to the part of the roof where I thought the problem might be. She thought she'd found something, so she tried to lift a tiny camera up there to photograph the problem. That didn't work, as the wind kept blowing it away. Then it got caught by a passing swallow.

I called in a local roofer. He's a young fellow, quite enthusiastic and very cheap. I discovered that although he'd passed all the required exams, he didn't have much experience with real-world roofing problems. I kept a close eye on him. I often advised him on how to do things and what not to do. He (we) got the job done, eventually. He sometimes asks for my advice.

I have a small orchard at the bottom end of my garden. There's a tall fence next to it, as it's close to the road. I think Lisa quite likes it (the orchard, not the fence). It's a pity she can't taste the apples. They're rather good.

Unfortunately, some troublesome young locals like them too. The previous year, most of the apples were gone before I could get at them myself. I tried putting up higher fencing, but the young scrumpers just cut a big hole in it.

I knew a little about force fields, so early the next spring, I set one up around the apple trees. It was solar powered, so it didn't cost me anything to run. It was possible to get through it if one pushed very hard, but that's not easy when you're on top of a fence or partway through it. It would also keep the wasps out when the apples were ripe. I had high hopes.

Lisa, being smarter than me, had noticed a slight problem. If the force field could keep the wasps out, it would also stop the bees from pollinating the apple blossom. Oops. It had to be left switched off until the apples had started to form. I've used a rain sensor from a car to deactivate the force field when it rains.

Robocat doesn't like the force field. It makes his circuits go haywire. He won't go near it.

Lisa sometimes uses Robocat to try to keep the garden tidy, although there's a limit to how much she can do.

When I built the force field, I needed an extra multimeter. I drove to John's house to see if he could lend me one. He handed me an old one that he'd had sitting on a shelf for years.

It looked familiar. In fact, it looked just like one of the two that disappeared from my house, long ago. While John wasn't looking, I looked in the battery compartment. I found the tracking device still in it.

I didn't say anything, but I guessed that some of John's early time travel experiments had something to do with it. I considered asking him where he'd got it from but thought better of it.

When the apples were ripe, the troublesome youngsters were back. They tried to reach the apples but failed. I felt pleased with myself. Unfortunately, the would-be thieves discovered they could get in when it rained, so I still lost a few apples.

I'd have to come up with a better solution. I'd been given some homemade jam a year earlier, by someone local, after I'd fixed her TV. I didn't like the stuff, but didn't have the heart to throw it out. I'd have to find some other use for it.

I remembered the sausage drive from my Spacemaker days. It could fire food products at high velocities. I built a much smaller version and set it up behind a small knothole in the fence, near the apple trees. I loaded it with the unwanted jam.

The next time it rained, I was ready. I left the force field switched on this time so I wouldn't get wet. When the scrumpers turned up, I blasted them with jam. They were covered with the stuff. The wasps wouldn't leave them alone. I don't think I ever saw them again.

Cat Capers

I had to be away for a few days recently. When Lisa was alive, she had always accompanied me on such trips. This time, it wasn't so easy.

She'd tried to come with me on a previous occasion. She sat on the passenger seat of my car. When I drove away, she disappeared through the back of the car, still sitting in the air. She couldn't keep up with me, so she had to stay behind.

With me away, Lisa was bored. She'd always been technically minded, so she wondered if she could do something to improve Robocat. She found it much easier to use him to do things than trying to do things herself with her limited energy.

She went into the basement and had a good look around. I've stored all sorts of electronic junk in there, as it's dry inside. I still had that old Andy version of her. She had thought it creepy when she first saw it, but she understood my reasons for building it. She wondered if she could occupy it instead of Robocat.

She got Robocat to plug it in to charge it. The batteries were extremely weak, so she couldn't get much charge into them.

Lisa tried for hours to make the android do anything useful. It had limited power and all the joints were stiff. She managed to get its eyelids to blink. Then she tried to move the arms. One was stuck, the other moved a little.

She got it to raise one arm a little, then rudely stick one finger in the air. When she tried to retract the finger and lower the arm, she couldn't. Not enough power. The arm had jammed anyway, so the Andy was stuck like that.

Then she had another idea. Maybe she could upgrade Robocat using parts from the android. Most of it was incompatible, but the memory and speech systems looked small enough to fit into Robocat.

It took her about two days to complete the work. I could have done it in about half an hour. So could she, if she was still alive. As a ghost, it wasn't so easy.

She re-initialised Robocat and tried him out. She tested all his usual functions first, to check she hadn't broken anything. Everything looked good, so she activated the modified systems.

Robocat's capabilities had made a giant leap forward. So did Robocat himself, crashing into the basement wall. She'd made the control systems much more sensitive than they had been previously.

She found it much easier to control him than before. With the extra memory, she could add new abilities. She tried to make him speak.

Robocat produced some dreadful noises initially, but Lisa managed to get that under control. Each time Robocat made a sound that sounded like a word, she would store that in his memory. Gradually, his speech improved. Lisa set him up so he behaved normally most of the time, only behaving differently when she occupied him.

She had intended to wait until I returned before putting Robocat through his paces, but she had always been impatient. She took Robocat down the street, looking for a way to test him.

She saw a man sitting on a park bench, obviously drunk. He was a local tramp (vagrant). He'd been causing trouble in the area for weeks, rummaging through bins, stealing and generally annoying people. People wanted him gone from the area, but they couldn't (legally) do much about it.

Lisa knew this. To her, this was too good a chance to miss. As a cat, she could do whatever she liked. She got Robocat to jump up on the bench next to him.

The drunk liked cats. He stroked Robocat.

"Who's a nice kitty?" said the drunk. "You wanna be my friend? (hic!)"

"Not blooming likely," said Robocat. The drunk jumped backwards and fell off the bench. He got up, staggered to the nearest bin and threw his bottle into it. Robocat chased him away, growling loudly, his eyes glowing bright blue.

Lisa was having far too much fun. She soon realised that her own energies were getting low. She took Robocat back home and rested until I returned. Then she told me all about it.

I was impressed with her work. Between us, we made further improvements. Lisa likes being a cat from time to time, but it's not as good as being human.

We haven't seen the tramp since.

A short while later, my son John visited me. I hadn't seen him for some time, as he'd been working overseas. He seemed quite excited about something he'd just invented and wanted my opinion.

I greeted him at my front door and asked him in. I sent him to my conservatory while I fetched a couple of beers. As he walked past the kitchen, he heard a voice.

"Hello John," said Lisa.

"Hi Mum," said John, his mind still full of ideas about what he planned to tell me. We met in the conservatory and started talking. John seemed puzzled about something.

"Who was that in your kitchen?" asked John. "I mistook her for Mum. I hope she won't be offended."

"That was your mother," I said carefully.

"Dad, that's cruel. You know how I felt about Mum. Nobody could replace her," he said. His face changed as Lisa walked into the room. He could see and hear her far better than I could, perhaps because he's thirty years older than me and directly related. I could see and hear her by that time without the mirrors, but not as well as John could.

We talked for most of the day. Much of it was rather emotional. Lisa said she'd been watching us both and was proud of us. John found it difficult to accept what he was seeing and hearing. I assured him he wasn't imagining things. It was late in the evening by the time he left. He never did tell me what he'd invented.

Epilogue

Well, that should have been it... the end of my story. It was time to send my recording to the publishers. I had picked it up and was looking around for suitable packaging when I heard a strange noise coming from outside my front door.

It was an odd, scratching sound. I wondered if I was going to be burgled again. I hid my recording somewhere safe and then cautiously returned to my front door. I could hear quiet voices outside. They didn't sound aggressive.

The scratching got louder. Then I heard whimpering and whining, followed by a bark. I didn't think a burglar would bring a dog, so I cautiously opened the door.

A black Labrador rushed in, jumped up at me and licked my face, nearly knocking me over. I didn't know any black Labradors, yet this dog clearly knew me well. I looked down and noticed a name tag on his collar. It said 'Muttley'. I thought that bark sounded familiar. But how could he be here after all this time?

I was so busy making a fuss of Muttley that I'd failed to notice two people standing in the doorway. They called out to me. They were Barry and Sue. Behind them stood Penny, Muttley's owner. All were grinning at me.

I was amazed to see them. I had thought they were all long gone. I asked them in. We went through the house to my garden and sat on the wooden chairs. Lisa was already there, tinkering with the rockery. The look on her face was indescribable. Only I could see her, or so I thought. I noticed her moving into Robocat.

We talked for ages. Sue and Barry had recently married. Sue proudly showed me the ring on her finger. They all looked older than I remembered, but not by much. Muttley looked just the same. I still had an old tennis ball lying around, so I threw it for him a few times to keep him busy. I didn't want him digging in my garden. It wasn't long before he'd chewed it up (the ball, I mean).

We talked about Lisa. I told them about how happy we had been, and about John. They had all liked Lisa. They said they wished she was still around. I didn't say anything, which I think they thought a little odd.

Robocat jumped onto Barry's lap, curled up and started purring as Barry stroked him. Barry liked cats. Lisa was clearly up to something, waiting for an opportunity. That worried me.

We talked about my wedding on Kebea and had a good laugh about it. Then Robocat lifted his head up, looked Barry straight in the eyes and said,

"Holy cats, Batman!"

Batman, I mean Barry, jumped out of his chair, leaving Robocat there. Robocat appeared to be grinning. I had some explaining to do. Lisa had left Robocat by then and had returned to the rockery, so I pushed him off the chair and asked Barry to sit back down.

I told them about Lisa's ghost. I also told them how she could occupy Robocat, as he was artificial. I explained that John and I could see and hear Lisa, but nobody else could. They didn't believe me, so Lisa moved a coin on the table in an L-shaped movement to prove she was there. Then she went back to what she'd been doing.

Sue thought she could see Lisa at the rockery, very slightly, so she walked over to her and tried to talk to her. She found that she could see and hear Lisa well enough to have a reasonable conversation with her. The two of them had always got along well. They talked for ages. I think Muttley could see Lisa too, but he couldn't understand why she had no smell.

Barry told me why they had come to see me. He and Sue wanted to leave Spacemakers and settle down, as Lisa and I had. They wanted to sell the business. They had found possible buyers for everything, but there were some major financial and legal issues to sort out. Much of the ownership was still with me. They had thought me long gone, so they'd tried to track down my son, John. Maybe he would have offspring who were still alive.

They were surprised to find him still living. They were even more surprised to find that I still am. John had told them where to find me.

I asked them why they didn't seem to have aged much. Barry told me that although the boffins had tried to compensate for time travel, they still hadn't quite got the hang of it. My visitors really were as young as they looked.

Spacemakers was still doing business, but not as much as before. Competitors had caught up. Most of the original production staff had left, replaced by less experienced people. Lorna had met and married a man on Kebea. They were both still alive, but very old. The older boffins had also left, including the triplets.

Ned had returned to Australia, to help his son look for more gold. Ron had retired a few years after I left with Lisa. People had noticed that time passed more slowly on Spacemakers than everywhere else. That had caused real problems. Ron had passed away, at a considerable age.

I still had my documents hidden in an old filing cabinet. I dug them out. They looked ancient. We devised a plan.

Over the next couple of weeks, working with a local firm of solicitors, we agreed to sell Spacemakers, the spaceship and most of the land to a large business in the local town. We would disable the ability to fly the entire factory.

The force field at the site would be dismantled. We sold Ivor and the railway line to a local railway preservation society.

We had one other matter to sort out. Lisa wanted a better body than Robocat. She used Robocat to speak to us about it in great detail. She wanted an up-to-date version of the Andy, but with all the human features that current ones don't have. It wouldn't be cheap.

By that time, all the remaining alien diamonds I'd collected before I married Lisa were gone. I'd sometimes used them to pay my living costs when I'd been unemployed.

Lisa reminded me about those crystals she'd picked up from the planet where the imitation Dougals were. She'd guessed they were diamonds, so she'd buried them on public land on Kebea before we left there. She felt it was about time we got them back.

We talked about it. Spacemaker One was still operational and in good shape. We agreed to use it to travel to Kebea and retrieve the diamonds. Lisa explained to us where she'd hidden them. She couldn't travel with us. She insisted that we not write anything down.

A week later, Barry and I set off for Kebea. It seemed strange to me, being back on Spacemaker One after all that time. The craft looked old by today's standards. Sue and Penny remained at my house to look after the place for me. Sue and Lisa had much catching up to do.

We landed on Kebea, about half a mile from where we thought the diamonds were and then walked to the site. We had backpacks and collapsible shovels with us.

The diamonds took some finding. Lisa had been careful to hide them well away from any buildings, to avoid being seen. We dug them up and filled in the hole.

While we were there, we took the opportunity to take photos, mostly for Lisa's benefit. We photographed the site where we had dug up the diamonds and then went to where Lisa used to live and photographed the village. We also tidied up her grave and took a photo of it.

We'd been told where Lorna lived, so we went to see her. She looked very old, but we still recognised her. She was amazed to see us. We talked for ages.

By the time we returned to Earth, the documents to sell Spacemakers were ready to sign, so we did. Barry and Sue were sad to leave Spacemakers.

We said our goodbyes, and then Barry, Sue, Penny and Muttley left. I know where they all live, so I'll probably visit them occasionally.

One thing I'd forgotten about until after Barry and the others had left was the Moonbase. There had never been any mention of it in the ownership documents. I considered keeping it, although Lisa wasn't so keen. There would be little point in having a Moonbase if you can't reach it.

We've already started working on the plans for Lisa's new artificial body. It won't be easy and we'll have to keep the work secret, but I'm sure we'll succeed, eventually. The Andy Lisa I built long ago might do temporarily, but it'll need work.

I had thought that keeping other spirits out of it might be a problem, but Lisa's spirit is different somehow. Maybe her being born on a different planet has something to do with it. She seems to be gaining strength all the time, perhaps from me.

The end (sort of)

Zzzzzz... WHAT?

Darkness.
An illuminated circle appears on the floor.
Ned fades into view, standing in the middle of it.

Ned: What's happening? Where am I?

He looks around but sees nothing.
Then a second light circle appears.
On it, stands Alan.

Alan: Hey! What's going on?
Ned: Beats me. Last thing I remember, I was chasing a 'roo off my gold patch.

Smythe appears, like the other two.

Smythe: Oi! What are you two up to?
Ned: It's not me!
Alan: Me neither.

Smythe: It must've been you two layabouts. There's nobody else here!
Layton: That's not quite true. I brought you here.
Alan: Who are you?
Layton: I'm the author.
Ned: Of what?
Layton: This book. You're in it.
Smythe: You're the one who's in it!

Ned laughs. Smythe looks annoyed. He walks towards Ned and tries to hit him. He misses. Ned runs away. Smythe gives chase. Ned stops and trips up Smythe. Smythe falls to the floor.

Alan: Now, now, ladies!
Bertha and Connie: It wasn't us! (They'd appeared without anyone noticing. Not easy, for those two.)
Layton: Calm down you lot, or I'll write you out of the book.
Connie: Like you did with us? We didn't even make it to the end!
Layton: You didn't deserve to!
Bertha: Now you've done it! Let's get him!

Bertha and Connie move towards Layton, who runs away.

Alastair: Behave, you lot! I'm trying to sleep!

Alastair wakes up.

About the author

Layton is an odd character. He likes to take the credit for things he hasn't done. Some call him a professional scapegoat. He thinks if he takes the credit for enough things, he'll eventually become famous. He wants to take the credit for this book. I suppose I might as well let him, for now.

I've decided that Layton is just a figment of his own imagination.

Yes, I've been a bit silly. Layton Bushel is the pen name of Alastair Warren. Since Layton doesn't actually exist, I've chosen to make fun of him.

Alastair is a retired former engineer, living in Scotland. This is his second attempt to write a book. He succeeded the first time, with a title called Forgotten Erf, using the same pen name.